One
Corpse
Too Many

The Complete Brother Cadfael Series

One
Corpse
Too Many

ELLIS
PETERS

Book-of-the-Month Club
New York

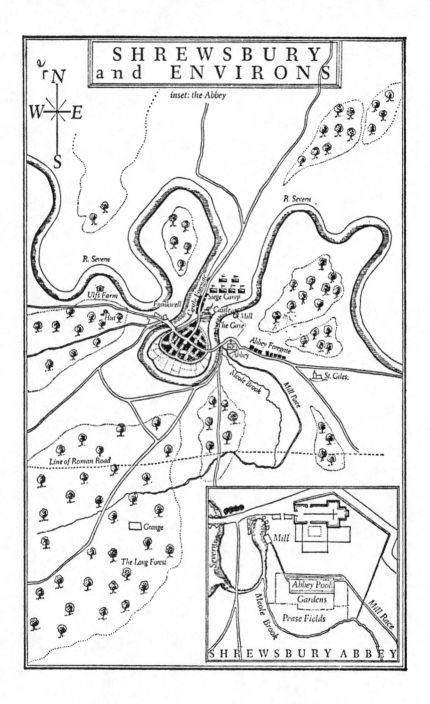

SHREWSBURY and ENVIRONS

inset: the Abbey

N
W E
S

R. Severn

R. Severn

Ulf's Farm

Frankwell

Siege Camp

Castle

The Gate

Mill

Abbey

Abbey Foregate

St. Giles

Meole Brook

Mill Race

Line of Roman Road

Grange

The Long Forest

Mill

Severn

Meole Brook

Abbey Pool

Gardens

Pease Fields

Mill Race

SHREWSBURY ABBEY

CHAPTER ONE

Brother Cadfael was working in the small kitchen garden by the abbot's fish-ponds when the boy was first brought to him. It was hot August noon, and if he had had his proper quota of helpers they would all have been snoring in the shade at this hour, instead of sweating in the sun; but one of his regular assistants, not yet out of his novitiate, had thought better of the monastic vocation and taken himself off to join his elder brother in arms on King Stephen's side, in the civil war for the crown of England, and the other had taken fright at the approach of the royal army because his family were of the Empress Maud's faction, and their manor in Cheshire seemed a far safer place to be than Shrewsbury under siege. Cadfael was left to do everything alone, but he had in his time laboured under far hotter suns than this, and was doggedly determined not to let his domain run wild, whether the outside world fell into chaos or no.

In this early summer of 1138 the fratricidal strife, hitherto somewhat desultory, was already two years old, but never before had it approached Shrewsbury so closely. Now its threat hung over castle and town like the shadow of death. But for all that, Brother Cadfael's mind was firmly upon life and growth, rather than destruction and war, and certainly he had no suspicion that another manner of killing, simple murder, furtive and unlicensed even in these anarchic times, was soon to disrupt the calm of his chosen life.

August should not, in normal circumstances, have been one of his busiest times in the gardens, but there was more than enough for one man to do properly, and the only relief they had to offer him was Brother Athanasius, who was deaf, half-senile, and not to be relied upon to know a useful herb from a weed, and the offer had been firmly declined. Better by far manage alone. There was a bed to be prepared for planting out late cabbages for succession, and fresh seed to be sown for the kind that can weather the winter, as well as pease to be gathered, and the dead, dried haulms of the early crop to be cleared away for fodder and litter. And in his wooden work-shed in the herbarium, his own particular pride, he had half a dozen preparations working in glass vessels and mortars on the shelves, all of them needing

1

attention at least once a day, besides the herb wines that bubbled busily on their own at this stage. It was high harvest time among the herbs, and all the medicines for the winter demanding his care.

However, he was not the man to let any part of his kingdom slip out of his control, however wastefully the royal cousins Stephen and Maud contended for the throne of England outside the abbey walls. If he lifted his head from digging compost into the cabbage bed he could see the sluggish plumes of smoke hanging over the abbey roofs and the town and castle beyond, and smell the acrid residue of yesterday's fires. That shadow and stink had hung like a pall over Shrewsbury for almost a month, while King Stephen stamped and raged in his camp beyond the Castle Foregate, the one dry-foot way into the town unless he could get possession of the bridges, and William Fitz-Alan within the fortress held on grimly, keeping an anxious eye on his dwindling supplies, and left the thundering of defiance to his incorrigible uncle, Arnulf of Hesdin, who had never learned to temper valour with discretion. The townspeople kept their heads low, locked their doors, shuttered their shops, or, if they could, made off westwards into Wales, to old, friendly enemies less to be feared than Stephen. It suited the Welsh very well that Englishmen should fear Englishmen – if either Maud or Stephen could be regarded as English! – and let Wales alone, and they would not grudge a helping hand to the fleeing casualties, provided the war went on merrily.

Cadfael straightened his back and mopped the sweat from a tonsured scalp burned to the colour of a ripe hazel-nut; and there was Brother Oswald the almoner bustling along the path towards him, with skirts flapping, and propelling before him by the shoulder a boy of about sixteen, in the coarse brown cotte and short summer hose of the countryside, barelegged but very decently shod in leather, and altogether looking carefully scrubbed and neat for a special occasion. The boy went where he was directed, and kept his eyes lowered with nervous meekness. Another family taking care to put its children out of reach of being pressed for either side, thought Cadfael, and small blame to them.

'Brother Cadfael, I think you have need of a helper, and here is a youngster who says he's not afraid of hard work. A good woman of the town has brought him in to the porter, and asked

2

that he be taken and taught as a lay servant. Her nephew from Hencot, she says, and his parents dead. There's a year's endowment with him. Prior Robert has given leave to take him, and there's room in the boys' dortoir. He'll attend school with the novices, but he'll not take vows unless he himself comes to wish it. What do you say, will you have him?'

Cadfael looked the boy over with interest, but said yes without hesitation, glad enough to be offered someone young, able-bodied and willing. The lad was slenderly built, but vigorous and firm on his feet, and moved with a spring. He looked up warily from under a cropped tangle of brown curls, and his eyes were long-lashed and darkly blue, very shrewd and bright. He was behaving himself meekly and decorously, but he did not look intimidated.

'Very heartily I'll have you,' said Cadfael, 'if you'll take to this outdoor work with me. And what's your name, boy?'

'Godric, sir,' said the young thing, in a small, gruff voice, appraising Cadfael just as earnestly as he was being appraised.

'Good, then, Godric, you and I will get on well enough. And first, if you will, walk around the gardens here with me and see what we have in hand, and get used to being within these walls. Strange enough I daresay you'll find it, but safer than in the town yonder, which I make no doubt is why your good aunt brought you here.'

The blue, bright eyes flashed him one glance and were veiled again.

'See you come to Vespers with Brother Cadfael,' the almoner instructed, 'and Brother Paul, the master of the novices, will show you your bed, and tell you your duties after supper. Pay attention to what Brother Cadfael tells you, and be obedient to him as you should.'

'Yes, sir,' said the boy virtuously. Under the meek accents a small bubble of laughter seemed to be trying, though vainly, to burst. When Brother Oswald hurried away, the blue eyes watched him out of sight, and then turned their intent gaze upon Cadfael. A demure, oval face, with a wide, firm mouth shaped properly for laughter, but quick to revert to a very sombre gravity. Even for those meant to be light-hearted, these were grave times.

'Come, see what manner of labour you're taking on yourself,' said Cadfael cheerfully, and downed his spade to take his new boy round the enclosed garden, showing him the vegetables, the herbs that made the noon air heady and drunken with fragrance, the fish ponds and the beds of pease that ran down almost to the brook. The early field was already dried and flaxen in the sun, all its harvest gathered, even the later-sown hung heavy and full in pod.

'These we should gather today and tomorrow. In this heat they'll pass their best in a day. And these spent ones have to be cleared. You can begin that for me. Don't pull them up, take the sickle and cut them off low to the ground, and the roots we plough in, they're good food for the soil.' He was talking in an easy, good-humoured flow, to pass off peacefully whatever residue of regret and strangeness there might be in this abrupt change. 'How old are you, Godric?'

'Seventeen,' said the husky voice beside him. He was on the small side for seventeen; let him try his hand at digging later on, the ground Cadfael was working was heavy to till. 'I can work hard,' said the boy, almost as though he had guessed at the thought, and resented it. 'I don't know much, but I can do whatever you tell me.'

'So you shall, then, and you can begin with the pease. Stack the dry stuff aside here, and it goes to provide stable litter. And the roots go back to the ground.'

'Like humankind,' said Godric unexpectedly.

'Yes, like humankind.' Too many were going back to the earth prematurely now in this fratricidal war. He saw the boy turn his head, almost involuntarily, and look across the abbey grounds and roofs to where the battered towers of the castle loomed in their pall of smoke. 'Have you kin within there, child?' asked Cadfael gently.

'No!' said the boy, too quickly. 'But I can't but think of them. They're saying in the town it can't last long – that it may fall tomorrow. And surely they've done only rightly! Before King Henry died he made his barons acknowledge the Empress Maud as his heir, and they all swore fealty. She was his only living child, she *should* be queen. And yet when her cousin, Count Stephen, seized the throne and had himself crowned, all too many of them took it meekly and forgot their oaths. That can't be right. And it can't be wrong to stand by the empress faithfully. How can they excuse changing sides? How can they justify Count Stephen's claim?'

'Justify may not be the apt word, but there are those among

the lords, more by far than take the opposite view, who would say, better a man for overlord than a woman. And if a man, why, Stephen was as near as any to the throne. He is King William's grandchild, just as Maud is.'

'But not son to the last king. And in any case, through his mother, who was a woman like Maud, so where's the difference?' The young voice had emerged from its guarded undertone, and rang clear and vehement. 'But the real difference was that Count Stephen rushed here and took what he wanted, while the empress was far away in Normandy, thinking no evil. And now that half the barons have recollected their oaths and declared for her, after all, it's late, and what's to come of it but bloodshed and deaths? It begins here, in Shrewsbury, and this won't be the end.'

'Child,' said Cadfael mildly, 'are you not trusting me to extremes?'

The boy, who had picked up the sickle and was swinging it in a capable, testing hand, turned and looked at him with blue eyes suddenly wide open and unguarded. 'Well, so I do,' he said.

'And so you may, for that matter. But keep your lips locked among others. We are in the battlefield here, as sure as in the town, our gates never being closed to any. All manner of men rub shoulders here, and in rough times some may try to buy favour with carrying tales. Some may even be collectors of such tales for their living. Your thoughts are safe in your head, best keep them there.'

The boy drew back a little, and hung his head. Possibly he felt himself reproved. Possibly not! 'I'll pay you trust for trust,' said Cadfael. 'In my measure there's little to choose between two such monarchs, but much to be said for keeping a man's fealty and word. And now let me see you hard at work, and when I've finished my cabbage patch I'll come and help you.'

He watched the boy set to work, which he did with immense vigour. The coarse tunic was cut very full, turning a lissome body into a bundle of cloth tied at the waist; possibly he had got it from some older and larger relative after the best of the wear was out of it. My friend, thought Cadfael, in this heat you won't keep up that pace very long, and then we shall see!

By the time he joined his assistant in the rustling field of bleached pea-stems, the boy was red in the face and sweating, and puffing audibly with the strokes of the sickle, but had not relaxed his efforts. Cadfael swept an armful of cut haulms to the edge of the field, and said earnestly: 'No need to make a penance of it, lad. Strip off to the waist and be comfortable.' And he slid his own frock, already kilted to the knee, down from powerful brown shoulders, and let the folds hang at his middle.

The effect was complex, but by no means decisive. The boy checked momentarily in his stroke, said: 'I'm well enough as I am!' with admirable composure, but several tones above the gruff, young-mannish level of his earlier utterances, and went on resolutely with his labours, at the same time as a distinct wave of red arose from his collar to engulf his slender neck and the curve of his cheek. Did that necessarily mean what it seemed to mean? He might have lied about his age, his voice might be but newly broken and still unstable. And perhaps he wore no shirt beneath the cotte, and was ashamed to reveal his lacks to a new acqaint- ance. Ah, well, there were other tests. Better make sure at once. If what Cadfael suspected was true, the matter was going to require very serious thought.

'There's that heron that robs our hatcheries, again!' he cried suddenly, pointing across the Meole brook, where the unsuspect- ing bird waded, just folding immense wings. 'Toss a stone across at him, boy, you're nearer than I!' The heron was an innocent stranger, but if Cadfael was right he was unlikely to come to any harm.

Godric stared, clawed up a sizeable stone, and heaved it heartily. His arm swung far back, swung forward with his slight weight willingly behind it, and hurled the stone under-arm across the brook and into the shallows, with a splash that sent the heron soaring, certainly, but several feet from where he had been standing.

'Well, well!' said Cadfael silently, and settled down to do some hard thinking.

In his siege camp, deployed across the entire land approach to the Castle Foregate, between broad coils of the river Severn, King Stephen fretted, fumed and feasted, celebrating the few loyal Salopians – loyal to him, that is! – who came to offer him aid, and planning his revenge upon the many disloyal who absented themselves.

He was a big, noisy, handsome, simple-minded man, very fair in colouring, very comely in countenance, and at this stage in his fortunes totally bewildered by the contention between his natural

6

good nature and his smarting sense of injury. He was said to be slow-witted, but when his Uncle Henry had died and left no heir but a daughter, and she handicapped by an Angevin husband and far away in France, no matter how slavishly her father's vassals had bowed to his will and accepted her as queen, Stephen for once in his life had moved with admirable speed and precision, and surprised his potential subjects into accepting him at his own valuation before they even had time to consider their own interests, much less remember reluctant vows. So why had such a successful coup abruptly turned sour? He would never understand. Why had half of his more influential subjects, apparently stunned into immobility for a time, revived into revolt now? Conscience? Dislike of the king imposed upon them? Superstitious dread of King Henry and his influence with God?

Forced to take the opposition seriously and resort to arms, Stephen had opened in the way that came naturally to him, striking hard where he must, but holding the door cheerfully open for penitents to come in. And what had been the result? He had spared, and they had taken advantage and despised him for it. He had invited submission without penalty, as he moved north against the rebel holds, and the local baronage had held off from him with contempt. Well, tomorrow's dawn attack should settle the fate of the Shrewsbury garrison, and make an example once for all. If these midlanders would not come peacefully and loyally at his invitation, they should come scurrying like rats to save their own skins. As for Arnulf of Hesdin . . . The obscenities and defiances he had hurled from the towers of Shrewsbury should be regretted bitterly, if briefly.

The king was conferring in his tent in the meads in the late afternoon, with Gilbert Prestcote, his chief aide and sheriff-designate of Salop, and Willem Ten Heyt, the captain of his Flemish mercenaries. It was about the time that Brother Cadfael and the boy Godric were washing their hands and tidying their clothing to go to Vespers. The failure of the local gentry to bring in their own levies to his support had caused Stephen to lean heavily upon his Flemings, who in consequence were very well hated, both as aliens and as impervious professionals, who would as soon burn down a village as get drunk, and were not at all averse to doing both together. Ten Heyt was a huge, well-favoured man with reddish-fair hair and long moustaches, barely thirty years old but a veteran in warfare. Prestcote was a quiet, laconic knight past fifty, experienced and formidable in battle, cautious in counsel, not a man to go to extremes, but even he was arguing for severity.

'Your Grace has tried generosity, and it has been shamelessly exploited to your loss. It's time to strike terror.'

'First,' said Stephen drily, 'to take castle and town.'

'That your Grace may consider as done. What we have mounted for the morning will get you into Shrewsbury. Then, if they survive the assault, your Grace may do what you will with FitzAlan, and Adeney, and Hesdin, and the commons of the garrison are no great matter, but even there you may be well advised to consider an example.'

The king would have been content enough then with his revenge on those three who led the resistance here. William FitzAlan owed his office as sheriff of Salop to Stephen, and yet had declared and held the castle for his rival. Fulke Adeney, the greatest of FitzAlan's vassal lords, had connived at the treason and supported his overlord wholeheartedly. And Hesdin had condemned himself over and over out of his own arrogant mouth. The rest were pawns, expendable but of no importance.

'They are noising it abroad in the town, as I've heard,' said Prestcote, 'that FitzAlan had already sent his wife and children away before we closed the way north out of the town. But Adeney also has a child, a daughter. She's said to be still within the walls. They got the women out of the castle early.' Prestcote was a man of the shire himself, and knew the local baronage at least by name and repute. 'Adeney's girl was betrothed from a child to Robert Beringar's son, of Maesbury, by Oswestry. They had lands neighbouring in those parts. I mention it because this is the man who is asking audience of you now, Hugh Beringar of Maesbury. Use him as you find, your Grace, but until today I would have said he was FitzAlan's man, and your enemy. Have him in and judge for yourself. If he's changed his coat, well and good, he has men enough at his command to be useful, but I would not let him in too easily.'

The officer of the guard had entered the pavilion, and stood waiting to be invited to speak; Adam Courcelle was one of Prestcote's chief tenants and his right-hand man, a tested soldier at thirty years old.

'Your Grace has another visitor,' he said, when the king turned to acknowledge his presence. 'A lady. Will you see her first? She has no lodging here as yet, and in view of the hour . . . She gives her name as Aline Siward, and says that her father, whom she has only recently buried, was always your man.'

'Time presses,' said the king. 'Let them both come, and the lady shall have first word.'

Courcelle led her by the hand into the royal presence, with every mark of deference and admiration, and she was indeed well worth any man's attention. She was slender and shy, and surely no older than eighteen, and the austerity of her mourning, the white cap and wimple from which a few strands of gold hair crept out to frame her cheeks, only served to make her look younger still, and more touching. She had a child's proud, shy dignity. Great eyes the colour of dark irises widened wonderingly upon the king's large comeliness as she made her reverence.

'Madam,' said Stephen, reaching a hand to her, 'I am sorry indeed for your loss, of which I have this minute heard. If my protection can in any way serve you, command me.'

'Your Grace is very kind,' said the girl in a soft, awed voice. 'I am now an orphan, and the only one of my house left to bring you the duty and fealty we owe. I am doing what my father would have wished, and but for his illness and death he would have come himself, or I would have come earlier. Until your Grace came to Shrewsbury we had no opportunity to render you the keys of the two castles we hold. As I do now!'

Her maid, a self-possessed young woman a good ten years older than her mistress, had followed into the tent and stood withdrawn. She came forward now to hand the keys to Aline, who laid them formally in the king's hands.

'We can raise for your Grace five knights, and more than forty men-at-arms, but at this time I have left all to supply the garrisons at home, since they may be of more use to your Grace so.' She named her properties and her castellans. It was like hearing a child recite a lesson learned by heart, but her dignity and gravity were those of a general in the field. 'There is one more thing I should say plainly, and to my much sorrow. I have a brother, who should have been the one to perform this duty and service.' Her voice shook slightly, and gallantly recovered. 'When your Grace assumed the crown, my brother Giles took the part of the Empress Maud, and after an open quarrel with my father, left home to join her party. I do not know where he is now, though we have heard rumours that he

9

made his way to her in France. I could not leave your Grace in
ignorance of the dissension that grieves me as it must you. I
hope you will not therefore refuse what I can bring, but use it
freely, as my father would have wished, and as I wish.'

She heaved a great sigh, as if she had thrown off a weight.
The king was enchanted. He drew her by the hand and kissed
her heartily on the cheek. To judge by the look on his face,
Courcelle was envying him the opportunity.

'God forbid, child,' said the king, 'that I should add any
morsel to your sorrows, or fail to lift what I may of them. With
all my heart I take your fealty, as dear to me as that of earl or
baron, and thank you for your pains taken to help me. And now
show me what I can do to serve you, for there can be no fit
lodging for you here in a military camp, and I hear you have
made no provision as yet for yourself. It will soon be evening.'

'I had thought,' she said timidly, 'that I might lodge in the
abbey guest house, if we can get a boat to put us across the
river.'

'Certainly you shall have safe escort over the river, and our
request to the abbot to give you one of the grace houses belonging to the abbey, where you may be private but protected, until
we can spare a safe escort to see you to your home.' He looked
about him for a ready messenger, and could not well miss Adam
Courcelle's glowing eagerness. The young man had bright chestnut hair, and eyes of the same burning brown, and knew that he
stood well with his king. 'Adam, will you conduct Mistress
Siward, and see her safely installed?'

'With all my heart, your Grace,' said Courcelle fervently, and
offered an ardent hand to the lady.

Hugh Beringar watched the girl pass by, her hand submissive
in the broad brown hand that clasped it, her eyes cast down, her
small, gentle face with its disproportionately large and noble
brow tired and sad now that she had done her errand faithfully.
From outside the royal tent he had heard every word. She
looked now as if she might melt into tears at any moment, like a
little girl after a formal ordeal, a child-bride dressed up to
advertise her riches or her lineage, and then as briskly dismissed
to the nursery when the transaction was assured. The king's
officer walked delicately beside her, like a conqueror conquered,
and no wonder.

'Come, the lord king waits,' said the guttural voice of Willem

Ten Heyt in his ear, and he turned and ducked his head beneath the awning of the tent. The comparative dimness within veiled the large, fair presence of the king.

'I am here, my liege,' said Hugh Beringar, and made his obeisance. 'Hugh Beringar of Maesbury, at your Grace's service with all that I hold. My muster is not great, six knights and some fifty men-at-arms, but half of them bowmen, and skilled. And all are yours.'

'Your name, Master Beringar, is known to us,' said the king drily. 'Your establishment also. That it was devoted to our cause was not so well known. As I have heard of you, you have been an associate of FitzAlan and Adeney, our traitors, until very recently. And even this change of heart comes rather belatedly. I have been some four weeks in these parts, without word from you.'

'Your Grace,' said Beringar, without haste to excuse himself or apparent discomfort at his cool reception, 'I grew up from a child regarding these men whom you understandably name your traitors, as my peers and friends, and in friendship have never found them wanting. Your Grace is too fair-minded a man not to admit that for one like me, who has not so far sworn fealty to any, the choice of a path at this moment may require a deal of thought, if it is to be made once for all. That King Henry's daughter has a reasonable claim is surely beyond question, I cannot call a man traitor for choosing that cause, though I may blame him for breaking his oath to you. As for me, I came into my lands only some months ago, and I have so far sworn fealty to none. I have taken my time in choosing where I will serve. I am here. Those who flock to you without thought may fall away from you just as lightly.'

'And you will not?' said the king sceptically. He was studying this bold and possibly over-fluent young man with critical attention. A lightweight, not above the middle height and slenderly built, but of balanced and assured movement; he might well make up in speed and agility what he lacked in bulk and reach. Perhaps two or three years past twenty, black-avised, with thin, alert features and thick, quirky dark brows. An unchancy fellow, because there was no guessing from his face what went on behind the deep-set eyes. His forthright speech might be honest, or it might be calculated. He looked quite subtle enough to have weighed up his sovereign and reasoned that boldness might not be displeasing.

11

'And I will not,' he said firmly. 'But that need not pass on my word. It can be put to the proof hereafter. I am on your Grace's probation.'

'You have not brought your force with you?'

'Three men only are with me. It would have been folly to leave a good castle unmanned or half-manned, and small service to you to ask that you feed fifty more without due provision for the increase. Your Grace has only to tell me where you would have me serve, and it shall be done.'

'Not so fast,' said Stephen. 'Others may also have need of time and thought before they embrace you, young man. You were close and in confidence with FitzAlan, some time ago.'

'I was. I still have nothing against him but that he has chosen one way, and I the other.'

'And as I hear, you are betrothed to Fulke Adeney's daughter.'

'I hardly know whether to say to that: I am! or: I was! The times have altered a great many plans previously made, for others as well as for me. As at this time, I do not know where the girl is, or whether the bargain still holds.'

'There are said to be no women now in the castle,' said the king, eyeing him closely. 'FitzAlan's family may well be clean away, perhaps out of the country by now. But Adeney's daughter is thought to be in hiding in the town. It would not be displeasing to me,' he said with soft emphasis, 'to have so valuable a lady in safe-keeping – in case even my plans should need to be altered. You were of her father's party, you must know the places likely to be sheltering her now. When the way is clear, you, of all people, should be able to find her.'

The young man gazed back at him with an inscrutable face, in which shrewd black eyes signalled understanding, but nothing more, neither consent nor resistance, no admission at all that he knew he was being set a task on which acceptance and favour might well depend. His face was bland and his voice guileless as he said: 'That is my intent, your Grace. I came from Maesbury with that also in mind.'

'Well,' said Stephen, warily content, 'you may remain in attendance against the town's fall, but we have no immediate work for you here. Should I have occasion to call you, where will you be found?'

'If they have room,' said Beringar, 'at the abbey guest house.'

12

The boy Godric stood through Vespers among the pupils and the novices, far back among the small fry of the house, and close to the laity, such as lived here outside the walls on the hither bank of the river, and could still reach this refuge. He looked, as Brother Cadfael reflected when he turned his head to look for the child, very small and rather forlorn, and his face, bright and impudent enough in the herbarium, had grown very solemn indeed here in church. Night was looming, his first night in this abode. Ah well, his affairs were being taken in hand more consolingly than he supposed, and the ordeal he was bracing himself to master need not confront him at all, if things went right, and at all events not tonight. Brother Paul, the master of the novices, had several other youngsters to look after, and was glad to have one taken firmly off his hands.

Cadfael reclaimed his protégé after supper, at which meal he was glad to see that Godric ate heartily. Evidently the boy was of a mettle to fight back against whatever fears and qualms possessed him, and had the good sense to fortify himself with the things of the flesh for the struggles of the spirit. Even more reassuringly, he looked up with relief and recognition when Cadfael laid a hand on his shoulder as they left the refectory.

'Come, we're free until Compline, and it's cool out in the gardens. No need to stay inside here, unless you wish.'

The boy Godric did not wish, he was happy to escape into the summer evening. They went down at leisure towards the fish ponds and the herbarium, and the boy skipped at Cadfael's side, and burst into a gay whistling, abruptly broken off.

'He said the master of the novices would want me, after supper. Is it really proper for me to come with you, like this?'

'All approved and blessed, child, don't be afraid. I've spoken with Brother Paul, we have his good word. You are my boy, and I am responsible for you.' They had entered the walled garden, and were suddenly engulfed and drowned in all those sun-drenched fragrances, rosemary, thyme, fennel, dill, sage, lavender, a whole world of secret sweetness. The heat of the sun lingered, heady with scent, even into the cool of the evening. Over their heads swifts wheeled and screamed in ecstasy.

They had arrived at the wooden shed, its oiled timbers radiated warmth towards them. Cadfael opened the door. 'This is your sleeping-place. Godric.'

There was a low bench-bed neatly arrayed at the end of the room. The boy stared, and quaked under Cadfael's hand.

'I have all these medicines brewing here, and some of them need tending regularly, some very early, they'd spoil if no one minded them. I'll show you all you have to do, it's not so heavy a task. And here you have your bed, and here a grid you may open for fresh air.' The boy had stopped shaking, the dark blue eyes were large and measuring, and fixed implacably upon Cadfael. There seemed to be a smile pending, but there was also a certain aura of offended pride. Cadfael turned to the door, and showed the heavy bar that guarded it within, and the impossibility of opening it from without, once that was dropped into its socket. 'You may shut out the world and me until you're ready to come out to us.'

The boy Godric, who was not a boy at all, was staring now in direct accusation, half-offended, half-radiant, wholly relieved.

'How did you know?' she demanded, jutting a belligerent chin.

'How were you going to manage in the dortoir?' responded Brother Cadfael mildly.

'I would have managed. Boys are not so clever, I could have cozened them. Under a wall like this,' she said, hoisting handfuls of her ample tunic, 'all bodies look the same, and men are blind and stupid.' She laughed then, viewing Cadfael's placid competence, and suddenly she was all woman, and startlingly pretty in her gaiety and relief. 'Oh, not *you*! How *did* you know? I tried so hard, I thought I could pass all trials. Where did I go wrong?'

'You did very well,' said Cadfael soothingly. 'But, child, I was forty years about the world, and from end to end of it, before I took the cowl and came to my green, sweet ending here. Where did you go wrong? Don't take it amiss, take it as sound advice from an ally, if I answer you. When you came to argument, and meant it with all your heart, you let your voice soar. And never a crack in it, mind you, to cover the change. That can be learned, I'll show you when we have leisure. And then, when I bade you strip and be easy – ah, never blush, child, I was all but certain then! – of course you put me off. And last, when I got you to toss a stone across the brook, you did it like a girl, under-arm, with a round swing. When did you ever see a boy throw like that? Don't let anyone else trick you into such another throw, not until you master the art. It betrays you at once.'

He stood patiently silent then, for she had dropped on to the bed, and sat with her head in her hands, and first she began to laugh, and then to cry, and then both together; and all the while he let her alone, for she was no more out of control than a man tossed between gain and loss, and manfully balancing his books. Now he could believe she was seventeen, a budding woman, and a fine one, too.

When she was ready, she wiped her eyes on the back of her hand, and looked up alertly, smiling like sunlight through a rainbow. 'And did you mean it?' she said. 'That you're responsible for me? I *said* I trusted you to extremes!'

'Daughter dear,' said Cadfael patiently, 'what should I do with you now but serve you as best I can, and see you safe out of here to wherever you would be?'

'And you don't even know who I am,' she said, marvelling. 'Who is trusting too far now?'

'What difference should it make to me, child, what your name may be? A lass left forlorn here to weather out this storm and be restored to her own people – is not that enough? What you want to tell, you'll tell, and I need no more.'

'I think I want to tell you everything,' said the girl simply, looking up at him with eyes wide and candid as the sky. 'My father is either in Shrewsbury castle this minute with his death hanging over him, or out of it and running for his life with William FitzAlan for the empress's lands in Normandy, with a hue and cry ready to be loosed after him any moment. I'm a burden to anyone who befriends me now, and likely to be a hunted hostage as soon as I'm missed from where I should be. Even to you, Brother Cadfael, I could be dangerous. I'm daughter to FitzAlan's chief ally and friend. My name is Godith Adeney.'

Lame Osbern, who had been born with both legs withered, and scuttled around at unbelievable speed on hands provided with wooden pattens, dragging his shrivelled knees behind him on a little wheeled trolley, was the humblest of the king's camp-followers. Normally he had his pitch by the castle gates in the town, but he had forsaken in time a spot now so dangerous, and transferred his hopeful allegiance to the edge of the siege camp, as near as he was allowed to get to the main guard, where the great went in and out. The king was notoriously open-handed, except towards his enemies-at-arms, and the pickings were good. The chief military officers, perhaps, were too preoccupied to waste thought or alms on a beggar, but some of those who came belatedly seeking favour, having decided which way fortune was tending, were apt to give to the poor as a kind of sop to God for luck, and the common bowmen and even the Flemings, when off-duty and merry, tossed Osbern a few coppers, or the scraps from their mess.

He had his little wagon backed well into the lee of a clump of half-grown trees, close to the guard-post, where he might come in for a crust of bread or a drink, and could enjoy the glow of the field-fire at night. Even summer nights can strike chill after the heat of the August day, when you have only a few rags to cover you, and the fire was doubly welcome. They kept it partially turfed, to subdue the glow, but left themselves light enough to scrutinise any who came late.

It was close to midnight when Osbern stirred out of an uneasy sleep, and straining his ears for the reason, caught the rustling of the bushes behind and to his left, towards the Castle Foregate but well aside from the open road. Someone was approaching from the direction of the town, and certainly not from the main gates, but roundabout in cover from along the riverside. Osbern knew the town like his own callused palm. Either this was a scout returning from reconnaissance – but why keep up this stealth right into the camp? – or else someone had crept out of town or castle by the only other way through the wall on this side, the water-port that led down to the river.

A dark figure, visible rather as movement than matter in a moonless night, slid out from the bushes and made at a crouching, silent scurry for the guard-post. At the sentry's challenge he halted immediately, and stood frozen but eager, and Osbern saw the faint outline of a slight, willowy body, wrapped closely in a black cloak, so that only a gleam of pale face showed. The voice that answered the challenge was young, high-pitched, torment-edly afraid and desperately urgent.

'I beg audience – I am not armed! Take me to your officer. I have something to tell – to the king's advantage. . . .'

They hauled him in and went over him roughly to ensure he bore no weapons; and whatever was said between them did not reach Osbern's ears, but the upshot of it was that he had his will. They led him within the camp, and there he vanished from view.

Osbern did not doze again, the cold of the small hours was gnawing through his rags. Such a cloak as that, he thought, shivering, I wish the good God would send me! Yet even the owner of so fine a garment had been shaking, the quavering voice had betrayed his fear, but also his avid hope. A curious incident, but of no profit to a poor beggar. Not, that is, until he saw the same figure emerge from the shadowy alleys of the camp and halt once more at the gate. His step was lighter and longer now, his bearing less furtive and fearful. He bore some token from the authorities that was enough to let him out again as he had entered, unharmed and unmolested. Osbern heard a few words pass: 'I am to go back, there must be no suspicion . . . I have my orders!'

Ah, now, in pure thankfulness for some alleviating mercy, he might be disposed to give. Osbern wheeled himself forward hurriedly into the man's path, and extended a pleading hand.

'For God's love, master! If he has been gracious to you, be gracious to the poor!'

He caught a glimpse of a pale face much eased, heard long breaths of relief and hope. A flicker of firelight caught the elaborate shape of a metal clasp that fastened the cloak at the throat. Out of the muffling folds a hand emerged, and dropped a coin into the extended palm. 'Say some prayers for me to-morrow,' said a low, breathless whisper, and the stranger flitted away as he had come, and vanished into the trees before Osbern had done blessing him for his alms.

Before dawn Osbern was roused again from fitful sleep, to withdraw himself hastily into the bushes out of all men's way. For it was still only the promise of a clear dawn, but the royal camp was astir, so quietly and in such practical order that he felt rather than heard the mustering of men, the ordering of ranks, the checking of weapons. The air of the morning seemed to shake to the tramping of regiments, while barely a sound could be heard. From curve to curve of Severn, across the neck of land that afforded the only dry approach to the town, the steady murmur of activity rippled, awesome and exhilarating, as King Stephen's army turned out and formed its divisions for the final assault of Shrewsbury castle.

CHAPTER TWO

Long before noon it was all over, the gates fired with brush-wood and battered down, the baileys cleared one by one, the last defiant bowman hunted down from the walls and towers, smoke heavy and thick like a pall over fortress and town. In the streets not a human creature or even a dog stirred. At the first assault every man had gone to earth with wife and family and beasts behind locked and barred doors, and crouched listening with stretched ears to the thunder and clash and yelling of battle. It lasted only a short while. The garrison had reached exhaustion, ill-supplied, thinned by desertions as long as there was any possi-bility of escape. Everyone had been certain the next determined attack must carry the town. The merchants of Shrewsbury waited with held breath for the inevitable looting, and heaved sighs of relief when it was called to heel peremptorily by the king himself – not because he grudged his Flemings their booty, but because he wanted them close about his person. Even a king is vulnerable, and this had been an enemy town, and was still unpacified. Moreover, his urgent business was with the garrison of the castle, and in particular with FitzAlan, and Adeney, and Arnulf of Hesdin.

Stephen stalked through the smoky, bloody, steel-littered bailey into the hall, and despatched Courcelle and Ten Heyt and their men with express orders to isolate the ring leaders and bring them before him. Prestcote he kept at his side; the keys were in the new lieutenant's hands, and provisions for the royal garrison were already in consideration.

'In the end,' said Prestcote critically, 'it has cost your Grace fairly low. In losses, certainly. In money – the delay was costly, but the castle is intact. Some repairs to the walls – new gates . . . This is a stronghold you need never lose again, I count it worth the time it took to win it.'

'We shall see,' said Stephen grimly, thinking of Arnulf of Hesdin bellowing his lordly insults from the towers. As though he courted death!

Courcelle came in, his helmet off and his chestnut hair blazing.

A promising officer, alert, immensely strong in personal combat, commanding with his men: Stephen approved him. 'Well, Adam. Are they run to earth? Surely FitzAlan is not hiding somewhere among the barns, like a craven servant?'

'No, your Grace, by no means!' said Courcelle ruefully. 'We have combed this fortress from roof to dungeons, I promise you we have missed nothing. But FitzAlan is clean gone! Give us time, and we'll find for you the day, the hour, the route they took, their plans....'

'*They?*' blazed Stephen, catching at the plural.

'Adeney is away with him. Not a doubt of it, they're loose. Sorry I am to bring your Grace such news, but truth is truth.' And give him his due, he had the guts to utter such truths. 'Hesdin,' he said, 'we have. He is here without. Wounded, but not gravely, nothing but scratched. I put him in irons for safety, but I think he is hardly in such heart as when he lorded it within here, and your Grace was well outside.'

'Bring him in,' ordered the king, enraged afresh to find he had let two of his chief enemies slip through his fingers.

Arnulf of Hesdin came in limping heavily, and dragging chains at wrist and ankle; a big, florid man nearing sixty, soiled with dust, smoke and blood. Two of the Flemings thrust him to his knees before the king. His face was fixed and fearful, but defiant still.

'What, are you tamed?' exulted the king. 'Where's your insolence now? You had plenty to say for yourself only a day or two ago, are you silenced? Or have you the wit to talk another language now?'

'Your Grace,' said Hesdin, grating out words evidently hateful to him, 'you are the victor, and I am at your mercy, and at your feet, and I have fought you fair, and I look to be treated honourably now. I am a nobleman of England and of France. You have need of money, and I am worth an earl's ransom, and I can pay it.'

'Too late to speak me fair, you who were loud-mouthed and foul-mouthed when there were walls between us. I swore to have your life then, and have it I will. An earl's ransom cannot buy it back. Shall I quote you my price? Where is FitzAlan? Where is Adeney? Tell me in short order where I may lay hands on those two, and better pray that I succeed, and I may – *may!* – consider letting you keep your miserable life.'

19

Hesdin reared his head and stared the king in the eyes. 'I find your price too high,' he said. 'Only one thing I'll tell you concerning my comrades, they did not run from you until all was already lost. And live or die, that's all you'll get from me. Go hunt your own noble game!'

'We shall see!' flared the king, infuriated. 'We shall see whether we get no more from you! Have him away, Adam, give him to Ten Heyt, and see what can be done with him. Hesdin, you have until two of the clock to tell us everything you know concerning their flight, or else I hang you from the battlements. Take him away!'

They dragged him out still on his knees. Stephen sat fuming and gnawing his knuckles. 'Is it true, you think, Prestcote, the one thing he did say? That they fled only when the fight was already lost? Then they may well be still in the town. How could they break through? Not by the Foregate, clean through our ranks. And the first companies within were sped straight for the two bridges. Somewhere in this island of a town they must be hiding. Find them!'

'They could not have reached the bridges,' said Prestcote positively. 'There's only one other way out, and that's by the water-gate to the river. I doubt if they could have swum Severn there without being seen, I am sure they had no boat. Most likely they are in hiding somewhere in the town.'

'Scour it! Find them! No looting until I have them safe in hold. Search everywhere, but find them.'

While Ten Heyt and his Flemings rounded up the prisoners taken in arms, and disposed the new garrison under Prestcote's orders, Courcelle and others with their companies pressed on through the town, confirmed the security of the two bridges, and set about searching every house and shop within the walls. The king, his conquest assured, returned to his camp with his own bodyguard, and waited grimly for news of his two fugitives. It was past two o'clock when Courcelle reported back to him.

'Your Grace,' he said bluntly, 'there is no better word than failure to bring you. We have searched every street, every officer and merchant of the town has been questioned, all premises ransacked. It is not such a great town, and unless by some miracle I do not see how they can well have got outside the walls unseen. But we have not found them, neither FitzAlan nor Adeney, nor trace nor word of them. In case they've swum the river and got clear beyond the Abbey Foregate, I've sent out a fast patrol that way, but I doubt if we shall hear of them now. And Hesdin is obdurate still. Not a word to be got from him, and Ten Heyt has done his best, short of killing too soon. We shall get nothing from him. He knows the penalty. Threats will do nothing.'

'He shall have what he was promised,' said Stephen grimly. 'And the rest? How many were taken of the garrison?'

'Apart from Hesdin, ninety-three in arms.' Courcelle watched the handsome, frowning face; bitterly angry and frustrated as the king was, he was unlikely to keep his grudges hot too long. They had been telling him for weeks that it was a fault in him to forgive too readily. 'Your Grace, clemency now would be taken for weakness,' said Courcelle emphatically.

'Hang them!' said Stephen, jerking out sentence harshly before he wavered.

'All?'

'All! And at once. Have them all out of the world before tomorrow.'

They gave the grisly work to the Flemings to do. It was what mercenaries were for, and it kept them busy all that day, and out of the houses of the town, which otherwise would have been pillaged of everything of value. The interlude, dreadful as it was, gave the guilds and the reeve and the bailiffs time to muster a hasty delegation of loyalty to the king, and obtain at least a grim and sceptical motion of grace. He might not believe in their sudden devotion, but he could appreciate its urgency.

Prestcote deployed his new garrison and made all orderly in the castle below, while Ten Heyt and his companies despatched the old garrison wholesale from the battlements. Arnulf of Hesdin was the first to die. The second was a young squire who had had a minor command under him; he was in a state of frenzied dread, and was hauled to his death yelling and protesting that he had been promised his life. The Flemings who handled him spoke little English, and were highly diverted by his pleadings, until the noose cut them off short.

Adam Courcelle confessed himself only too glad to get away from the slaughter, and pursue his searches to the very edges of the town, and across the bridges into the suburbs. But he found no trace of William FitzAlan or Fulke Adeney.

From the morning's early alarm to the night's continuing slaughter, a chill hush of horror hung over the abbey of St Peter and St Paul. Rumours flew thick as bees in swarm, no one knew what was really happening, but everyone knew that it would be terrible. The brothers doggedly pursued their chosen régime, service after service, chapter and Mass and the hours of work, because life could only be sustained by refusing to let it be disrupted, by war, catastrophe or death. To the Mass after chapter came Aline Siward with her maid Constance, pale and anxious and heroically composed; and perhaps as a result, Hugh Beringar also attended, for he had observed the lady passing from the house she had been given in the Foregate, close to the abbey's main mill. During the service he paid rather more attention to the troubled, childish profile beneath the white mourning wimple than to the words of the celebrant.

Her small hands were devoutly folded, her resolute, vulnerable lips moved silently, praying piteously for all those dying and being hurt while she knelt here. The girl Constance watched her closely and jealously, a protective presence, but could not drive the war away from her.

Beringar followed at a distance until she re-entered her house. He did not seek to overtake her, nor attempt as yet to speak to her. When she had vanished, he left his henchmen behind, and went out along the Foregate to the end of the bridge. The section that drew up was still lifted, sealing in the town, but the clamour and shrieking of battle was already subsiding to his right, where the castle loomed in its smoky halo beyond the river. He would still have to wait before he could carry out his promised search for his affianced bride. Within the hour, if he had read the signs aright, the bridge should be down, and open. Meantime, he went at leisure to take his midday meal. There was no hurry.

Rumours flew in the guest house, as everywhere else. Those who had business of unimpeachable honesty elsewhere were all seeking to pack their bags and leave. The consensus of opinion was that the castle had certainly fallen, and the cost would run very high. King Stephen's writ had better be respected henceforth, for he was here, and victorious, and the Empress Maud, however legitimate her claim, was far away in Normandy, and unlikely to provide any adequate protection. There were whispers, also, that FitzAlan and Adeney, at the last moment, had broken out of the trap and were away. For which many breathed thanks, though silently.

When Beringar went out again, the bridge was down, the way open, and King Stephen's sentries manning the passage. They were strict in scrutinising his credentials, but passed him within respectfully when they were satisfied. Stephen must have given orders concerning him. He crossed, and entered at the guarded but open gate in the wall. The street rose steeply, the island town sat high. Beringar knew it well, and knew where he was bound. At the summit of the hill the row of the butchers' stalls and houses levelled out, silent and deserted.

Edric Flesher's shop was the finest of the row, but it was shuttered and still like all the rest. Hardly a head looked out, and even then only briefly and fearfully, and was withdrawn as abruptly behind barred doors. By the look of the street, they had not so far been ravaged. Beringar thudded at the shut door, and when he heard furtive stirrings within, lifted his voice: 'Open to me, Hugh Beringar! Edric – Petronilla – Let me in, I'm alone!'

He had half expected that the door would remain sealed like a tomb, and those within silent, and he would not have blamed them; but, instead, the door was flung wide, and there was Petronilla beaming and opening her arms to him as if to a saviour. She was getting old, but still plump, succulent and kindly, the most wholesome thing he had seen in this siege town so far. Her grey hair was tight and neat under its white cap, and her twinkling grey eyes bright and intelligent as ever, welcoming him in.

'Master Hugh – to see a known and trusted face here now!' Beringar was instantly sure that she did not quite trust him! 'Come in, and welcome! Edric, here's Hugh – Hugh Beringar!' And there was her husband, prompt to her call, large and rubicund and competent, the master of his craft in this town, and a councillor.

They drew him within, and closed the door firmly, as he noted and approved. Beringar said what a lover should say, without preamble: 'Where is Godith? I came to look for her, to provide for her. Where has he hidden her?'

It seemed they were too intent on making sure the shutters were fast, and listening for hostile footsteps outside, to pay

23

immediate attention to what he was saying. And too ready with questions of their own to answer his questions.

'Are you hunted?' asked Edric anxiously. 'Do you need a place to hide?'

And: 'Were you in the garrison?' demanded Petronilla, and patted him concernedly in search of wounds. As though she had been his nurse once, instead of Godith's, and seen him every day of his life instead of twice or thrice since the childhood betrothal. A little too much solicitude! And a neat, brief breathing-space while they considered how much or how little to tell him!

'They've been hunting here already,' said Edric. 'I doubt if they'll come again, they had the place to pieces after the sheriff and the Lord Fulke. You're welcome to a shelter here if you need it. Are they close on your heels?'

He was sure by that time that they knew he had never been inside the castle, nor committed in any way to FitzAlan's stand. This clever, trusted old servant and her husband had been deep in Adeney's confidence, they knew very well who had held with him, and who had held aloof.

'No, it's not that, I'm in no danger and no need. I came only to look for Godith. They're saying he left it too late to send her away with FitzAlan's family. Where can I find her?'

'Did someone send you here to look for her?' asked Edric.

'No, no, none . . . But where else would he place her? Who is there to be trusted like her nurse? Of course I came first to you! Never tell me she was not here!'

'She was here,' said Petronilla. 'Until a week ago we had her. But she's gone, Hugh, you're too late. He sent two knights to fetch her away, and not even we were told where she was bound. What we don't know we can't be made to tell, he said. But it's my belief they got her away out of the town in good time, and she's far off by now, and safe, pray God!' No doubt about the fervency of that prayer, she would fight and die for her nurseling. And lie for her, too, if need be!

'But for God's sake, friends, can you not help me to her at all? I'm her intended husband. I'm responsible for her if her father is dead, as by now, for all I know, he may well be. . . .'

That got him something for his trouble, at any rate, if it was no more than the flicker of a glance passing between them, before they exclaimed their 'God forbid!' in unison. They knew

24

very well, by the frenzied search, that FitzAlan and Adeney had been neither killed nor taken. They could not yet be sure that they were clean away and safe, but they were staking their lives and loyalty on it. So now he knew he would get nothing more from them, he, the renegade. Not, at any rate, by this direct means.

'Sorry I am, lad,' said Edric Flesher weightily, 'to have no better comfort for you, but so it is. Take heart that at least no enemy has laid hand on her, and we pray none ever will.' Which could well be taken, reflected Beringar whimsically, as a thrust at me.

'Then I must away, and try what I can discover elsewhere,' he said dejectedly. 'I'll not put you in further peril. Open, Petronilla, and look if the street's empty for me.' Which she did, nothing loth, and reported it as empty as a beggar's palm. Beringar clasped Edric's hand, and leaned and kissed Edric's wife, and was rewarded and avenged by a vivid, guilty blush.

'Pray for her,' he said, asking one thing at least they would not grudge him, and slipped through the half-open door, and heard it closed firmly behind him. Not too loudly, since he was supposed to be affecting stealth, but still audibly, he tramped with hasty steps along the street as far as the corner of the house. Then, whirling, he skipped back silently on his toes to lay an ear to the shutter.

'Hunting for his bride!' Petronilla was saying scornfully. 'Yes, and a fair price he'd pay for her, too, and she a certain decoy for her father's return, if not for FitzAlan's! He has his way to make with Stephen now, and my girl's his best weapon.'

'Maybe we're too hard on him,' responded Edric mildly. 'Who's to say he doesn't truly want to see the girl safe? But I grant you we dared take no chances. Let him do his own hunting.'

'Thank God,' she said fiercely, 'he can't well know I've hid my lamb away in the one place where no sane man will look for her!' And she chuckled at the word 'man'. 'There'll be a time to get her out of there later, when all the hue and cry's forgotten. Now I pray her father's miles from here and riding hard. And that those two lads in Frankwell will have a lucky run westward with the sheriff's treasury tonight. May they all come safe to Normandy, and be serviceable to the empress, bless her!'

'Hush, love!' said Edric chidingly. 'Even behind locked doors . . .'

They had moved away into an inner room; a door closed between. Hugh Beringar abandoned his listening-post and walked demurely away down the long, curving hill to the town gate and the bridge, whistling softly and contentedly as he went. He had got more even than he had bargained for. So they were hoping to smuggle out FitzAlan's treasury, as well as his person, and this very night, westward into Wales! And had had the forethought to stow it away meantime, against this desperate contingency, outside the walls of the town, somewhere in the suburb of Frankwell. No gates to pass, no bridges to cross. As for Godith – he had a shrewd idea now where to look for her. With the girl *and* the money, he reflected, a man could buy the favour of far less corruptible men than King Stephen!

Godith was in the herbarium workshop, obstinately stirring, diluting and mixing as she had been shown, an hour before Vespers, with her heart in anguished suspense, and her mind in a twilight between hope and despair. Her face was grubby from smearing away tears with a hand still soiled from the garden, and her eyes were rimmed with the washed hollows and grimed uplands of her grief and tension. Two tears escaped from her angry efforts at damming them, while both hands were occupied, and fell into a brew which should not have been weakened. Godith swore, an oath she had learned in the mews, long ago, when the falconers were suffering from a careless and impudent apprentice who had been her close friend.

'Rather say a blessing with them,' said Brother Cadfael's voice behind her shoulder, gently and easily. 'That's likely to be the finest tisane for the eyes I ever brewed. Never doubt God was watching.' She had turned her dirty, dogged, appealing face to him in silence, finding encouragement in the very tone of his voice. 'I've been to the gate house, and the mill, and the bridge. Such ill news as there is, is ill indeed, and presently we'll go pray for the souls of those quitting this world. But all of us quit it at last, by whatever way, that's not the worst of evils. And there is some news not all evil. From all I can hear this side Severn, and at the bridge itself – there's an archer among the guard there was with me in the Holy Land – your father and FitzAlan are neither dead, wounded nor captive, and all search of the town

26

has failed to find them. They're clear away, Godric, my lad. I doubt if Stephen for all his hunting will lay hand on them now. And now you may tend to that wine you're watering, and practise your young manhood until we can get you safely out of here after your sire.'

Just for a moment she rained tears like the spring thaw, and then she glinted radiance like the spring sun. There was so much to grieve over, and so much to celebrate, she did not know which to do first, and essayed both together, like April. But her age was April, and the hopeful sunshine won.

'Brother Cadfael,' she said when she was calm, 'I wish my father could have known you. And yet you are not of his persuasion, are you?'

'Child dear,' said Cadfael comfortably, 'my monarch is neither Stephen nor Maud, and in all my life and all my fighting I've fought for only one king. But I value devotion and fidelity, and doubt if it matters whether the object falls short. What you do and what you are is what matters. Your loyalty is as sacred as mine. Now wash your face and bathe your eyes, and you can sleep for half an hour before Vespers – but no, you're too young to have the gift!'

She had not the gift that comes with age, but she had the exhaustion that comes of youthful stress, and she fell asleep on her bench-bed within seconds, drugged with the syrup of relief. He awoke her in time to cross the close for Vespers. She walked beside him discreetly, her shock of clipped curls combed forward on her brow to hide her still reddened eyes.

Driven to piety by shock and terror, all the inhabitants of the guest house were also converging on the church, among them Hugh Beringar; not, perhaps, a victim of fear, but drawn by the delicate bait of Aline Siward, who came hastening from her house by the mill with lowered eyes and heavy heart. Beringar had, none the less, a quick eye for whatever else of interest might be going on round about him. He saw the two oddly contrasted figures coming in from the gardens, the squat, solid, powerful middle-aged monk with the outdoor tan and the rolling, seaman's gait, with his hand protectively upon the shoulder of a slip of a boy in a cotte surely inherited from an older and larger kinsman, a barelegged, striding youth squinting warily through a bush of brown hair. Beringar looked, and considered;

27

he smiled, but so inwardly that on his long, mobile mouth the smile hardly showed.

Godith controlled both her face and her pace, and gave no sign of recognition. In the church she strolled away to join her fellow-pupils, and even exchange a few nudges and grins with them. If he was still watching, let him wonder, doubt, change his mind. He had not seen her for more than five years. Whatever his speculations, he could not be sure. Nor was he watching this part of the church, she noted; his eyes were on the unknown lady in mourning most of the time. Godith began to breathe more easily, and even allowed herself to examine her affianced bridegroom almost as attentively as he was observing Aline Siward. When last seen, he had been a coltish boy of eighteen, all elbows and knees, not yet in full command of his body. Now he had a cat's assured and contemptuous grace, and a cool, aloof way with him. A presentable enough fellow, she owned critically, but no longer of interest to her, or possessed of any rights in her. Circumstances alter fortunes. She was relieved to see that he did not look in her direction again.

All the same, she told Brother Cadfael about it, as soon as they were alone together in the garden after supper, and her evening lesson with the boys was over. Cadfael took it gravely.

'So that's the fellow you were to marry! He came here straight from the king's camp, and has certainly joined the king's party, though according to Brother Dennis, who collects all the gossip that's going among his guests, he's on sufferance as yet, and has to prove himself before he'll get a command.' He scrubbed thoughtfully at his blunt, brown nose, and pondered. 'Did it seem to you that he recognised you? Or even looked over-hard at you, as if you reminded him of someone known?'

'I thought at first he did give me a hard glance, as though he might be wondering. But then he never looked my way again, or showed any interest. No, I think I was mistaken. He doesn't know me. I've changed in five years, and in this guise . . . In another year,' said Godith, astonished and almost alarmed at the thought, 'we should have been married.'

'I don't like it!' said Cadfael, brooding. 'We shall have to keep you well out of his sight. If he wins his way in with the king, maybe he'll leave here with him in a week or so. Until then, keep far from the guest house or the stables, or the gate house, or anywhere he may be. Never let him set eyes on you if you can avoid.'

'I know!' said Godith, shaken and grave. 'If he does find me he may turn me to account for his own advancement. I do know! Even if my father had reached shipboard, he would come back and surrender himself, if I were threatened. And then he would die, as all those poor souls over there have died. . . .' She could not bear to turn her head to look towards the towers of the castle, hideously ornamented. They were dying there still, though she did not know it; the work went on well into the hours of darkness. 'I will avoid him, like the plague,' she said fervently, 'and pray that he'll leave soon.'

Abbot Heribert was an old, tired and peace-loving man, and disillusionment with the ugly tendencies of the time, combined with the vigour and ambition of his prior, Robert, had disposed him to withdraw from the world ever deeper into his own private consolations of the spirit. Moreover, he knew he was in disfavour with the king, like all those who had been slow to rally to him with vociferous support. But confronted with an unmistakable duty, however monstrous, the abbot could still muster courage enough to rise to the occasion. There were ninety-four dead or dying men being disposed of like animals, and every one had a soul, and a right to proper burial, whatever his crimes and errors. The Benedictines of the abbey were the natural protectors of those rights, and Heribert did not intend King Stephen's felons to be shovelled haphazard and nameless into an unmarked grave. All the same, he shrank from the horror of the task, and looked about him for someone more accomplished in these hard matters of warfare and bloodshed than himself, to lend support. And the obvious person was Brother Cadfael, who had crossed the world in the first Crusade, and afterwards spent ten years as a sea captain about the coasts of the Holy Land, where fighting hardly ever ceased.

After Compline, Abbot Heribert sent for Cadfael to his private parlour.

'Brother, I am going – now, this night – to ask King Stephen for his leave and authority to give Christian burial to all those slaughtered prisoners. If he consents, tomorrow we must take up their poor bodies, and prepare them decently for the grave.

There will be some who can be claimed by their own families, the rest we shall bury honourably with the rites due to them. Brother, you have yourself been a soldier. Will you – if I speed with the king – will you take charge of this work?'

'Not gladly, but with all my heart, for all that,' said Brother Cadfael, 'yes, Father, I will.'

CHAPTER THREE

'Yes, I will,' said Godith, 'if that's how I can best be useful to you. Yes, I will go to my morning lesson and my evening lesson, eat my dinner without a word or a look to anyone, and then make myself scarce and shut myself up here among the potions. Yes, and drop the bar on the door, if need be, and wait until I hear your voice before I open again. Of course I'll do as you bid. But for all that, I wish I could go with you. These are my father's people and my people, I wish I could have some small part in doing them these last services.'

'Even if it were safe for you to venture there,' said Cadfael firmly, 'and it is not, I would not let you go. The ugliness that man can do to man might cast a shadow between you and the certainty of the justice and mercy God can do to him hereafter. It takes half a lifetime to reach the spot where eternity is always visible, and the crude injustice of the hour shrivels out of sight. You'll come to it when the time's right. No, you stay here and keep well out of Hugh Beringar's way.'

He had even thought of recruiting that young man into his working-party of able-bodied and devoutly inclined helpers, to make sure that he spent the day away from anywhere Godith might be. Whether in a bid to acquire merit for their own souls, out of secret partisan sympathy with the dead men's cause, or to search anxiously for friends or kin, three of the travellers in the guest house had volunteered their aid, and it might have been possible, with such an example, to inveigle others, even Beringar, into feeling obliged to follow suit. But it seemed that the young man was already out and away on horseback, perhaps dancing hopeful attendance on the king; a newcomer seeking office can't afford to let his face be forgotten. He had also ridden out the previous evening, as soon as Vespers was over, so said the lay brothers in the stables. His three men-at-arms were here, idling their day away with nothing to do once the horses were groomed, fed and exercised, but they saw no reason why they should involve themselves in an activity certainly unpleasant, and possibly displeasing to the king. Cadfael could not blame them. He had a muster of twenty, brothers, lay brothers and the three benevolent travellers, when they set out across the bridge and through the streets of the town to the castle.

Probably King Stephen had been glad enough to have a service offered voluntarily which he might otherwise have had to impose by order. Someone had to bury the dead, or the new garrison would be the first to suffer, and in an enclosed fortress in a tightly walled town disease can fester and multiply fearfully. All the same, the king would perhaps never forgive Abbot Heribert for the implied reproach, and the reminder of his Christian duty. Howbeit, the old man had brought back the needful authority; Cadfael's party was passed through the gates without question, and Cadfael himself admitted to Prestcote's presence.

'Your lordship will have had orders about us,' he said briskly. 'We are here to take charge of the dead, and I require clean and adequate space where they may be decently laid until we take them away for burial. If we may draw water from the well, that's all besides that we need ask. Linen we have brought with us.'

'The inner ward has been left empty,' said Prestcote indifferently. 'There is room there, and there are boards you may use if you need them.'

'The king has also granted that such of these unfortunates as were men of this town, and have families or neighbours here, can be claimed and taken away for private burial. Will you have that cried through the town, when I am satisfied that all is ready? And give them free passage in and out?'

'If there are any bold enough to come,' said Prestcote drily, 'they may have their kin and welcome. The sooner all this carrion is removed, the better shall I be pleased.'

'Very well! Then what have you done with them?' For the walls and towers had been denuded before dawn of their sudden crop of sorry fruit. The Flemings must have worked half the night to put the evidence out of sight, which was surely not their idea, but might well be Prestcote's. He had approved these deaths, he did not therefore have to take pleasure in them, and he was an old soldier of strict and orderly habits, who liked a clean garrison.

'We cut them down, when they were well dead, and dropped them over the parapet into the green ditch under the wall. Go out by the Foregate, and between the towers and the road you'll find them.'

Cadfael inspected the small ward offered him, and it was at least clean and private, and had room for all. He led his party out through the gate in the town wall, and down into the deep, dry ditch beneath the towers. Long, fruiting grasses and low bushes partially hid what on closer approach looked like a battle-field. The dead lay piled deep at one spot close under the wall, and were sprawled and scattered like broken toys for yards on either side. Cadfael and his helpers tucked up their gowns and went to work in pairs, without word spoken, disentangling the knotted skein of bodies, carrying away first the most accessible, lifting apart those shattered into boneless embraces by their fall from above. The sun climbed high, and the heat was reflected upon them from the stone of the walls. The three pious travellers shed their cottes. In the deep hollow the air grew heavy and stifling, and they sweated and laboured for breath, but never flagged.

'Pay close attention always,' said Cadfael warningly, 'in case some poor soul still breathes. They were in haste, they may have cut someone down early. And in this depth of cushioning below, a man could survive even the fall.'

But the Flemings, for all their hurry, had been thorough. There was no live man salvaged out of that massacre.

They had started work early, but it was approaching noon by the time they had all the dead laid out in the ward, and were beginning the work of washing and composing the bodies as becomingly as possible, straightening broken limbs, closing and weighting eyelids, even brushing tangled hair into order, and binding fallen jaws, so that the dead face might be no horror to some unfortunate parent or wife who had loved it in life. Before he would go to Prestcote and ask for the promised proclamation to be made, Cadfael walked the range of his salvaged children, and checked that they were as presentable as they could well be made. And as he paced, he counted. At the end he frowned, and stood to consider, then went back and counted again. And that done, he began a much closer scrutiny of all those he had not himself handled, drawing down the linen wrappings that covered the worst ravages. When he rose from the last of them, his face was grim, and he marched away in search of Prestcote without a word to any.

33

'How many,' demanded Cadfael, 'did you say you despatched at the king's order?'

'Ninety-four,' said Prestcote, puzzled and impatient.

'Either you did not count,' said Cadfael, 'or you miscounted. There are ninety-five here.'

'Ninety-four or ninety-five,' said Prestcote, exasperated, 'one more or less, what does it matter? Traitors all, and condemned, am I to tear my hair because the number does not tally?'

'Not you, perhaps,' said Cadfael simply, 'but God will require an accounting. Ninety-four, including Arnulf of Hesdin, you had orders to slay. Justified or not, that at least was ordered, you had your sanction, the thing is registered and understood. Any accounting for those comes later and in another court. But the ninety-fifth is not in the reckoning, no king authorised his removal out of this world, no castellan had orders to kill him, never was he accused or convicted of rebellion, treason or any other crime, and the man who destroyed him is guilty of murder.'

'God's wounds!' exploded Prestcote violently. 'An officer in the heat of fighting miscounts by one, and you would make a *coram rege* case out of it! He was omitted in the count delivered, but he was taken in arms and hanged like the rest, and no more than his deserts. He rebelled like the rest, he is hanged like the rest, and that's an end of it. In God's name, man, what do you want me to do?'

'It would be well,' said Cadfael flatly, 'if you would come and look at him, to begin with. For he is *not* like the rest. He was not hanged like the rest, his hands were not bound like the rest – he is in no way comparable, though someone took it for granted we would all see and think as you, and omit to count. I am telling you, my lord Prestcote, there is a murdered man among your executed men, a leaf hidden in your forest. And if you regret that my eyes found him, do you think God had not seen him long before? And supposing you could silence me, do you think God will keep silence?'

Prestcote had stopped pacing by that time, and stood staring very intently. 'You are in good earnest,' he said, shaken. 'How could there be a man there dead in some other way? Are you sure of what you say?'

'I am sure. Come and see! He is there because some felon

34

put him there, to pass for one among the many, and arouse no curiosity, and start no questions.'

'Then he would need to know that the many would be there.'

'Most of this town and all this garrison would know that, by nightfall. This was a deed of night. Come and see!'

And Prestcote went with him, and showed every sign of consternation and concern. But so would a guilty man, and who was better placed to know all a guilty man needed to know, to protect himself? Still, he kneeled with Cadfael beside the body that was different, there in the confines of the ward, between high walls, with the odour of death just spreading its first insidious pall over them.

A young man, this. No armour on him, but naturally the rest had been stripped of theirs, mail and plate being valuable. But his dress was such as to suggest that he had worn neither mail nor leather, he was clad in lightweight, dark cloth, but booted, the manner of dress a man would wear for a journey in summer weather, to ride light, be warm enough by night, and shed the short cotte to be cool enough by day. He looked about twenty-five years old, no more, reddish brown in colouring and round and comely of face, if the eye could make allowance for the congestion of strangulation, now partially smoothed out by Cadfael's experienced fingers. The bulge and stare of the eyes was covered, but the lids stood large.

'He died strangled,' said Prestcote, relieved to see the signs.

'He did, but not by a rope. And not with hands bound, like these others. Look!' Cadfael drew down the folds of the capuchon from the round young throat, and showed the sharp, cruel line that seemed to sever head from body. 'You see the thinness of this cord that took his life? No man ever dangled from such a noose. It runs level round his neck, and is fine as fishing line. It may well have been fishing line. You see the edges of this furrow in his flesh, discoloured, and shiny? The cord that killed him was waxed, to bite smooth and deep. And you see this pit here behind?' He raised the lifeless head gently on his arm, and showed, close to the knotted cord of the spine, a single, deep, bruised hollow, with a speck of black blood at its heart. 'The mark of one end of a wooden peg, a hand-hold to twist when the cord was round the victim's throat. Stranglers use such waxed cords, with two hand-holds at the ends – killers by stealth, highway birds of prey. Given strength of hand and

35

wrist, it is a very easy way of seeing your enemies out of this world. And do you see, my lord, how his neck, where the thong bites, is lacerated and beaded with dried blood? Now see here, both hands – Look at his nails, black at the tips with his own blood. He clawed at the cord that was killing him. His hands were free. Did you hang any whose hands were not tied?'

'No!' Prestcote was so fascinated by the details he could not deny that the answer escaped him involuntarily. It would have been futile to snatch it back. He looked up at Brother Cadfael across the unknown young man's body, and his face sharpened and hardened into hostility. 'There is nothing to be gained,' he said deliberately, 'by making public so wild a tale. Bury your dead and be content. Let the rest be!'

'You have not considered,' said Cadfael mildly, 'that as yet there is no one who can put a name or a badge to this boy. He may as well be an envoy of the king as an enemy. Better treat him fairly, and keep your peace with both God and man. Also,' he said, in a tone even more cloistrally innocent, 'you may raise doubts of your own integrity if you meddle with truth. If I were you, I would report this faithfully, and send out that proclamation to the townsfolk at once, for we are ready. Then, if any can claim this young man, you have delivered your soul. And if not, then clearly you have done all man can do to right a wrong. And your duty ends there.'

Prestcote eyed him darkly for some moments, and then rose abruptly from his knees. 'I will send out the word,' he said, and stalked away into the hall.

The news was cried through the town, and word sent formally to the abbey, so that the same announcement might be made at the guest house there. Hugh Beringar, riding in from the east on his return from the king's camp, having forded the river at an island downstream, heard the proclamation at the gate house of the abbey, and saw among those anxiously listening the slight figure of Aline Siward, who had come out from her house to hear the news. For the first time he saw her with head uncovered. Her hair was the light, bright gold he had imagined it would be, and shed a few curling strands on either side her oval face. The long lashes shadowing her eyes were many shades darker, a rich bronze. She stood listening intently, gnawed a doubtful lip, and

36

knotted her small hands together. She looked hesitant, and burdened, and very young.

Beringar dismounted only a few paces from her, as if he had by mere chance chosen that spot in order to be still and hear to the end what Prior Robert was saying.

' – and his Grace the king gives free warranty to any who may wish, to come and claim their kin, if there be any such among the executed, and give them burial in their own place and at their own charge. Also, since there is one in particular whose identity is not known, he desires that all who come may view him, and if they can, name him. All which may be done without fear of penalty or disfavour.'

Not everyone would take that at its face value, but she did. What was troubling her was not fear of any consequences to herself, but a desperate feeling that she ought to make this dolorous pilgrimage, while equally earnestly she shrank from the horrors she might have to see. She had, Beringar remembered, a brother who had defied his father and run off to join the empress's adherents; and though she had heard rumours that he might have reached France, she had no means of knowing if they were true. Now she was struggling to escape the conviction that wherever there were garrisons of her brother's faction fallen victims of this civil war, she ought to go and assure herself that he was not among them. She had the most innocent and eloquent of faces, her every thought shone through.

'Madam,' said Beringar, very softly and respectfully, 'if there is any way I can be of service to you, I beg you command me.'

She turned to look at him, and smiled, for she had seen him in church, and knew him to be a guest here like herself, and stress had turned Shrewsbury into a town where people behaved to one another either as loyal neighbours or potential informers, and of the latter attitude she was incapable. Nevertheless, he saw fit to establish his credentials. 'You will remember I came to offer the king my troth when you did. My name is Hugh Beringar of Maesbury. It would give me pleasure to serve you. And it seemed to me that you were finding cause for perplexity and distress in what we have just heard. If there is any errand I can do for you, I will, gladly.'

'I do remember you,' said Aline, 'and I take your offer very kindly, but this is something only I can do, if it must be done. No one else here would know my brother's face. To tell the truth, I was hesitating . . . But there will be women from the town, I know, going there with certain knowledge to find their sons. If they can do it, so can I.'

'But you have no good reason,' he said, 'to suppose that your brother may be among these unfortunates.'

'None, except that I don't know *where* he is, and I do know he embraced the empress's cause. It would be better, wouldn't it, to be sure? Not to miss any possibility? As often as I do not find him dead, I may hope to see him again alive.'

'Was he very dear to you?' asked Beringar gently.

She hesitated to answer that, taking it very gravely. 'No, I never knew him as sister should know brother. Giles was always for his own friends and his own way, and five years my elder. By the time I was eleven or twelve he was for ever away from home, and came back only to quarrel with my father. But he is the only brother I have, and *I* have not disinherited him. And they're saying there's one there more than they counted, and unknown.'

'It will not be Giles,' he said firmly.

'But if it were? Then he needs his name, and his sister to do what's right.' She had made up her mind. 'I must go.'

'I think you should not. But I am sure you should not go alone.' He thought ruefully that her answer to that would be that she had her maid to accompany her, but instead she said at once: 'I will not take Constance into such a scene! She has no kin there, and why should she have to suffer it as well as I?'

'Then, if you will have me, I will go with you.'

He doubted if she had any artifice in her; certainly at this pass she showed none. Her anxious face brightened joyfully, she looked at him with the most ingenuous astonishment, hope and gratitude. But she still hesitated. 'That is kind indeed, but I can't let you do it. Why should you be subjected to such pain, just because I have a duty?'

'Oh, come now!' he said indulgently, sure of himself and of her. 'I shall not have a moment's peace if you refuse me and go alone. But if you tell me I shall only be adding to your distress by insisting, then I'll be silent and obey you. On no other condition.'

It was more than she could do. Her lips quivered. 'No – it would be a lie. I am not very brave!' she said sadly. 'I shall be grateful indeed.'

He had what he had wanted; he made the most of it. Why ride, when the walk through the town could be made to last so much longer, and provide so much more opportunity to get to know her better? Hugh Beringar sent his horse to the stables, and set out with Aline along the highway and over the bridge into Shrewsbury.

Brother Cadfael was standing guard over his murdered man in a corner of the inner ward, beside the archway, where every citizen who came in search of child or kinsman must pass close, and could be questioned. But all he got so far was mute shaking of heads and glances half-pitying, half-relieved. No one knew the young man. And how could he expect great concern from these poor souls who came looking, every one, for some known face, and barely saw the rest?

Prestcote had made good his word, there was no tally kept of those who came, and no hindrance placed in their way, or question asked of them. He wanted his castle rid of its grim reminders as quickly as possible. The guard, under Adam Courcelle, had orders to remain unobtrusive, even to help if that would get the unwelcome guests off the premises by nightfall.

Cadfael had persuaded every man of the guard to view his unknown, but none of them could identify him. Courcelle had frowned down at the body long and sombrely, and shaken his head.

'I never saw him before, to my knowledge. What can there possibly have been about a mere young squire like this, to make someone hate him enough to kill?'

'There can be murders without hate,' said Cadfael grimly. 'Footpads and forest robbers take their victims as they come, without any feeling of liking or disliking.'

'Why, what can such a youth have had to make him worth killing for gain?'

'Friend,' said Cadfael, 'there are those in the world would kill for the few coins a beggar has begged during the day. When they see kings cut down more than ninety in one sweep, whose fault was only to be in arms on the other side, is it much wonder rogues take that for justification? Or at least for licence!' He saw the colour burn high in Courcelle's face, and a momentary spark of anger in his eye, but the young man made no protest. 'Oh, I know you had your orders, and no choice but to obey

39

them. I have been a soldier in my time, and borne the same discipline, and done things I would be glad now to think I had not done. That's one reason I've accepted, in the end, another discipline.'

'I doubt,' said Courcelle drily, 'if I shall ever come to that.'

'So would I have doubted it, then. But here I am, and would not change again to your calling. Well, we do the best we can with our lives!' And the worst, he thought, viewing the long lines of motionless forms laid out along the ward, with other men's lives, if we have power.

There were some gaps in the silent ranks by then. Some dozen or so had been claimed by parents and wives. Soon there would be piteous little hand-carts pushed up the slope to the gate, and brothers and neighbours lifting limp bodies to carry them away. More of the townspeople were still coming timidly in through the archway, women with shawls drawn close over their heads and faces half-hidden, gaunt old men trudging resignedly to look for their sons. No wonder Courcelle, whose duties could hardly have encompassed this sort of guard before, looked almost as unhappy as the mourners.

He was frowning down at the ground in morose thought when Aline came into view in the archway, her hand drawn protectively through Hugh Beringar's arm. Her face was white and taut, her eyes very wide and her lips stiffly set, and her fingers clutched at her escort's sleeve as drowning men clutch at floating twigs, but she kept her head up and her step steady and firm. Beringar matched his pace attentively to hers, made no effort to divert her eyes from the sorry spectacle in the ward, and cast only few and brief, but very intent, side-glances at her pale countenance. It would certainly have been a tactical error, Cadfael thought critically, to attempt the kind of protective ardour that claims possession; young and ingenuous and tender as she might be, this was a proud patrician girl of old blood, not to be trifled with if once that blood was up. If she had come here on her own family business, like these poor, prowling citizens, she would not thank any man to try and take it out of her hands. She might, none the less, be deeply thankful for his considerate and reticent presence.

Courcelle looked up, almost as though he had felt a breath of unease moving before them, and saw the pair emerge into the sunlight in the ward, cruel afternoon sunlight that spared no detail. His head jerked up and caught the light, his bright hair burning up like a furze fire. 'Christ God!' he said in a hissing undertone, and went plunging to intercept them on the threshold.

'Aline! – Madam, should you be here? This is no place for you, so desolate a spectacle. I marvel,' he said furiously to Beringar, 'that you should brinʒ her here, to face a scene so harrowing.'

'He did not bring me,' said Aline quickly. 'It was I insisted on coming. Since he could not prevent me, he has been kind enough to come with me.'

'Then, dear lady, you were foolish to impose such a penance on yourself,' said Courcelle fiercely. 'Why, how can you have business here? Surely there's none here belonging to you.'

'I pray you may be right,' she said. Her eyes, huge in the white face, ranged in fearful fascination over the shrouded ranks at her feet, and visibly the first horror and revulsion changed gradually into appalled human pity. 'But I must know! Like all these others! I have only one way of being certain, and it's no worse for me than for them. You know I have a brother – you were there when I told the king. . . .'

'But he cannot be here. You said he was fled to Normandy.'

'I said it was rumoured so – but how can I be sure? He *may* have won to France, he may have joined some company of the empress's men nearer home, how can I tell? I must see for myself whether he chose Shrewsbury or not.'

'But surely the garrison here were known. Your name is very unlikely to have been among them.'

'The sheriff's proclamation,' said Beringar mildly, speaking up for the first time in this encounter, 'mentioned that there was one here, at least, who was not known. One more, apparently, than the expected tally.'

'You must let me see for myself,' said Aline, gently and firmly, 'or how can I have any peace?'

Courcelle had no right to prevent, however it grieved and enraged him. And at least this particular corpse was close at hand, and could bring her nothing but reassurance. 'He lies here,' he said, and turned her towards the corner where Brother Cadfael stood. She gazed, and was surprised into the faint brightness of a smile, a genuine smile though it faded soon.

'I think I should know you. I've seen you about the abbey, you are Brother Cadfael, the herbalist.'

41

'That is my name,' said Cadfael. 'Though why you should have learned it I hardly know.'

'I was asking the porter about you,' she owned, flushing. 'I saw you at Vespers and Compline, and – Forgive me, brother, if I have trespassed, but you had such an air – as though you had lived adventures before you came to the cloister. He told me you were in the Crusade – with Godfrey of Bouillon at the siege of Jerusalem! I have only dreamed of such service . . . Oh!' She had lowered her eyes from his face, half abashed by her own ardour, and seen the young, dead face exposed at his feet. She gazed and gazed, in controlled silence. The face was not offensive, rather its congestion had subsided; the unknown lay youthful and almost comely.

'This is a most Christian service you are doing now,' said Aline, low-voiced, 'for all these here. This is the unexpected one? The one more than was counted?'

'This is he.' Cadfael stooped and drew down the linen to show the good but simple clothing, the absence of anything warlike about the young man. 'But for the dagger, which every man wears when he travels, he was unarmed.'

She looked up sharply. Over her shoulder Beringar was gazing down with frowning concentration at the rounded face that must have been cheerful and merry in life. 'Are you saying,' asked Aline, 'that he was not in the fight here? Not captured with the garrison?'

'So it seems to me. You don't know him?'

'No.' She looked down with pure, impersonal compassion. 'So young! It's great pity! I wish I could tell you his name, but I never saw him before.'

'Master Beringar?'

'No. A stranger to me.' Beringar was still staring down very sombrely at the dead. They were almost of an age, surely no more than a year between them. Every man burying his twin sees his own burial.

Courcelle, hovering solicitously, laid a hand on the girl's arm, and said persuasively: 'Come now, you've done your errand, you should quit this sad place at once, it is not for you. You see your fears were groundless, your brother is not here.'

'No,' said Aline, 'this is not he, but for all that he *may* – How can I be sure unless I see them all?' She put off the urging touch, but very gently. 'I've ventured this far, and how is it worse for me than for any of these others?' She looked round appealingly. 'Brother Cadfael, this is your charge now. You know I must ease my mind. Will you come with me?'

'Very willingly,' said Cadfael, and led the way without more words, for words were not going to dissuade her, and he thought her right not to be dissuaded. The two young men followed side by side, neither willing to give the other precedence. Aline looked down at every exposed face, wrung but resolute.

'He was twenty-four years old – not very like me, his hair was darker . . . Oh, here are all too many no older than he!'

They had traversed more than half of the dolorous passage when suddenly she caught at Cadfael's arm, and froze where she stood. She made no outcry, she had breath only for a soft moan, audible as a word only to Cadfael, who was nearest. 'Giles!' she said again more strongly, and what colour she had drained from her face and left her almost translucent, staring down at a face once imperious, wilful and handsome. She sank to her knees, stooping to study the dead face close, and then she uttered the only cry she ever made over her brother, and that very brief and private, and swooped breast to breast with him, gathering the body into her arms. The mass of her hair slipped out of its coils and spilled gold over them both.

Brother Cadfael, who was experienced enough to let her alone until she seemed to need comfort for her grief instead of decent reticence, would have waited quietly, but he was hurriedly thrust aside, and Adam Courcelle fell on his knees beside her, and took her beneath the arms to lift her against his shoulder. The shock of discovery seemed to have shaken him fully as deeply as it had Aline, his face was stricken and dismayed, his voice an appalled stammer.

'Madam! – Aline – Dear God, is this indeed your brother? If I'd known . . . if I'd known, I'd have saved him for you. . . . Whatever the cost, I would have delivered him . . . God forgive me!'

She lifted a tearless face from the curtain of her yellow hair, and looked at him with wonder and compunction, seeing him so shattered. 'Oh, hush! How can this be any fault of yours? You could not know. You did only what you were ordered to do. And how could you have saved one, and let the rest die?'

'Then truly this *is* your brother?'

'Yes,' she said, gazing down at the dead youth with a face

43

now drained even of shock and grief. 'This is Giles.' Now she knew the worst, and now she had only to do what was needful, what fell to her for want of father and brothers. She crouched motionless in Courcelle's arm, earnestly regarding the dead face. Cadfael, watching, was glad he had managed to mould some form back into features once handsome, but in death fallen into a total collapse of terror. At least she was not viewing that hardly human disintegration.

Presently she heaved a short, sharp sigh, and made to rise, and Hugh Beringar, who had shown admirably judicious restraint throughout, reached a hand to her on the other side, and lifted her to her feet. She was mistress of herself as perhaps she had never been before, never having had to meet such a test until now. What was required of her she could and would do.

'Brother Cadfael, I do thank you for all you have done, not only for Giles and me, but for all these. Now, if you permit, I will take my brother's burial into my charge, as is only fitting.'

Close and anxious at her shoulder, still deeply shaken, Courcelle asked: 'Where would you have him conveyed? My men shall carry him there for you, and be at your orders as long as you need them. I wish I might attend you myself, but I must not leave my guard.'

'You are very kind,' she said, quite composed now. 'My mother's family has a tomb at St Alkmund's church, here in the town. Father Elias knows me. I shall be grateful for help in taking my brother there, but I need not keep your men from their duties longer. All the rest I will do.' Her face had grown intent and practical, she had work to do, all manner of things to take into account, the need for speed, the summer heat, the provision of all the materials proper to decent preparation for the grave. She made her dispositions with authority.

'Messire Beringar, you have been kind, and I do value it, but now I must stay to see to my family's rites. There is no need to sadden all the rest of your day, I shall be safe enough.'

'I came with you,' said Hugh Beringar, 'and I shall not return without you.' The very way to talk to her now, without argument, without outward show of sympathy. She accepted his resolve simply, and turned to her duty. Two of the guards brought a narrow litter, and lifted Giles Siward's body into it, and she herself steadied and straightened the lolling head.

At the last moment Courcelle, frowning down distressfully at

44

the corpse, said abruptly: 'Wait! I have remembered – I believe there is something here that must have belonged to him.'

He went hastily through the archway and across the outer ward to the guard-towers, and in a few moments came back carrying over his arm a black cloak. 'This was among the gear they left behind in the guardroom at the end. I think it must have been his – this clasp at the neck has the same design, see, as the buckle of his belt.'

It was true enough, there was the same dragon of eternity, tail in mouth, lavishly worked in bronze. 'I noticed it only now. That cannot be by chance. Let me at least restore him this.' He spread out the cloak and draped it gently over the litter, covering the dead face. When he looked up, it was into Aline's eyes, and for the first time they regarded him through a sheen of tears.

'That was very kindly done,' she said in a low voice, and gave him her hand. 'I shall not forget it.'

Cadfael went back to his vigil by the unknown, and continued his questioning, but it brought no useful response. In the coming night all these dead remaining must be taken on carts down the Wyle and out to the abbey; this hot summer would not permit further delay. At dawn Abbot Heribert would consecrate a new piece of ground at the edge of the abbey enclosure, for a mass grave. But this unknown, never condemned, never charged with any crime, whose dead body cried aloud for justice, should not be buried among the executed, nor should there be any rest until he could go to his grave under his own rightful name, and with all the individual honours due to him.

In the house of Father Elias, priest of St Alkmund's church, Giles Siward was reverently stripped, washed, composed and shrouded, all by his sister's hands, the good father assisting. Hugh Beringar stood by to fetch and carry for them, but did not enter the room where they worked. She wanted no one else, she was quite sufficient to the task laid on her, and if she was robbed of any part of it now she would feel deprivation and resentment, not gratitude. But when all was done, and her brother laid ready for rest before the altar of the church, she was suddenly weary to death, and glad enough of Beringar's almost silent company and ready arm back to her house by the mill.

On the following morning Giles Siward was interred with all due ceremony in the tomb of his maternal grandfather in the church of St Alkmund, and the monks of the abbey of St Peter and St Paul buried with due rites all the sixty-six soldiers of the defeated garrison still remaining in their charge.

CHAPTER FOUR

Aline brought back with her the cotte and hose her brother had worn, and the cloak that had covered him, and herself carefully brushed and folded them. The shirt no one should ever wear again, she would burn it and forget; but these stout garments of good cloth must not go to waste, in a world where so many went half-naked and cold. She took the neat bundle, and went in at the abbey gate house, and finding the whole courtyard deserted, crossed to the ponds and the gardens in search of Brother Cadfael. She did not find him. The digging out of a grave large enough to hold sixty-six victims, and the sheer repetitive labour of laying them in it, takes longer than the opening of a stone tomb to make room for one more kinsman. The brothers were hard at work until past two o'clock, even with every man assisting.

But if Cadfael was not there, his garden-boy was, industriously clipping off flower-heads dead in the heat, and cutting leaves and stems of blossoming savory to hang up in bunches for drying. All the end of the hut, under the eaves, was festooned with drying herbs. The diligent boy worked barefoot and dusty from the powdery soil, and a smear of green coloured one cheek. At the sound of approaching footsteps he looked round, and came out in haste from among his plants, in a great wave of fragrance, which clung about him and distilled from the folds of his coarse tunic like the miraculous sweetness conferred upon some otherwise unimpressive-looking saint. The hurried swipe of a hand over his tangle of hair only served to smear the other cheek and half his forehead.

'I was looking,' said Aline, almost apologetically, 'for Brother Cadfael. You must be the boy called Godric, who works for him.'

'Yes, my lady,' said Godith gruffly. 'Brother Cadfael is still busy, they are not finished yet.' She had wanted to attend, but he would not let her; the less she was seen in full daylight, the better.

'Oh!' said Aline, abashed. 'Of course, I should have known. Then may I leave my message with you? It is only – I've

47

brought these, my brother's clothes. He no longer needs them, and they are still good, someone could be glad of them. Will you ask Brother Cadfael to dispose of them somewhere they can do good? However he thinks best.'

Godith had scrubbed grubby hands down the skirts of her cotte before extending them to take the bundle. She stood suddenly very still, eyeing the other girl and clutching the dead man's clothes, so startled and shaken that she forgot for a moment to keep her voice low. 'No longer needs . . . You had a brother in there, in the castle? Oh, I am sorry! Very sorry!'

Aline looked down at her own hands, empty and rather lost now that even this last small duty was done. 'Yes. One of many,' she said. 'He made his choice. I was taught to think it the wrong one, but at least he stood by it to the end. My father might have been angry with him, but he would not have had to be ashamed.'

'I am sorry!' Godith hugged the folded garments to her breast and could find no better words. 'I'll deliver your message to Brother Cadfael as soon as he comes. And he would want me to give you his thanks for your most feeling charity, until he can do it for himself.'

'And give him this purse, too. It is for Masses for them all. But especially a Mass for the one who should not have been there – the one nobody knows.'

Godith stared in bewilderment and wonder. 'Is there one like that? One who did not belong? I didn't know!' She had seen Cadfael for only a few hurried moments when he came home late and weary, and he had had no time to tell her anything. All she knew was that the remaining dead had been brought to the abbey for burial; this mysterious mention of one who had no place in the common tragedy was new to her.

'So he said. There were ninety-five where there should have been only ninety-four, and one did not seem to have been in arms. Brother Cadfael was asking all who came, to look and see if they knew him, but I think no one has yet put a name to him.'

'And where, then, is he now?' asked Godith, marvelling.

'That I don't know. Though they must have brought him here to the abbey. Somehow I don't think Brother Cadfael will let him be put into the earth with all the rest, and he nameless and unaccounted for. You must know his ways better than I. Have you worked with him long?'

'No, a very short time,' said Godith, 'but I do begin to know him.' She was growing a little uneasy, thus innocently studied at close quarters by those clear iris eyes. A woman might be more dangerous to her secret than a man. She cast a glance back towards the beds of herbs where she had been working.

'Yes,' said Aline, taking the allusion, 'I must not keep you from your proper work.'

Godith watched her withdraw, almost regretting that she dared not prolong this encounter with another girl in this sanctuary of men. She laid the bundle of clothing on her bed in the hut, and went back to work, waiting in some disquiet for Cadfael to come; and even when he did appear he was tired, and still burdened with business.

'I'm sent for to the king's camp. It seems his sheriff has thought best to let him know what sort of unexpected hare I've started, and he wants an accounting from me. But I'm forgetting,' he said, passing a hard palm over cheeks stiff with weariness, 'I've had no time to talk to you at all, you've heard nothing of all that −'

'Ah, but I have,' said Godith. 'Aline Siward was here looking for you. She brought these, see, for you to give as alms, wherever you think best. They were her brother's. She told me. And this money is for Masses − she said especially a Mass for this one man more than was looked for. Now tell me, what is this mystery?'

It was pleasant to sit quietly for a while and let things slide, and therefore he relaxed and sat down with her, and told her. She listened intently, and when he was done she asked at once: 'And where is he now, this stranger nobody knows?'

'He is in the church, on a bier before the altar. I want all who come to services to pass by him, in the hope that someone must know him, and give him a name. We can't keep him beyond tomorrow,' he said fretfully, 'the season is too hot. But if we must bury him unknown, I intend it to be where he can as easily be taken up again, and to keep his clothes and a drawing of his face, until we discover the poor lad.'

'And you truly believe,' she questioned, awed, 'that he was murdered? And then cast in among the king's victims, to hide the crime away for ever?'

'Child, I've told you! He was taken from behind, with a strangler's cord ready prepared for the deed. And it was done in the same night that the others died and were flung over into

49

the ditch. What better opportunity could a murderer have? Among so many, who was to count, and separate, and demand answers? He had been dead much the same time as some of those others. It should have been a certain cover.'

'But it was not!' she said, vengefully glowing. 'Because *you* came. Who else would have cared to be so particular among ninety-five dead men? Who else would have stood out alone for the rights of a man not condemned – killed without vestige of law? Oh, Brother Cadfael, you have made me as irreconcilable as you are on this. Here am I, and have not seen this man. Let the king wait a little while! Let me go and see! Or go with me, if you must, but let me look at him.'

Cadfael considered and got to his feet, groaning a little at the effort. He was not so young as he once had been, and he had had a hard day and night. 'Come, then, have your will, who am I to shut you out where I invite others in? It should be quiet enough there now, but keep close to me. Oh, girl, dear, I must also be about getting you safe out of here as soon as I may.'

'Are you so eager to get rid of me?' she said, offended. 'And just when I'm getting to know sage from marjoram! What would you do without me?'

'Why, train some novice I can expect to keep longer than a few weeks. And speaking of herbs,' said Cadfael, drawing out a little leather bag from the breast of his habit, and shaking out a six-inch sprig of sun-dried herbage, a thin, square stem studded at intervals with pairs of spreading leaves, with tiny brown balls set in the joints of them, 'do you know what this one is?'

She peered at it curiously, having learned much in a few days. 'No. We don't grow it here. But I might know it if I saw it growing fresh.'

'It's goose-grass – cleavers it's also called. A queer, creeping thing that grows little hooks to hold fast, even on these tiny seeds you see here. And you see it's broken in the middle of this straight stem?'

She saw, and was curiously subdued. There was something here beyond her vision; the thing was a wisp of brown, bleached and dry, but indeed folded sharply in the midst by a thin fracture. 'What is it? Where did you find it?'

'Caught into the furrow in this poor lad's throat,' he said, so gently that she could take it in without shock, 'broken here by the ligament that strangled him. And it's last year's crop, not

50

new. The stuff is growing richly at this season, seeding wild everywhere, this was in fodder, or litter, grass cut last autumn and dried out. Never turn against the herb, it's sovereign for healing green wounds that are stubborn to knit. All the things of the wild have their proper uses, only misuse makes them evil.' He put the small slip of dryness away carefully in his bosom, and laid an arm about her shoulders. 'Come, then, let's go and look at this youngster, you and I together.'

It was mid-afternoon, the time of work for the brothers, play for the boys and the novices, once their limited tasks were done. They came down to the church without meeting any but a few half-grown boys at play, and entered the cool dimness within.

The mysterious young man from the castle ditch lay austerely shrouded on his bier in the choir end of the nave, his head and face uncovered. Dim but pure light fell upon him; it needed only a few minutes to get accustomed to the soft interior glow in this summer afternoon, and he shone clear to view. Godith stood beside him and gazed in silence. They were alone there, but for him, and they could speak, in low voices. But when Cadfael asked softly: 'Do you know him?' he was already sure of the answer.

A fine thread of a whisper beside him said: 'Yes.'

'Come!' He led her out as softly as they had come. In the sunlight he heard her draw breath very deep and long. She made no other comment until they were secure together in the herbarium, in the drowning summer sweetness, sitting in the shade of the hut.

'Well, who is he, this young fellow who troubles both you and me?'

'His name,' she said, very low and wonderingly, 'is Nicholas Faintree. I've known him, by fits and starts, since I was twelve years old. He is a squire of FitzAlan's, from one of his northern manors, he's ridden courier for his lord several times in the last few years. He would not be much known in Shrewsbury, no. If he was waylaid and murdered here, he must have been on his lord's business. But FitzAlan's business was almost finished in these parts.' She hugged her head between her hands, and thought passionately. 'There are some in Shrewsbury could have named him for you, you know, if they had had reason to come looking for men of their own. I know of some who may be able

51

to tell you what he was doing here that day and that night. If you can be sure no ill will come to them?'

'Never by me,' said Cadfael, 'that I promise.'

'There's my nurse, the one who brought me here and called me her nephew. Petronilla served my family all her grown life, until she married late, too late for children of her own, and she married a good friend to FitzAlan's house and ours, Edric Flesher, the chief of the butchers' guild in town. The two of them were close in all the plans when FitzAlan declared for the empress Maud. If you go to them from me,' she said confidently, 'they'll tell you anything they know. You'll know the shop, it has the sign of the boar's head, in the butchers' row.'

Cadfael scrubbed thoughtfully at his nose. 'If I borrow the abbot's mule, I can make better speed, and spare my legs, too. There'll be no keeping the king waiting, but on the way back I can halt at the shop. Give me some token, to show you trust me, and they can do as much without fear.'

'Petronilla can read, and knows my hand. I'll write you a line to her, if you'll lend me a little leaf of vellum, a mere corner will do.' She was alight with ardour, as intent as he. 'He was a merry person, Nicholas, he never did harm to anyone, that I know, and he was never out of temper. He laughed a great deal . . . But if you tell the king he was of the opposite party, he won't care to pursue the murderer, will he? He'll call it a just fate, and bid you leave well alone.'

'I shall tell the king,' said Cadfael, 'that we have a man plainly murdered, and the method and time we know, but not the place or the reason. I will also tell him that we have a name for him – it's a modest name enough, it can mean nothing to Stephen. As at this moment there's no more to tell, for I know no more. And even if the king should shrug it off and bid me let things lie, I shall not do it. By my means or God's means, or the both of us together, Nicholas Faintree shall have justice before I let this matter rest.'

Having the loan of the abbot's own mule, Brother Cadfael took with him in this errand the good cloth garments Aline had entrusted to him. It was his way to carry out at once whatever tasks fell him, rather than put them off until the morrow, and there were beggars enough on his way through the town. The hose he gave to an elderly man with eyes whitened over with thick cauls, who sat with stick beside him and palm extended in the shade of the town gate. He looked of a suitable figure, and was in much-patched and threadbare nethers that would certainly fall apart very soon. The good brown cotte went to a frail creature no more than twenty years old who begged at the high cross, a poor feeble-wit with hanging lip and a palsied shake, who had a tiny old woman holding him by the hand and caring for him jealously. Her shrill blessings followed Cadfael down towards the castle gate. The cloak he still had folded before him when he came to the guard-post of the king's camp, and saw Lame Osbern's little wooden trolley tucked into the bole of a tree close by, and marked the useless, withered legs, and the hands callused and muscular from dragging all that dead weight about by force. His wooden pattens lay beside him in the grass. Seeing a frocked monk approaching on a good riding mule, Osbern seized them and propelled himself forward into Cadfael's path. And it was wonderful how fast he could move, over short distances and with intervals for rest, but all the same so immobilised a creature, half his body inert, must suffer cold in even the milder nights, and in the winter terribly.

'Good brother,' coaxed Osbern, 'spare an alms for a poor cripple, and God will reward you!'

'So I will, friend,' said Cadfael, 'and better than a small coin, too. And you may say a prayer for a gentle lady who sends it to you by my hand.' And he unfolded from the saddle before him, and dropped into the startled, malformed hands, Giles Siward's cloak.

'You did right to report truly what you found,' said the king consideringly. 'Small wonder that my castellan did not make the same discovery, he had his hands full. You say this man was taken from behind by stealth, with a strangler's cord? It's a footpad's way, and foul. And above all, to cast his victim in among my executed enemies to cover the crime – that I will not bear! How dared he make me and my officers his accomplices! That I count an affront to the crown, and for that alone I would wish the felon taken and judged. And the young man's name – Faintree, you said?'

'Nicholas Faintree. So I was told by one who came and saw him, where we had laid him in the church. He comes from a family in the north of the county. But that is all I know of him.'

'It is possible,' reflected the king hopefully, 'that he had ridden to Shrewsbury to seek service with us. Several such young men from north of the county have joined us here.'

'It is possible,' agreed Cadfael gravely; for all things are possible, and men do turn their coats.

'And to be cut off by some forest thief for what he carried – it happens! I wish I could say our roads are safe, but in this new anarchy, God knows, I dare not claim it. Well, you may pursue such enquiries as can be made into this matter, if that's your wish, and call upon my sheriff to do justice if the murderer can be found. He knows my will. I do not like being made use of to shield so mean a crime.'

And that was truth, and the heart of the matter for him, and perhaps it would not have changed his attitude, thought Cadfael, even if he had known that Faintree was FitzAlan's squire and courier, even if it were proved, as so far it certainly was not, that he was on FitzAlan's rebellious business when he died. By all the signs, there would be plenty of killing in Stephen's realm in the near future, and he would not lose his sleep over most of it, but to have a killer-by-stealth creeping for cover into his shadow, that he would take as a deadly insult to himself, and avenge accordingly. Energy and lethargy, generosity and spite, shrewd action and incomprehensible inaction, would always alternate and startle in King Stephen. But somewhere within that tall, comely, simple-minded person there was a grain of nobility hidden.

'I accept and value your Grace's support,' said Brother Cadfael truthfully, 'and I will do my best to see justice done. A man cannot lay down and abandon the duty God has placed in his hands. Of this young man I know only his name, and the appearance of his person, which is open and innocent, and that he was accused of no crime, and no man has complained of wrong by him, and he is dead unjustly. I think this as unpleasing to your Grace as ever it can be to me. If I can right it, so I will.'

At the sign of the boar's head in the butchers' row he was received with the common wary civility any citizen would show to a monk of the abbey. Petronilla, rounded and comfortable and grey, bade him in and would have offered all the small attentions that provide a wall between suspicious people, if he had not at once given her the worn and much-used leaf of vellum on which Godith had, somewhat cautiously and laboriously, inscribed her trust in the messenger, and her name. Petronilla peered and flushed with pleasure, and looked up at this elderly, solid, homely brown monk through blissful tears.

'The lamb, she's managing well, then, my girl? And you taking good care of her! Here she says it, I know that scrawl, I learned to write with her. I had her almost from birth, the darling, and she the only one, more's the pity, she should have had brothers and sisters. It was why I wanted to do everything with her, even the letters, to be by her whatever she needed. Sit down, brother, sit down and tell me of her, if she's well, if she needs anything I can send her by you. Oh, and, brother, how are we to get her safely away? Can she stay with you, if it runs to weeks?'

When Cadfael could wedge a word or two into the flow he told her how her nurseling was faring, and how he would see to it that she continued to fare. It had not occurred to him until then what a way the girl had of taking hold of hearts, without at all designing it. By the time Edric Flesher came in from a cautious skirmish through the town, to see how the land lay, Cadfael was firmly established in Petronilla's favour, and vouched for as a friend to be trusted.

Edric settled his solid bulk into a broad chair, and said with a gusty breath of cautious relief: 'Tomorrow I'll open the shop. We're fortunate! Ask me, he rues the vengeance he took for those he failed to capture. He's called off all pillage here, and for once he's enforcing it. If only his claims were just, and he had more spine in his body, I think I'd be for him. And to look like a hero, and be none, that's hard on a man.' He gathered his great legs under him, and looked at his wife, and then, longer, at Cadfael. 'She says you have the girl's good word, and that's enough. Name your need, and if we have it, it's yours.'

'For the girl,' said Cadfael briskly, 'I will keep her safe as long as need be, and when the right chance offers, I'll get her away to where she should be. For my need, yes, there you may help me. We have in the abbey church, and we shall bury there tomorrow, a young man you may know, murdered on the night after the castle fell, the night the prisoners were hanged and thrown into the ditch. But he was killed elsewhere, and thrown among the rest to have him away into the ground unquestioned. I can tell you how he died, and when. I cannot tell you where, or why, or who did this thing. But Godith tells me that his name is Nicholas Faintree, and he was a squire of FitzAlan.'

All this he let fall between them in so many words, and heard and felt their silence. Certainly there were things they knew, and equally certainly this death they had not known, and it struck at them like a mortal blow.

'One more thing I may tell you,' he said. 'I intend to have the truth out into the open concerning this thing, and see him avenged. And more, I have the king's word to pursue the murderer. He likes the deed no more than I like it.'

After a long moment Edric asked: 'There was only one, dead after this fashion? No second?'

'Should there have been? Is not one enough?'

'There were two,' said Edric harshly. 'Two who set out together upon the same errand. How did this death come to light? It seems you are the only man who knows.'

Brother Cadfael sat back and told them all, without haste. If he had missed Vespers, so be it. He valued and respected his duties, but if they clashed, he knew which way he must go. Godith would not stir from her safe solitude without him, not until her evening schooling.

'Now,' he said, 'you had better tell me. I have Godith to protect, and Faintree to avenge, and I mean to do both as best I can.'

The two of them exchanged glances, and understood each other. It was the man who took up the tale.

'A week before the castle and the town fell, with FitzAlan's family already away, and our plans made to place the girl with your abbey in hiding, FitzAlan also took thought for the end, if he died. He never ran until they broke in at the gates, you know that? By the skin of his teeth he got away, swam the river with Adeney at his shoulder, and got clear. God be thanked! But the day before the end he made provision for whether he lived or died. His whole treasury had been left with us here, he wanted it to reach the empress if he were slain. That day we moved it out into Frankwell, to a garden I hold there, so that there need be no bridge to pass if we had to convey it away at short notice. And we fixed a signal. If any of his party came with a certain token – a trifle it was, a drawing, but private to us who knew – they should be shown where the treasury was, provided with horses, all they might need, and put over there to pick up the valuables and make their break by night.'

'And so it was done?' said Cadfael.

'On the morning of the fall. It came so early, and in such force, we'd left it all but too late. Two of them came. We sent them over the bridge to wait for night. What could they have done by daylight?'

'Tell me more. What time did these two come to you that morning, what had they to say, how did they get their orders? How many may have known what was toward? How many would have known the way they would take? When did you last see them both alive?'

'They came just at dawn. We could hear the din by then, the assault had begun. They had the parchment leaf that was the signal, the head of a saint drawn in ink. They said there had been a council the night before, and FitzAlan had said then he would have them go the following day, whatever happened and whether he lived or no, get the treasury away safe to the empress, for her use in defending her right.'

'Then all who were at that council would know those two would be on the road the following night, as soon as it was dark enough. Would they also know the road? Did they know where the treasury was hidden?'

'No, where we had put it, beyond that it was in Frankwell, no one had been told. Only FitzAlan and I knew that. Those two squires had to come to me.'

'Then any who had ill designs on the treasury, even if they knew the time of its removal, could not go and get it for themselves, they could only waylay it on the road. If all those officers close to FitzAlan knew that it was to be taken westward into Wales from Frankwell, there'd be no doubt about the road. For the first mile and more there is but one, by reason of the coils of the river on either side.'

'You are thinking that one of those who knew thought to get the gold for himself, by murder?' said Edric. 'One of FitzAlan's own men? I cannot believe it! And surely all, or most, stayed to the end, and died. Two men riding by night could well be waylaid by pure chance, by men living wild in the forest . . .'

'Within a mile of the town walls? Don't forget, whoever

57

killed this lad did so close enough to Shrewsbury castle to have ample time and means to take his body and toss it among all those others in the ditch, long before the night was over. Knowing very well that all those others would be there. Well, so they came, they showed their credentials, they told you the plan had been made the previous evening, come what might. But what came, came earlier and more fiercely than anyone had expected, and all done in haste. Then what? You went with them over to Frankwell?'

'I did. I have a garden and a barn there, where they and their horses lay in hiding until dark. The valuables were packed into two pairs of saddle-bags – one horse with his rider and that load would have been overdone – in a cavity in a dry well on my land there. I saw them safe under cover, and left them there about nine in the morning.'

'And at what time would they venture to start?'

'Not until full dark. And do you truly tell me Faintree was murdered, soon after they set out?'

'Past doubt he was. Had it been done miles away, he would have been disposed of some other way. This was planned, and ingenious. But not ingenious enough. You knew Faintree well – or so Godith gave me to think. Who was the other? Did you also know him?'

Heavily and slowly, Edric said 'No! It seemed to me that Nicholas knew him well enough, they were familiar together like good comrades, but Nicholas was one open to any new friend. I had never seen this lad before. He was from another of Fitz-Alan's northern manors. He gave his name as Torold Blund.'

They had told him all they knew, and something more than had been said in words. Edric's brooding frown spoke for him. The young man they knew and trusted was dead, the one they did not know vanished, and with him FitzAlan's valuables, plate and coin and jewellery, intended for the empress's coffers. Enough to tempt any man. The murderer clearly knew all he needed to know in order to get possession of that hoard; and who could have known half so well as the second courier himself? Another might certainly waylay the prize on the road. Torold Blund need not even have waited for that. Those two had been in hiding together all that day in Edric's barn. It was possible that Nicholas Faintree had never left it until he was dead, draped over a horse for the short ride back to the castle ditch, before two horses with one rider set out westward into Wales.

'There was one more thing happened that day,' said Petronilla, as Cadfael rose to take his leave. 'About two of the clock, after the king's men had manned both bridges and dropped the draw-bridge, *he* came – Hugh Beringar, he that was betrothed to my girl from years back – making pretence to be all concern for her, and asking where he could find her. Tell him? No, what do you take me for? I told him she'd been taken away a good week before the town fell, and we were not told where, but I thought she was far away by now, and safe out of Stephen's country. Right well we knew he must have come to us with Stephen's authority, or he would never have been let through so soon. He'd been to the king's camp before ever he came hunting for my Godith, and it's not for love he's searching for her. She's worth a fat commission, as bait for her father, if not for Fitz-Alan himself. Don't let my lamb get within his sight, for I hear he's living in the abbey now.'

'And he was here that very afternoon?' pressed Cadfael, concerned. 'Yes, yes, I'll take good care to keep her away from him, I've seen that danger. But there could not have been any mention when he came here, could there, of Faintree's mission? Nothing to make him prick his ears? He's very quick, and very private! No – no, I ask your pardon, I know you'd never let out word. Ah, well, my thanks for your help, and you shall know if I make progress.'

He was at the door when Petronilla said grievingly at his shoulder: 'And he seemed such a fine young lad, this Torold Blund! How can a body tell what lies behind the decent, ordinary face?'

'Torold Blund!' said Godith, testing the name slow syllable by syllable. 'That's a Saxon name. There are plenty of them up there in the northern manors, good blood and old. But I don't know him. I think I can never have seen him. And Nicholas was on good, close terms with him? Nicholas was easy, but not stupid, and they sound much of an age, he must have known him well. And yet...'

'Yes,' said Cadfael, 'I know! And yet! Girl dear, I am too tired to think any more. I'm going to Compline, and then to my bed, and so should you. And tomorrow...'

'Tomorrow,' she said, rising to the touch of his hand, 'we shall bury Nicholas. *We!* He was in some measure my friend, and I shall be there.'

'So you shall, my heart,' said Cadfael, yawning, and led her away in his arm to celebrate, with gratitude and grief and hope, the ending of the day.

CHAPTER FIVE

Nicholas Faintree was laid, with due honours, under a stone in the transept of the abbey church, an exceptional privilege. He was but one, after so many, and his singleness was matter for celebration, besides the fact that there was room within rather than without, and the labour involved was less. Abbot Heribert was increasingly disillusioned and depressed with all the affairs of this world, and welcomed a solitary guest who was not a symbol of civil war, but the victim of personal malice and ferocity. Against all the probabilities, in due course Nicholas might find himself a saint. He was mysterious, feloniously slain, young, to all appearances clean of heart and life, innocent of evil, the stuff of which martyrs are made.

Aline Siward was present at the funeral service, and had brought with her, intentionally or otherwise, Hugh Beringar. That young man made Cadfael increasingly uneasy. True, he was making no inimical move, nor showing any great diligence in his search for his affianced bride, if, indeed, he was in search of her at all. But there was something daunting in the very ease and impudence of his carriage, the small, sardonic turn of his lip, and the guileless clarity of the black eyes when they happened to encounter Cadfael's. No doubt about it, thought Cadfael, I shall be happier when I've got the girl safely away from here, but in the meantime at least I can move her away from anywhere he's likely to be.

The main orchards and vegetable gardens of the abbey were not within the precinct, but across the main road, stretched along the rich level beside the river, called the Gaye; and at the far end of this fertile reach there was a slightly higher field of corn. It lay almost opposite the castle, and no great distance from the king's siege camp, and had suffered some damage during the siege; and though what remained had been ripe for cutting for almost a week, it had been too dangerous to attempt to get it in. Now that all was quiet, they were in haste to salvage a crop that could not be spared, and all hands possible were mustered to do the work in one day. The second of the abbey's mills was at the end of the field, and because of the same dangers had been abandoned for the season, just when it was beginning to be needed, and had suffered damage which would keep it out of use until repairs could be undertaken.

'You go with the reapers,' said Cadfael to Godith. 'My thumbs prick, and rightly or wrongly, I'd rather have you out of the enclave, if only for a day.'

'Without you?' said Godith, surprised.

'I must stay here and keep an eye on things. If anything threatens, I'll be with you as fast as legs can go. But you'll be well enough, no one is going to have leisure to look hard at you until that corn is in the barns. But stay by Brother Athanasius, he's as blind as a mole, he wouldn't know a stag from a hind. And take care how you swing a sickle, and don't come back short of a foot!'

She went off quite happily among the crowd of reapers in the end, glad of an outing and a change of scene. She was not afraid. Not afraid enough, Cadfael considered censoriously, but then, she had an old fool here to do the fearing for her, just as she'd once had an old nurse, protective as a hen with one chick. He watched them out of the gate house and over the road towards the Gaye, and went back with a relieved sigh to his own labours in the inner gardens. He had not been long on his knees, weeding, when a cool, light voice behind him, almost as quiet as the steps he had not heard in the grass, said: 'So this is where you spend your more peaceful hours. A far cry and a pleasant change from harvesting dead men.'

Brother Cadfael finished the last corner of the bed of mint before he turned to acknowledge the presence of Hugh Beringar. 'A pleasant change, right enough. Let's hope we've finished with that kind of crop, here in Shrewsbury.'

'And you found a name for your stranger in the end. How was that? No one in the town seemed to know him.'

'All questions get their answers,' said Brother Cadfael sententiously, 'if you wait long enough.'

'And all searches are bound to find? But of course,' said Beringar, smiling, 'you did not say how long is long enough. If a man found at eighty what he was searching for at twenty, he might prove a shade ungrateful.'

'He might well have stopped wanting it long before that,' said Brother Cadfael drily, 'which is in itself an answer to any want. Is there anything you are looking for here in the herbarium, that I can help you to, or are you curious to learn about these simples of mine?'

'No,' owned Beringar, his smile deepening, 'I would hardly say it was any simplicity I came to study.' He pinched off a sprig of mint, crushed it between his fingers, and set it first to his nose and then closed fine white teeth upon its savour. 'And what should such as I be looking for here? I may have *caused* a few ills in my time, I'm no hand at healing them. They tell me, Brother Cadfael, you have had a wide-ranging career before you came into the cloister. Don't you find it unbearably dull here, after such battles, with no enemy left to fight?'

'I am not finding it at all dull, these days,' said Cadfael, plucking out willowherb from among the thyme. 'And as for enemies, the devil makes his way in everywhere, even into cloister, and church, and herbarium.'

Beringar threw his head back and laughed aloud, until the short black hair danced on his forehead. 'Vainly, if he comes looking for mischief where you are! But he'd hardly expect to blunt his horns against an old crusader here! I take the hint!'

But all the time, though he scarcely seemed to turn his head or pay much attention to anything round him, his black eyes were missing nothing, and his ears were at stretch while he laughed and jested. By this time he knew that the well-spoken and well-favoured boy of whom Aline had innocently spoken was not going to make his appearance, and more, that Brother Cadfael did not care if he poked his nose into every corner of the garden, sniffed at every drying herb and peered at every potion in the hut, for they would tell him nothing. The bench-bed was stripped of its blanket, and laden with a large mortar and a gently bubbling jar of wine. There was no trace of Godith anywhere to be found. The boy was simply a boy like the rest, and no doubt slept in the dortoir with the rest.

'Well, I'll leave you to your cleansing labours,' said Beringar, 'and stop hampering your meditations with my prattle. Or have you work for me to do?'

'The king has none?' said Cadfael solicitously.

Another ungrudging laugh acknowledged the thrust. 'Not yet, not yet, but that will come. Such talent he cannot afford to hold off suspiciously for ever. Though to be sure, he did lay one testing task upon me, and I seem to be making very little progress in that.' He plucked another tip of mint, and bruised and bit it with pleasure. 'Brother Cadfael, it seems to me that you are the most practical man of hand and brain here. Supposing I should have need of your help, you would not refuse it without due thought – would you?'

Brother Cadfael straightened up, with some creaking of back muscles, to give him a long, considering look. 'I hope,' he said cautiously, 'I never do anything without due thought – even if the thought sometimes has to shift its feet pretty briskly to keep up with the deed.'

'So I supposed,' said Beringar, sweet-voiced and smiling. 'I'll bear that in mind as a promise.' And he made a small, graceful obeisance, and walked away at leisure to the courtyard.

The reapers came back in time for Vespers, sun-reddened, weary and sweat-stained, but with the corn all cut and stacked for carrying. After supper Godith slipped out of the refectory in haste, and came to pluck at Cadfael's sleeve.

'Brother Cadfael, you must come! Something vital!' He felt the quivering excitement of her hand, and the quiet intensity of her whispering voice. 'There's time before Compline – come back to the field with me.'

'What is it?' he asked as softly, for they were within earshot of a dozen people if they had spoken aloud, and she was not the woman to fuss over nothing. 'What has happened to you? What have you left down there that's so urgent?'

'A man! A wounded man! He's been in the river, he was hunted into it upstream and came down with the current. I dared not stay to question, but I know he's in need. And hungry! He's been there a night and a day. . . .'

'How did you find him? You alone? No one else knows?'

'No one else.' She gripped Cadfael's sleeve more tightly, and her whisper grew gruff with shyness. 'It was a long day . . . I went aside, and had to go far aside, into the bushes near the mill. Nobody saw . . .'

'Surely, child! I know!' Please God all the boys, her contemporaries, were kept hard at it, and never noticed such daintiness. Brother Athanasius would not have noticed a thunderclap right behind him. 'He was there in the bushes? And is still?'

'Yes. I gave him the bread and meat I had with me, and told him I'd come back when I could. His clothes have dried on him – there's blood on his sleeve . . . But I think he'll do well, if *you* take care of him. We could hide him in the mill – no one goes there yet.' She had thought of all the essentials, she was towing him towards his hut in the herb garden, not directly towards the gate house. Medicines, linen, food, they would need all these.

'Of what age,' asked Cadfael, more easily now they were well away from listeners, 'is this wounded man of yours?'

'A boy,' she said on a soft breath. 'Hardly older than I am. And hunted! He thinks *I* am a boy, of course. I gave him the water from my bottle, and he called me Ganymede. . . .'

Well, well, thought Cadfael, bustling before her into the hut, a young man of some learning, it seems! 'Then, Ganymede,' he said, bundling a roll of linen, a blanket and a pot of salve into her arms, 'stow these about you, while I fill this little vial and put some vittles together. Wait here a few minutes for me, and we'll be off. And on the way you can tell me everything about this young fellow you've discovered, for once across the road no one is going to hear us.'

And on the way she did indeed pour out in her relief and eagerness what she could not have said so freely by daylight. It was not yet dark, but a fine neutral twilight in which they saw each other clear but without colours.

'The bushes there are thick. I heard him stir and groan, and I went to look. He looks like a young gentleman of family, some-one's squire. Yes, he talked to me, but – but told me nothing, it was like talking to a wilful child. So weak, and blood on his shoulder and arm, and making little jests . . . But he trusted me enough to know I wouldn't betray him.' She skipped beside Cadfael through the tall stubble into which the abbey sheep would soon be turned to graze, and to fertilise the field with their droppings. 'I gave him what I had, and told him to lie still, and I would bring help as soon as it grew dusk.'

'Now we're near, do you lead the way. You he'll know.'

There was already starlight before the sun was gone, a lovely August light that would still last them, their eyes being accus-tomed, an hour or more, while veiling them from other eyes. Godith withdrew from Cadfael's clasp the hand that had clung like a child's through the stubble, and waded forward into the low, loose thicket of bushes. On their left hand, within a few yards of them, the river ran, dark and still, only the thrusting

65

sound of its current like a low throb shaking the silence, and an occasional gleam of silver showing where its eddies swirled.

'Hush! It's me – Ganymede! And a friend to us both!'

In the sheltered dimness a darker form stirred, and raised into sight a pale oval of face and a tangled head of hair almost as pale. A hand was braced into the grass to thrust the half-seen stranger up from the ground. No broken bones there, thought Cadfael with satisfaction. The hard-drawn breath signalled stiffness and pain, but nothing mortal. A young, muted voice said: 'Good lad! Friends I surely need . . .'

Cadfael knelt beside him and lent him a shoulder to lean against. 'First, before we move you, where's the damage? Nothing out of joint – by the look of you, nothing broken.' His hands were busy about the young man's body and limbs, he grunted cautious content.

'Nothing but gashes,' muttered the boy laboriously, and gasped at a shrewd touch. 'I lost enough blood to betray me, but into the river . . . And half-drowned . . . they must think wholly . . .' He relaxed with a great sigh, feeling how confidently he was handled.

'Food and wine will put the blood back into you, in time. Can you rise and go?'

'Yes,' said his patient grimly, and all but brought his careful supporters down with him, proving it.

'No, let be, we can do better for you than that. Hold fast by me, and turn behind me. Now, your arms round my neck. . . .'

He was long, but a light weight. Cadfael stooped forward, hooked his thick arms round slim, muscular thighs, and shrugged the weight securely into balance on his solid back. The dank scent of the river water still hung about the young man's clothing. 'I'm too great a load,' he fretted feebly. 'I could have walked . . .'

'You'll do as you're bid, and no argument. Godric, go before, and see there's no one in sight.'

It was only a short way to the shadow of the mill. Its bulk loomed dark against the still lambent sky, the great round of the undershot wheel showing gaps here and there like breaks in a set of teeth. Godith heaved open the leaning door, and felt her way before them into gloom. Through narrow cracks in the floorboards on the left side she caught fleeting, spun gleams of the river water hurrying beneath. Even in this hot, dry season, lower

66

than it had been for some years, the Severn flowed fast and still. 'There'll be dry sacks in plenty piled somewhere by the landward wall,' puffed Cadfael at her back. 'Feel your way along and find them.' There was also a dusty, rustling layer of last harvest's chaff under their feet, sending up fine powder to tickle their noses. Godith groped her way to the corner, and spread sacks there in a thick, comfortable mattress, with two folded close for a pillow. 'Now take this long-legged heron of yours under the armpits, and help me ease him down. . . . There, as good a bed as mine in the dortoir! Now close the door, before I make light to see him by.'

He had brought a good end of candle with him, and a handful of the dry chaff spread on a millstone made excellent tinder for the spark he struck. When his candle was burning steadily he ground it into place on the flickering chaff, quenching the fire that might have blown and spread, and anchoring his light on a safe candlestick, as the wax first softened and then congealed again. 'Now let's look at you!'

The young man lay back gratefully and heaved a huge sigh, meekly abandoning the responsibility for himself. Out of a soiled and weary face, eyes irrepressibly lively gazed up at them, of some light, bright colour not then identifiable. He had a large, generous mouth, drawn with exhaustion but wryly smiling, and the tangle of hair matted and stained from the river would be as fair as corn-stalks when it was clean. 'One of them ripped your shoulder for you, I see,' said Cadfael, hands busy unfastening and drawing off the dark cotte encrusted down one sleeve with dried blood. 'Now the shirt – you'll be needing new clothes, my friend, before you leave this hostelry.'

'I'll have trouble paying my shot,' said the boy, valiantly grinning, and ended the grin with a sharp indrawn breath as the sleeve was detached painfully from his wound.

'Our charges are low. For a straight story you can buy such hospitality as we're offering. Godric, lad, I need water, and river water's better than none. See if you can find anything in this place to carry it in.'

She found the sound half of a large pitcher among the debris under the wheel, left by some customer after its handle and lip had got broken, scrubbed it out industriously with the skirt of her cotte, and went obediently to bring water, he hoped safely. The flow of the river here would be fresher than the leat, and

67

occupy her longer on the journey, while Cadfael undid the boy's belt, and stripped off his shoes and hose, shaking out the blanket to spread over his nakedness. There was a long but not deep gash, he judged from a sword-cut, down the right thigh, a variety of bruises showing bluish on his fair skin, and most strangely, a thin, broken graze on the left side of his neck, and another curiously like it on the outer side of his right wrist. Mere healed, dark lines, these, older by a day or two than his wounds. 'No question,' mused Cadfael aloud, 'but you've been living an interesting life lately.'

'Lucky to keep it,' murmured the boy, half-asleep in his new ease.

'Who was hunting you?'

'The king's men – who else?'

'And still will be?'

'Surely. But in a few days I'll be fit to relieve you of the burden of me . . .'

'Never mind that now. Turn a little to me – so! Let's get this thigh bound up, it's clean enough, it's knitting already. This will sting.' It did, the youth stiffened and gasped a little, but made no complaint. Cadfael had the wound bound and under the blanket by the time Godith came with the pitcher of water. For want of a handle she had to use two hands to carry it.

'Now we'll see to this shoulder. This is where you lost so much blood. An arrow did this!' It was an oblique cut sliced through the outer part of his left arm just below the shoulder, bone-deep, leaving an ugly flap of flesh gaping. Cadfael began to sponge away the encrustations of blood from it, and press it firmly together beneath a pad of linen soaked in one of his herbal salves. 'This will need help to knit clean,' he said, busy rolling his bandage tightly round the arm. 'There, now you should eat, but not too much, you're over-weary to make the best use of it. Here's meat and cheese and bread, and keep some by you for morning, you may well be ravenous when you wake.'

'If there's water left,' besought the young man meekly, 'I should like to wash my hands and face. I'm foul!'

Godith kneeled beside him, moistened a piece of linen in the pitcher, and instead of putting it into his hand, very earnestly and thoroughly did it for him, putting back the matted hair from his forehead, which was wide and candid, even teasing out some of the knots with solicitous fingers. After the first surprise

68

he lay quietly and submissively under her ministering touch, but his eyes, cleansed of the soiled shadows, watched her face as she bent over him, and grew larger and larger in respectful wonder. And all this while she had hardly said a word.

The young man was almost too worn out to eat at all, and flagged very soon. He lay for a few moments with lids drooping, peering at his rescuers in silent thought. Then he said, his tongue stumbling sleepily: 'I owe you a name, after all you've done for me. . . .'

'Tomorrow,' said Cadfael firmly. 'You're in the best case to sleep sound, and here I believe you may. Now drink this down – it helps keep wounds from festering, and eases the heart.' It was a strong cordial of his own brewing, he tucked away the empty vial in his gown. 'And here's a little flask of wine to bear you company if you wake. In the morning I'll be with you early.'

'We!' said Godith, low but firmly.

'Wait, one more thing!' Cadfael had remembered it at the last moment. 'You've no weapon on you – yet I think you did wear a sword.'

'I shed it,' mumbled the boy drowsily, 'in the river. I had too much weight to keep afloat – and they were shooting. It was in the water I got this clout . . . I had the wit to go down, I hope they believe I stayed down . . . God knows it was touch and go!'

'Yes, well, tomorrow will do. And we must find you a weapon. Now, good night!'

He was asleep before ever they put out the candle, and drew the door closed. They walked wordlessly through the rustling stubble for some minutes, the sky over them an arch of dark and vivid blue paling at the edges into a fringe of sea-green. Godith asked abruptly: 'Brother Cadfael, who was Ganymede?'

'A beautiful youth who was cup-bearer to Jove, and much loved by him.'

'Oh!' said Godith, uncertain whether to be delighted or rueful, this success being wholly due to her boyishness.

'But some say that it's also another name for Hebe,' said Cadfael.

'Oh! And who is Hebe?'

'Cup-bearer to Jove, and much loved by him – but a beautiful maiden.'

'Ah!' said Godith profoundly. And as they reached the road

and crossed towards the abbey, she said seriously: 'You know who he must be, don't you?'

'Jove? The most god-like of all the pagan gods . . .'

'*He!*' she said severely, and caught and shook Brother Cadfael's arm in her solemnity. 'A Saxon name, and Saxon hair, and on the run from the king's men. . . . He's Torold Blund, who set out with Nicholas to save FitzAlan's treasury for the empress. And of course he had nothing to do with poor Nicholas's death. I don't believe he ever did a shabby thing in his whole life!'

'That,' said Cadfael, 'I hesitate to say of any man, least of all myself. But I give you my word, child, this one most shabby thing he certainly did not do. You may sleep in peace!'

It was nothing out of the ordinary for Brother Cadfael, that devoted gardener and apothecary, to rise long before it was necessary for Prime, and have an hour's work done before he joined his brothers at the first service; so no one thought anything of it when he dressed and went out early on that particular morning, and no one even knew that he also roused his boy, as he had promised. They went out with more medicaments and food, and a cotte and hose that Brother Cadfael had filched from the charity offerings that came in to the almoner. Godith had taken away with her the young man's bloodstained shirt, which was of fine linen and not to be wasted, had washed it before she slept, and mended it on rising, where the arrow-head had sliced the threads asunder. On such a warm August night, spread out carefully on the bushes in the garden, it had dried well.

Their patient was sitting up in his bed of sacks, munching bread with appetite, and seemed to have total trust in them, for he made no move to seek cover when the door began to open. He had draped his torn and stained cotte round his shoulders, but for the rest was naked under his blanket, and the bared, smooth chest and narrow flanks were elegantly formed. Body and eyes still showed blue bruises, but he was certainly much restored after one long night of rest.

'Now,' said Cadfael with satisfaction, 'you may talk as much as you like, my friend, while I dress this wound of yours. The leg will do very well until we have more time, but this shoulder is a tricky thing. Godric, see to him on the other side while I uncover it, it may well stick. You steady bandage and arm while

70

I unbind. Now, sir . . .' And he added, for fair exchange: 'They call me Brother Cadfael, I'm as Welsh as Dewi Sant, and I've been about the world, as you may have guessed. And this boy of mine is Godric, as you've heard, and brought me to you. Trust us both, or neither.'

'I trust both,' said the boy. He had more colour this morning, or it was the flush of dawn reflected, his eyes were bright and hazel, more green than brown. 'I owe you more than trust can pay, but shew me more I can do, and I'll do it. My name is Torold Blund, I come from a hamlet by Oswestry, and I'm FitzAlan's man from head to foot.' The bandage stuck then, and Godith felt him flinch, and locked the fold until she could ease it free by delicate touches. 'If that puts you · in peril,' said Torold, suppressing the pain, 'I do believe I'm fit to go, and go I will. I would not for the world shrug off my danger upon you.'

'You'll go when you're let,' said Godith, and for revenge snatched off the last fold of bandage, but very circumspectly, and holding the anointed pad in place. 'And it won't be today.'

'Hush, let him talk, time's short,' said Cadfael. 'Go to it, lad. We're not in the business of selling Maud's men to Stephen, or Stephen's men to Maud. How did you come here in this pass?'

Torold took a deep breath, and talked to some purpose. 'I came to the castle here with Nicholas Faintree, who was also FitzAlan's man, from the next manor to my father's, we joined the garrison only a week before it fell. The evening before the assault there was a council – we were not there, we were small fry – and they resolved to get the FitzAlan treasury away the very next day for the use of the empress, not knowing then it would be the last day. Nicholas and I were told off to be the messengers because we were new to Shrewsbury, and not known, and might get through well enough where others senior to us might be known and cut down at sight. The goods – they were not too bulky, thank God, not much plate, more coin, and most of all in jewellery – were hidden somewhere no one knew but our lord and his agent who had them in guard. We had to ride to him when the word was given, take them from where he would show us, and get clear by night for Wales. FitzAlan had an accord with Owain Gwynedd – not that he's for either party here, he's for Wales, but civil war here suits him well, and he and FitzAlan are friends. Before it was well dawn they attacked, and it was plain we could not hold. So we were sent off on our

errand – it was to a shop in the town . . .' He wavered, uneasy at
giving any clue.

'I know,' said Cadfael, wiping away the exudation of the night
from the shoulder wound, and anointing a new pad. 'It was Edric
Flesher, who himself has told me his part in it. You were taken
out to his barn in Frankwell, and the treasury laid up with you
to wait for the cover of night. Go on!'

The young man, watching the dressing of his own hurts without emotion, went on obediently: 'We rode as soon as it was
dark. From there clear of the suburb and into trees is only a
short way. There's a herdsman's hut there in the piece where
the track is in woodland, though only along the edge, the fields
still close. We were on this stretch when Nick's horse fell lame. I
lit down to see, for he went very badly, and he had picked up a
caltrop, and was cut to the bone.'

'Caltrops?' said Brother Cadfael, startled. 'On such a forest
path, away from any field of battle?' For those unobtrusive
martial cruelties, made in such a shape as to be scattered under
the hooves of cavalry, and leaving always one crippling spike
upturned, surely had no part to play on a narrow forest ride.

'Caltrops,' said Torold positively. 'I don't speak simply
from the wound, the thing was there embedded, I know, I
wrenched it out. But the poor beast was foundered, he could go,
but not far, and not loaded. There's a farm I know of very close
there, I thought I could get a fresh horse in exchange for Nick's,
a poor exchange, but what could we do? We did not even unload, but Nick lighted down, to ease the poor creature of his
weight, and said he would wait there in the hut for me. And I
went, and I got a mount from the farm – it's off to the right,
heading west as we were, the man's name is Ulf, he's distant kin
to me on my mother's side – and rode back, with Nick's half the
load on this new nag.

'I came up towards the hut,' he said, stiffening at the recollec-
tion, 'and I thought he would be looking out for me, ready to
mount, and he was not. I don't know why that made me so uneasy.
Not a breath stirring, and for all I was cautious, I knew I could
be heard by any man truly listening. And he never showed face
or called out word. So I never went too near. I drew off, and
reined forward a little way, and made a single tether of the
horses, to be off as fast as might be. One knot to undo, and with
a single pluck. And then I went to the hut.'

'It was full dark then?' asked Cadfael, rolling bandage.

'Full dark, but I could see, having been out in it. Inside it was black as pitch. The door stood half open to the wall. I went inside stretching my ears, and not a murmur. But in the middle of the hut I fell over him. Over Nick! If I hadn't I might not be here to tell as much,' said Torold grimly, and cast a sudden uneasy glance at his Ganymede, so plainly some years his junior, and attending him with such sedulous devotion. 'This is not good hearing.' His eyes appealed eloquently to Cadfael over Godith's shoulder.

'You'd best go on freely,' said Cadfael with sympathy. 'He's deeper in this than you think, and will have your blood and mine if we dare try to banish him. No part of this matter of Shrewsbury has been good hearing, but something may be saved. Tell your part, we'll tell ours.'

Godith, all eyes, ears and serviceable hands, wisely said nothing at all.

'He was dead,' said Torold starkly. 'I fell on him, mouth to mouth, there was no breath in him. I held him, reaching forward to save myself as I fell, I had him in my arms and he was like an armful of rags. And then I heard the dry fodder rustle behind me, and started round, because there was no wind to stir it, and I was frightened . . .'

'Small blame!' said Cadfael, smoothing a fresh pad soaked in his herbal salve against the moist wound. 'You had good reason. Trouble no more for your friend, he is with God surely. We buried him yesterday within the abbey. He has a prince's tomb. You, I think, escaped the like very narrowly, when his murderer lunged from behind the door.'

'So I think, too,' said the boy, and drew in hissing breath at the bite of Cadfael's dressing. 'There he must have been. The grass warned me when he made his assay. I don't know how it is, every man throws up his right arm to ward off blows from his head, and so did I. His cord went round my wrist as well as my throat. I was not clever or a hero, I lashed out in fright and jerked it out of his hands. It brought him down on top of me in the dark. I know only too well,' he said, defensively, 'that you may not believe me.'

'There are things that go to confirm you. Spare to be so wary of your friends. So you were man to man, at least, better odds than before. How did you escape him?'

'More by luck than valour,' said Torold ruefully. 'We were rolling about in the hay, wrestling and trying for each other's throat, everything by feel and nothing by sight, and neither of us could get space or time to draw, for I don't know how long, but I suppose it was no more than minutes. What ended it was that there must have been an old manger there against the wall, half fallen to pieces, and I banged my head against one of the boards lying loose in the hay. I hit him with it, two-handed, and he dropped. I doubt I did him any lasting damage, but it knocked him witless long enough for me to run, and run I did, and loosed both the horses, and made off westward like a hunted hare. I still had work to do, and there was no one but me left to do it, or I might have stayed to try and even the account for Nick. Or I might not,' owned Torold with scowling honesty. 'I doubt I was even thinking about FitzAlan's errand then, though I'm thinking of it now, and have been ever since. I ran for my life. I was afraid he might have had others lying in ambush to come to his aid. All I wanted was out of there as fast as my legs would go.'

'No need to make a penance of it,' said Cadfael mildly, securing his bandage. 'Sound sense is something to be glad of, not ashamed. But my friend, it's taken you two full days, by your own account, to get to much the same spot you started from. I take it, by that, the king has allies pretty thick between here and Wales, at least by the roads.'

'Thick as bees in swarm! I got well forward by the more northerly road, and all but ran my head into a patrol where there was no passing. They were stopping everything that moved, what chance had I with two horses and a load of valuables? I had to draw off into the woods, and by that time it was getting light, there was nothing to be done but lie up until dark again and try the southerly road. And that was no better, they had loose companies ranging the countryside by then. I thought I might make my way through by keeping off the roads and close to the curve of the river, but it was another night lost. I lay up in a copse on the hill all day Thursday, and tried again by night, and that was when they winded me, four or five of them, and I had to run for it, with only one way to run, down towards the river. They had me penned, I couldn't get out of the trap. I took the saddle-bags from both horses, and turned the beasts loose, and started them off at a panic gallop, hoping they'd crash through and lead the pursuit away from me, but there was one of the fellows too near, he saw the trick, and made for me instead. He gave me this slash in the thigh, and his yell brought the others running. There was only one thing to do. I took to the water, saddle-bags and all. I'm a strong swimmer, but with that weight it was hard work to stay afloat, and let the current bring me downstream. That's when they started shooting. Dark as it was, they'd been out in it long enough to have fair vision, and there's always light from the water when there's something moving in it. So I got this shoulder wound, and had the sense to go under and stay under as long as I had breath. Severn's fast, even in summer water it carried me down well. They followed along the bank for a while, and loosed one or two more arrows, but then I think they were sure I was under for good. I worked my way towards the bank as soon as it seemed safe, to get a foot to ground and draw breath here and there, but I stayed in the water. I knew the bridge would be manned, I dared not drag myself ashore until I was well past. It was high time by then. I remember crawling into the bushes, but not much else, except rousing just enough to be afraid to stir when your people came reaping. And then Godric here found me. And that's the truth of it,' he ended firmly, and looked Cadfael unblinkingly in the eye.

'But not the whole truth,' said Cadfael, placidly enough. 'Godric found no saddle-bags along with you.' He eyed the young face that fronted him steadily, lips firmly closed, and smiled. 'No, never fret, we won't question you. You are the sole custodian of FitzAlan's treasury, and what you've done with it, and how, God knows, you ever managed to do anything sensible with it in your condition, that's your affair. You haven't the air of a courier who has failed in his mission, I'll say that for you. And for your better peace, all the talk in the town is that Fitz-Alan and Adeney were not taken, but broke out of the ring and are got clean away. Now we have to leave you alone here until afternoon, we have duties, too. But one of us, or both, will come and see how you're faring then. And here's food and drink, and clothes I hope will fit you well enough to pass. But lie quiet for today, you're not your own man yet, however wholeheartedly you may be FitzAlan's.'

Godith laid the washed and mended shirt on top of the folded garments, and was following Cadfael to the door when the look on Torold's face halted her, half uneasy, half triumphant. His eyes grew round with amazement as he stared at the crisp, clean linen, and the fine stitches of the long mend where the blood-stained gash had been. A soft whistle of admiration saluted the wonder.

'Holy Mary! Who did this? Do you keep an expert seamstress within the abbey walls? Or did you pray for a miracle?'

'That? That's Godric's work,' said Cadfael, not altogether innocently, and walked out into the early sushine, leaving Godith flushed to the ears. 'We learn more skills in the cloister than merely cutting wheat and brewing cordials,' she said loftily, and fled after Cadfael.

But she was grave enough on the way back, going over in her mind Torold's story, and reflecting how easily he might have died before ever she met him; not merely once, in the murderer's cord, nor the second time from King Stephen's roaming companies, but in the river, or from his wounds in the bushes. It seemed to her that divine grace was taking care of him, and had provided her as the instrument. There remained lingering anxieties.

'Brother Cadfael, you do believe him?'

'I believe him. What he could not tell truth about, he would not lie about, either. Why, what's on your mind still?'

'Only that before I saw him I said – I was afraid the companion who rode with Nicholas was far the most likely to be tempted to kill him. How simple it would have been! But you said yesterday, you *did* say, he did not do it. Are you quite sure? How do you know?'

'Nothing simpler, girl dear! The mark of the strangler's cord is on his neck and on his wrist. Did you not understand those thin scars? He was meant to go after his friend out of this world. No, you need have no fear on that score, what he told us is truth. But there may be things he could not tell us, things we ought to discover, for Nicholas Faintree's sake. Godith, this afternoon, when you've seen to the lotions and wines, you may leave the garden and go and keep him company if you please, and I'll come there as soon as I can. There are things I must look into, over there on the Frankwell side of Shrewsbury.'

CHAPTER SIX

From the Frankwell end of the western bridge, the suburb outside the walls and over the river, the road set off due west,
climbing steadily, leaving behind the gardens that fringed the
settlement. At first it was but a single road mounting the hill that
rose high above Severn, then shortly it branched into two, of
which the more southerly soon branched again, three spread
fingers pointing into Wales. But Cadfael took the road Nicholas
and Torold had taken on the night after the castle fell, the most
northerly of the three.

He had thought of calling on Edric Flesher in the town, and
giving him the news that one, at least, of the two young couriers
had survived and preserved his charge, but then he had decided
against it. As yet Torold was by no means safe, and until he was
well away, the fewer people who knew of his whereabouts the
better, the less likely was word of him to slip out in the wrong
place, where his enemies might overhear. There would be time
later to share any good news with Edric and Petronilla.

The road entered the thick woodland of which Torold had
spoken, and narrowed into a grassy track, within the trees but
keeping close to the edge, where cultivated fields showed between
the trunks. And there, withdrawn a little deeper into the woods,
lay the hut, low and roughly timbered. From this place it would
be a simple matter to carry a dead body on horseback as far as
the castle ditch. The river, as everywhere here, meandered in
intricate coils, and would have to be crossed in order to reach
the place where the dead had been flung, but there was a place
opposite the castle on this side where a central island made the
stream fordable even on foot in such a dry season, once the castle
itself was taken. The distance was small, the night had been long
enough. Then somewhere off to the right lay Ulf's holding, where
Torold had got his exchange of horses. Cadfael turned off in
that direction, and found the croft not a quarter of a mile from
the track.

Ulf was busy gleaning after carrying his corn, and not at first
disposed to be talkative to an unknown monk, but the mention

of Torold's name, and the clear intimation that here was someone Torold had trusted, loosened his tongue.

'Yes, he did come with a lamed horse, and I did let him have
the best of mine in exchange. I was the gainer, though, even so,
for the beast he left with me came from FitzAlan's stables. He's
still lame, but healing. Would you see him? His fine gear is well
hidden, it would mark him out for stolen or worse if it was seen.'

Even without his noble harness the horse, a tall roan, showed
suspiciously fine for a working farmer to possess, and undoubtedly he was still lame of one fore-foot. Ulf showed him the
wound.

'Torold said a caltrop did this,' mused Cadfael. 'Strange place
to find such.'

'Yet a caltrop it was, for I have it, and several more like it that
I went and combed out of the grass there next day. My beasts
cross there, I wanted no more of them lamed. Someone seeded
a dozen yards of the path at its narrowest there. To halt them
by the hut, what else?'

'Someone who knew in advance what they were about and the
road they'd take, and gave himself plenty of time to lay his trap,
and wait in ambush for them to spring it.'

'The king had got wind of the matter somehow,' Ulf opined
darkly, 'and sent some of his men secretly to get hold of whatever they were carrying. He's desperate for money – as bad as
the other side.'

Nevertheless, thought Cadfael, as he walked back to the hut in
the woods, for all that I can see, this was no party sent out by
the king, but one man's enterprise for his own private gain. If he
had indeed been the king's emissary he would have had a company with him. It was not King Stephen's coffers that were to
have profited, if all had gone according to plan.

To sum up, then, it was proven there had indeed been a third
here that night. Over and over Torold was cleared of blame. The
caltrops were real, a trail of them had been laid to ensure
laming one or other of the horses, and so far the stratagem had
succeeded, perhaps even better than expected, since it had
severed the two companions, leaving the murderer free to deal
with one first, and then lie in wait for the other.

Cadfael did not at once go into the hut; the surroundings
equally interested him. Somewhere here, well clear of the hut
itself, Torold had regarded the pricking of his thumbs, and

tethered the horses forward on the road, ready for flight. And somewhere here, too, probably withdrawn deeper into cover, the third man had also had a horse in waiting. It should still be possible to find their traces. It had not rained since that night, nor was it likely that many men had roamed these woods since. All the inhabitants of Shrewsbury were still keeping close under their own roof-trees unless forced to go abroad, and the king's patrols rode in the open, where they could ride fast.

It took him a little while, but he found both places. The solitary horse had been hobbled and left to graze, and by the signs he had been a fine creature, for the hoof-marks he had left in a patch of softer ground, a hollow of dried mud where water habitually lay after rain, and had left a smooth silt, showed large and well shod. The spot where two had waited together was well to westward of the hut, and in thick cover. A low branch showed the peeled scar where the tether had been pulled clear in haste, and two distinguishable sets of prints could be discerned where the grass thinned to bare ground.

Cadfael went into the hut. He had broad daylight to aid him, and with the door set wide there was ample light even within. The murderer had waited here for his victim, he must have left his traces.

The remains of the winter fodder, mown along the sunlit fringes of the woods, had been left here against the return of autumn, originally in a neat stack against the rear wall, but now a stormy sea of grass was spread and tossed over the entire earthen floor, as though a gale had played havoc within there. The decrepit manger from which Torold had plucked his loose plank was there, drunkenly leaning. The dry grass was well laced with small herbs now rustling and dead but still fragrant, and there was a liberal admixture of hooky, clinging goose-grass in it. That reminded him not only of the shred of stem dragged deep into Nick Faintree's throat by the ligature that killed him, but also of Torold's ugly shoulder wound. He needed goose-grass to make a dressing for it, he would look along the fringe of the fields, it must be plentiful here. God's even-handed justice, that called attention to one friend's murder with a dry stem of last year's crop, might well, by the same token, design to soothe and heal the other friend's injuries by the gift of this year's.

Meantime, the hut yielded little, except the evident chaos of a hand-to-hand struggle waged within it. But in the rough

79

timbers behind the door there were a few roving threads of deep blue woollen cloth, rather pile than thread. Someone had certainly lain in hiding there, the door drawn close to his body. There was also one clot of dried clover that bore a smaller clot of blood. But Cadfael raked and combed in vain among the rustling fodder in search of the strangler's weapon. Either the murderer had found it again and taken it away with him, or else it lay deeply entangled in some corner, evading search. Cadfael worked his way backwards on hands and knees from the manger to the doorway, and was about to give up, and prise himself up from his knees, when the hand on which he supported his weight bore down on something hard and sharp, and winced from the contact in surprise. Something was driven half into the earth floor under the thinning layers of hay, like another caltrop planted here for inquisitive monks to encounter to their grief and injury. He sat back on his heels, and carefully brushed aside the rustling grasses, until he could get a hand to the hidden thing and prise it loose. It came away into his hand readily, filling his palm, hard, encrusted and chill. He lifted it to the invading sunlight in the doorway behind him, and it glittered with pinpoints of yellow, a miniature sun.

Brother Cadfael rose from his knees and took it into the full daylight of afternoon to see what he had found. It was a large, rough-cut gem stone, as big as a crab-apple, a deep-yellow topaz still gripped and half-enclosed by an eagle's talon of silver-gilt. The claw was complete, finely shaped, but broken off at the stem, below the stone it clutched. This was the tip of some excellent setting in silver, perhaps the end of a brooch-pin – no, too large for that. The apex of a dagger-hilt? If so, a noble dagger, no common working knife. Beneath that jagged tip would have been the rounded hand-grip, and on the cross-piece, perhaps, some smaller topaz stones to match this master-stone. Broken off thus, it lay in his hand a sullen, faceted ball of gold.

One man had threshed and clawed here in his death-throes, two others had rolled and flailed in mortal combat; any one of the three, with a thrusting hip and the weight of a convulsed body, could have bored this hilt into the hard-packed earth of the floor, and snapped off the crown-stone thus at its most fragile point, and never realised the loss.

Brother Cadfael put it away carefully in the scrip at his girdle, and went to look for his goose-grass. In the thick herbage at the edge of the trees, where the sun reached in, he found sprawling, angular mats of it, filled his scrip, and set off for home with dozens of the little hooked seeds clinging in his skirts.

Godith slipped away as soon as all the brothers had dispersed to their afternoon work, and made her way by circumspect deviations to the mill at the end of the Gaye. She had taken with her some ripe plums from the orchard, the half of a small loaf of new bread, and a fresh flask of Cadfael's wine. The patient had rapidly developed a healthy appetite, and it was her pleasure to enjoy his enjoyment of food and drink, as though she had a proprietorial interest in him by reason of having found him in need.

He was sitting on his bed of sacks, fully dressed, his back against the warm timbers of the wall, his long legs stretched out comfortably before him with ankles crossed. The cotte and hose fitted reasonably well, perhaps a little short in the sleeves. He looked surprisingly lively, though still rather greyish in the face, and careful in his movements because of the lingering aches and pains from his wounds. She was not best pleased to see that he had struggled into the cotte, and said so.

'You should keep that shoulder easy, there was no need to force it into a sleeve yet. If you don't rest it, it won't heal.'

'I'm very well,' he said abstractedly. 'And I must bear whatever discomfort there may be, if I'm to get on my way soon. It will knit well enough, I dare say.' His mind was not on his own ills, he was frowning thoughtfully over other matters. 'Godric, I had no time to question, this morning, but – your Brother Cadfael said Nick's buried, and in the abbey. Is that truth?' He was not so much doubting their word as marvelling how it had come about. 'How did they ever find him?'

'That was Brother Cadfael's own doing,' said Godith. She sat down beside him and told him. 'There was one more than there should have been, and Brother Cadfael would not rest until he had found the one who was different, and since then he has not let anyone else rest. The king knows there was murder done, and has said it should be avenged. If anyone can get justice for your friend, Brother Cadfael is the man.'

'So whoever it was, there in the hut, it seems I did him little harm, only dimmed his wits for a matter of minutes. I was

81

afraid of it. He was fit enough and cunning enough to get rid of his dead man before morning.'

'But not clever enough to deceive Brother Cadfael. Every individual soul must be accounted for. Now at least Nicholas has had all the rites of the church in his own clean name, and has a noble tomb.'

'I'm glad,' said Torold, 'to know he was not left there to rot unhonoured, or put into the ground nameless among all the rest, though they were our comrades, too, and not deserving of such a death. If we had stayed, we should have suffered the same fate. If they caught me, I might suffer it yet. And yet King Stephen approves the hunt for the murderer who did his work for him! What a mad world!'

Godith thought so, too; but for all that, there was a difference, a sort of logic in it, that the king should accept the onus of the ninety-four whose deaths he had decreed, but utterly reject the guilt for the ninety-fifth, killed treacherously and without his sanction.

'He despised the manner of the killing, and he resented being made an accomplice in it. And no one is going to capture you,' she said firmly, and hoisted the plums out of the breast of her cotte, and tumbled them between them on the blanket. 'Here's a taste of something sweeter than bread. Try them!'

They sat companionably eating, and slipping the stones through a chink in the floorboards into the river below. 'I still have a task laid on me,' said Torold at length, soberly, 'and now I'm alone to see it done. And heaven knows, Godric, what I should have done without you and Brother Cadfael, and sad I shall be to set off and leave you behind, with small chance of seeing you again. Never shall I forget what you've done for me. But go I must, as soon as I'm fit and can get clear. It will be better for you when I'm gone, you'll be safer so.'

'Who is safe? Where?' said Godith, biting into another ripe purple plum. 'There is no safe place.'

'There are degrees in danger, at any rate. And I have work to do, and I'm fit to get on with it now.'

She turned and gave him a long, roused look. Never until that moment had she looked far enough ahead to confront the idea of his departure. He was something she had only newly discovered, and here he was, unless she was mistaking his meaning, threatening to take himself off, out of her hands and out of her life. Well, she had an ally in Brother Cadfael. With the authority of her master she said sternly: 'If you're thinking you're going to set off anywhere until you're fully healed, then think again, and smartly, too. You'll stay here until you're given leave to go, and that won't be today, or tomorrow, you can make up your mind to that!'

Torold gaped at her in startled and delighted amusement, laid his head back against the rough timber of the wall, and laughed aloud. 'You sound like my mother, the time I had a bad fall at the quintain. And dearly I love you, but so I did her, and I still went my own way. I'm fit and strong and able, Godric, and I'm under orders that came before your orders. I must go. In my place, you'd have been out of here before now, as fierce as you are.'

'I would not,' she said furiously, 'I have more sense. What use would you be, on the run from here, without even a weapon, without a horse – you turned your horses loose, remember, to baffle the pursuit, you told us so! How far would you get? And how grateful would FitzAlan be for your folly? Not that we need go into it,' she said loftily, 'seeing you're not fit even to walk out of here as far as the river. You'd be carried back on Brother Cadfael's shoulders, just as you came here the first time.'

'Oh, would I so, Godric, my little cousin?' Torold's eyes were sparkling mischief. He had forgotten for the moment all his graver cares, amused and nettled by the impudence of this urchin, vehemently threatening him with humiliation and failure. 'Do I look to you so feeble?'

'As a starving cat,' she said, and plunged a plum-stone between the boards with a vicious snap. 'A ten-year-old could lay you on your back!'

'You think so, do you?' Torold rolled sideways and took her about the middle in his good arm. 'I'll show you, Master Godric, whether I'm fit or no!' He was laughing for pure pleasure, feeling his muscles stretch and exult again in a sudden, sweet bout of horseplay with a trusted familiar, who needed taking down a little for everyone's good. He reached his wounded arm to pin the boy down by the shoulders. The arrogant imp had uttered only one muffled squeak as he was tipped on his back. 'One hand of mine can more than deal with you, my lovely lad!' crowed Torold, withdrawing half his weight, and flattening his left palm firmly in the breast of the over-ample cotte, to demonstrate.

He recoiled, stricken and enlightened, just as Godith got breath enough to swear at him, and strike out furiously with her right hand, catching him a salutary box on the ear. They fell apart in a huge, ominous silence, and sat up among the rumpled sacks with a yard or more between them.

The silence and stillness lasted long. It was a full minute before they so much as tilted cautious heads and looked sidewise at each other. Her profile, warily emerging from anger into guilty sympathy, was delicate and pert and utterly feminine, he must have been weak and sick indeed, or he would surely have known. The soft, gruff voice was only an ambiguous charm, a natural deceit. Torold scrubbed thoughtfully at his stinging ear, and asked at last, very carefully: 'Why didn't you tell me? I never meant to offend you, but how was I to know?'

'There was no need for you to know,' snapped Godith, still ruffled, 'if you'd had the sense to do as you're bid, or the courtesy to treat your friends gently.'

'But you goaded me! Good God,' protested Torold, 'it was only the rough play I'd have used on a young brother of my own, and you asked for it.' He demanded suddenly: 'Does Brother Cadfael know?'

'Of course he does! Brother Cadfael at least can tell a hart from a hind.'

There fell a second and longer silence, full of resentment, curiosity and caution, while they continued to study each other through lowered lashes, she furtively eyeing the sleeve that covered his wound, in case a telltale smear of blood should break through, he surveying again the delicate curves of her face, the jut of lip and lowering of brows that warned him she was still offended.

Two small, wary voices uttered together, grudgingly: 'Did I hurt you?'

They began to laugh at the same instant, suddenly aware of their own absurdity. The illusion of estrangement vanished utterly; they fell into each other's arms helpless with laughter, and nothing was left to complicate their relationship but the slightly exaggerated gentleness with which they touched each other.

'But you shouldn't have used that arm so,' she reproached at last, as they disentangled themselves and sat back, eased and content. 'You could have started it open again, it's a bad gash.' 'Oh, no, there's no damage. But you – I wouldn't for the world have vexed you.' And he asked, quite simply, and certain of his right to be told: 'Who are you? And how did you ever come into such a coil as this?'

She turned her head and looked at him long and earnestly; there would never again be anything with which she would hesitate to trust him.

'They left it too late,' she said, 'to send me away out of Shrewsbury before the town fell. This was a desperate throw, turning me into an abbey servant, but I was sure I could carry it off. And I did, with everyone but Brother Cadfael. *You* were taken in, weren't you? I'm a fugitive of your party, Torold, we're two of a kind. I'm Godith Adeney.'

'Truly?' He beamed at her, round-eyed with wonder and delight. 'You're Fulke Adeney's daughter? Praise God! We were anxious for you! Nick especially, for he knew you . . . I never saw you till now, but I, too . . .' He stooped his fair head and lightly kissed the small, none too clean hand that had just picked up the last of the plums. 'Mistress Godith, I am your servant to command! This is splendid! If I'd known, I'd have told you better than half a tale.'

'Tell me now,' said Godith, and generously split the plum in half, and sent the stone whirling down into the Severn. The riper half she presented to his open mouth, effectively closing it for a moment. 'And then,' she said, 'I'll tell you my side of it, and we shall have a useful whole.'

Brother Cadfael did not go straight to the mill on his return, but halted to check that his workshop was in order, and to pound up his goose-grass in a mortar, and prepare a smooth green salve from it. Then he went to join his young charges, careful to circle into the shadow of the mill from the opposite direction, and to keep an eye open for any observer. Time was marching all too swiftly, within an hour he and Godith would have to go back for Vespers.

They had both known his step; when he entered they were sitting side by side with backs propped against the wall, watching the doorway with rapt, expectant smiles. They had a certain serene, aloof air about them, as though they inhabited a world immune from common contacts or common cares, but generously accessible to him. He had only to look at them, and he knew they had no more secrets; they were so rashly and candidly man and woman together that there was no need even to ask anything. Though they were both waiting expectantly to tell him!

'Brother Cadfael . . .' Godith began, distantly radiant.

'First things first,' said Cadfael briskly. 'Help him out of cotte and shirt, and start unwinding the bandage until it sticks – as it will, my friend, you're not out of the wood yet. Then wait, and I'll ease it off.'

There was no disconcerting or chastening them. The girl was up in a moment, easing the seam of the cotte away from Torold's wound, loosening the ties of his shirt to slip it down from his shoulder, gently freeing the end of the linen bandage and beginning to roll it up. The boy inclined this way and that to help, and never took his eyes from Godith's face, as she seldom took hers from his absorbed countenance, and only to concentrate upon his needs.

'Well, well!' thought Cadfael philosophically. 'It seems Hugh Beringar will seek his promised bride to little purpose – if, indeed, he really is seeking her?'

'Well, youngster,' he said aloud, 'you're a credit to me and to yourself, as clean-healing flesh as ever I saw. This slice of you that somebody tried to sever will stay with you lifelong, after all, and the arm will even serve you to hold a bow in a month or so. But you'll have the scar as long as you live. Now hold steady, this may burn, but trust me, it's the best salve you could have for green wounds. Torn muscles hurt as they knit, but knit they will.'

'It doesn't hurt,' said Torold in a dream. 'Brother Cadfael . . .'

'Hold your tongue until we have you all bound up trim. Then you can talk your hearts out, the both of you.'

And talk they did, as soon as Torold was helped back into his shirt, and the cotte draped over his shoulders. Each of them took up the thread from the other, as though handed it in a fixed and formal ceremony, like a favour in a dance. Even their voices had grown somehow alike, as if they matched tones without understanding that they did it. They had not the least idea, as yet, that they were in love. The innocents believed they were involved in a partisan comradeship, which was but the lesser half of what had happened to them in his absence.

86

'So I have told Torold all about myself,' said Godith, 'and he has told me the only thing he did not tell us before. And now he wants to tell you.'

Torold picked up the tendered thread willingly. 'I have Fitz-Alan's treasury safely hidden,' he said simply. 'I had it in two pairs of linked saddle-bags, and I kept it afloat, too, all down the river, though I had to shed sword and sword-belt and dagger and all to lighten the load. I fetched up under the first arch of the stone bridge. You'll know it as well as I. That first pier spreads, there used to be a boat-mill moored under it, some time ago, and the mooring chain is still there, bolted to a ring in the stone. A man can hold on there and get his breath, and so I did. And I hauled up the chain and hooked my saddle-bags on to it, and let them down under the water, out of sight. Then I left them there, and drifted on down here just about alive, to where Godith found me.' He found no difficulty in speaking of her as Godith; the name had a jubilant sound in his mouth. 'And there all that gold is dangling in the Severn still, I hope and believe, until I can reclaim it and get it away to its rightful owner. Thank God he's alive to benefit by it.' A last qualm shook him suddenly and severely. 'There's been no word of anyone finding it?' he questioned anxiously. 'We should know if they had?'

'We should know, never doubt it! No, no one's hooked any such fish. Why should anyone look for it there? But getting it out again undetected may not be so easy. We three must put our wits together,' said Cadfael, 'and see what we can do between us. And while you two have been swearing your alliance, let me tell you what I've been doing.'

He made it brief enough. 'I found all as you told it. The traces of your horses are there, and of your enemy's, too. One horse only. This was a thief bent on his own enrichment, no zealot trying to fill the king's coffers. He had seeded the path for you liberally with caltrops, your kinsman collected several of them next day, for the sake of his own cattle. The signs of your struggle within the hut are plain enough. And pressed into the earth floor I found this.' He produced it from his scrip, a lump of deep yellow roughly faceted, and clenched in the broken silver-gilt claw. Torold took it from him and examined it curiously, but without apparent recognition.

'Broken off from a hilt, would you think?'

'Not from yours, then?'

'Mine?' Torold laughed. 'Where would a poor squire with his way to make get hold of so fine a weapon as this must have been? No, mine was a plain old sword my grandsire wore before me, and a dagger to match, in a heavy hide sheath. If it had been light as this, I'd have tried to keep it. No, this is none of mine.'

'Nor Faintree's, either?'

Torold shook his head decidedly. 'If he had any such, I should have known. Nick and I are of the same condition, and friends three years and more.' He looked up intently into Brother Cadfael's face. 'Now I remember a very small thing that may have meaning, after all. When I broke free and left the other fellow dazed, I trod on something under the hay where we'd been struggling, a small, hard thing that almost threw me. I think it could well have been this. It was *his*? Yes, it must have been his! Snapped off against the ground as we rolled.'

'His, almost certainly, and the only thing we have to lead us to him,' said Cadfael, taking back the stone and hiding it again from view in his pouch. 'No man would willingly discard so fine a thing because one stone was broken from it. Whoever owned it still has it, and will get it repaired when he dare. If we can find the dagger, we shall have found the murderer.'

'I wish,' said Torold fiercely, 'I could both go and stay! I should be glad to be the one to avenge Nick, he was a good friend to me. But my part is to obey my orders, and get Fitz-Alan's goods safely over to him in France. And,' he said, regarding Cadfael steadily, 'to take with me also Fulke Adeney's daughter, and deliver her safe to her father. If you will trust her to me.'

'And help us,' added Godith with immense confidence.

'Trust her to you – I might,' said Cadfael mildly. 'And help you both I surely will, as best I can. A very simple matter! All I have to do – and mark you, she has the assurance to demand it of me! – is to conjure you two good horses out of the empty air, where even poor hacks are gold, retrieve your hidden treasure for you, and see you well clear of the town, westward into Wales. Just a trifle! Harder things are done daily by the saints . . .'

He had reached this point when he stiffened suddenly, and spread a warning hand to enjoin silence. Listening with ears stretched, he caught for a second time the soft sound of a foot moving warily in the edge of the rustling stubble, close to the open door.

'What is it?' asked Godith in a soundless whisper, her eyes immense in alarm.

'Nothing!' said Cadfael as softly. 'My ears playing tricks.' And aloud he said: 'Well, you and I must be getting back for Vespers. Come! It wouldn't do to be late.'

Torold accepted his silent orders, and let them go without a word from him. If someone had indeed been listening . . . But he had heard nothing, and it seemed to him that even Cadfael was not sure. Why alarm Godith? Brother Cadfael was her best protector here, and once within the abbey walls she would again be in sanctuary. As for Torold, he was his own responsibility, though he would have been happier if he had had a sword!

Brother Cadfael reached down into the capacious waist of his habit, and drew out a long poniard in a rubbed and worn leather scabbard. Silently he put it into Torold's hands. The young man took it, marvelling, staring as reverently as at a first small miracle, so apt was the answer to his thought. He had it by the sheath, the cross of the hilt before his face, and was still gazing in wonder as they went out from him into the evening, and drew the door closed after them. Cadfael took the memory of that look with him into the fresh, saffron air of sunset. He himself must once have worn the same rapt expression, contemplating the same uplifted hilt. When he had taken the Cross, long ago, his vow had been made on that hilt, and the dagger had gone with him to Jerusalem, and roved the eastern seas with him for ten years. Even when he gave up his sword along with the things of this world, and surrendered all pride of possessions, he had kept the poniard. Just as well to part with it at last, to someone who had need of it and would not disgrace it.

He looked about him very cautiously as they rounded the corner of the mill and crossed the race. His hearing was sharp as a wild creature's, and he had heard no whisper or rustle from outside until the last few moments of their talk together, nor could he now be certain that what he had heard was a human foot, it might well have been a small animal slipping through the stubble. All the same, he must take thought for what might happen if they really had been spied upon. Surely, at the worst, only the last few exchanges could have been overheard, though those were revealing enough. Had the treasure been mentioned? Yes, he himself had said that all that was required of him was to obtain two horses, retrieve the treasure, and see them safely headed for Wales. Had anything been said then of *where* the treasure was hidden? No, that had been much earlier. But the listener, if listener there had been, could well have learned that a hunted fugitive of FitzAlan's party was in hiding there, and worse, that Adeney's daughter was being sheltered in the abbey.

This was getting too warm for comfort. Best get them away as soon as the boy was fit to ride. But if this evening passed, and the night, and no move was made to betray them, he would suspect he had been fretting over nothing. There was no one in sight here but a solitary boy fishing, absorbed and distant on the river bank.

'What was it?' asked Godith, meek and attentive beside him. 'Something made you uneasy, I know.'

'Nothing to worry your head about,' said Cadfael. 'I was mistaken. Everything is as it should be.'

From the corner of his eye, at that moment, he caught the sudden movement down towards the river, beyond the clump of bushes where she had found Torold. Out of the meagre cover a slight, agile body unfolded and stood erect, stretching lazily, and drifted at an oblique angle towards the path on which they walked, his course converging with theirs. Hugh Beringar, his stride nicely calculated to look accidental and yet bring him athwart their path at the right moment, showed them a placid and amiable face, recognising Cadfael with pleasure, accepting his attendant boy with benevolence.

'A very fair evening, brother! You're bound for Vespers? So am I. We may walk together?'

'Very gladly,' said Cadfael heartily. He tapped Godith on the shoulder, and handed her the small sacking bundle that held his herbs and dressings. 'Run ahead, Godric, and put these away for me, and come down to Vespers with the rest of the boys. You'll save my legs, and have time to give a stir to that lotion I have been brewing. Go on, child, run!'

And Godith clasped the bundle and ran, taking good care to run like an athletic boy, rattling one hand along the tall stubble, and whistling as she went, glad enough to put herself out of that young man's sight. Her own eyes and mind were full of another young man.

'A most biddable lad you have,' said Hugh Beringar benignly, watching her race ahead.

'A good boy,' said Cadfael placidly, matching him step for

step across the field blanched to the colour of cream. 'He has a year's endowment with us, but I doubt if he'll take the cowl. But he'll have learned his letters, and figuring, and a deal about herbs and medicines, it will stand him in good stead. You're at leisure today, my lord?'

'Not so much at leisure,' said Hugh Beringar with equal serenity, 'as in need of your skills and knowledge. I tried your garden first, and not finding you there, thought you might have business today over here in the main gardens and orchard. But for want of a sight of you anywhere, I sat down to enjoy the evening sunshine, here by the river. I knew you'd come to Vespers, but never realised you had fields beyond here. Is all the corn brought in now?'

'All that we have here. The sheep will be grazing the stubble very shortly. What was it you wanted of me, my lord? If I may serve you in accord with my duty, be sure I will.'

'Yesterday morning, Brother Cadfael, I asked you if you would give any request of mine fair consideration, and you told me you give fair consideration to all that you do. And I believe it. I had in mind what was then no more than a rumoured threat, now it's a real one. I have reason to know that King Stephen is already making plans to move on, and means to make sure of his supplies and his mounts. The siege of Shrewsbury has cost him plenty, and he now has more mouths to feed and more men to mount. It's not generally known, or too many would be taking thought to evade it, as I am,' owned Beringar blithely, 'but he's about to issue orders to have every homestead in the town searched, and a tithe of all fodder and provisions in store commandeered for the army's use. And all – mark that, *all* – the good horses to be found, no matter who owns them, that are not already in army or garrison service. The abbey stables will not be exempt.'

This Cadfael did not like at all. It came far too pat, a shrewd thrust at his own need of horses, and most ominous indication that Hugh Beringar, who had this information in advance of the general citizens, might also be as well informed of what went on in other quarters. Nothing this young man said or did would ever be quite what it seemed, but whatever game he played would always be his own game. The less said in reply, at this stage, the better. Two could play their own games, and both, possibly, benefit. Let him first say out what he wanted, even if what he said would have to be scrutinised from all angles, and subjected to every known test.

'That will be bad news to Brother Prior,' said Cadfael mildly.

'It's bad news to me,' said Beringar ruefully. 'For I have four horses in those same abbey stables, and while I might have a claim to retain them all for myself and my men, once the king has given me his commission, I can't make any such claim at this moment with security. It might be allowed, it might not. And to be open with you, I have no intention of letting my two best horses be drafted for the king's army. I want them out of here and in some private place, where they can escape Prestcote's foraging parties, until this flurry is over.'

'Only two?' said Cadfael innocently. 'Why not all?'

'Oh, come, I know you have more cunning than that. Would I be here without horses at all? If they found none of mine, they'd be hunting for all, and small chance I'd have left for royal favour. But let them take the two nags, and they won't question further. Two I can afford. Brother Cadfael, it takes no more than a few days in this place to know that you are the man to take any enterprise in hand, however rough and however risky.' His voice was brisk and bland, even hearty, he seemed to intend no double meanings. 'The lord abbot turns to you when he's faced with an ordeal beyond his powers. I turn to you for practical help. You know all this countryside. Is there a place of safety where my horses can lie up for a few days, until this round-up is over?'

So improbable a proposal Cadfael had not looked for, but it came as manna from heaven. Nor did he hesitate long over taking advantage of it for his own ends. Even if lives had not depended on the provision of those two horses, he was well aware that Beringar was making use of him without scruple, and he need have no scruples about doing as much in return. It went a little beyond that, even, for he had a shrewd suspicion that at this moment Beringar knew far too much of what was going on in his, Cadfael's mind, and had no objection whatever to any guesses Cadfael might be making as to what was going on in his, Beringar's. Each of us, he thought, has a hold of sorts upon the other, and each of us has a reasonable insight into the other's methods, if not motives. It will be a fair fight. And yet this debonair being might very well be the murderer of Nicholas Faintree. That would be a very different duel, with no quarter asked or offered. In the meantime, make the most of what might or might not be quite accidental circumstances.

'Yes,' said Cadfael, 'I do know of such a place.'

Beringar did not even ask him where, or question his judgment as to whether it would be remote enough and secret enough to be secure. 'Show me the way tonight,' he said outright, and smiled into Cadfael's face. 'It's tonight or never, the order will be made public tomorrow. If you and I can make the return journey on foot before morning, ride with me. Rather you than any!'

Cadfael considered ways and means; there was no need to consider what his answer would be.

'Better get your horses out after Vespers, then, out to St Giles. I'll join you there when Compline is over, it will be getting dark then. It wouldn't do for me to be seen riding out with you, but you may exercise your own horses in the evening as the fit takes you.'

'Good!' said Beringar with satisfaction. 'Where is this place? Have we to cross the river anywhere?'

'No, nor even the brook. It's an old grange the abbey used to maintain in the Long Forest, out beyond Pulley. Since the times grew so unchancy we've withdrawn all our sheep and cattle from there, but keep two lay brothers still in the house. No one will look for horses there, they know it's all but abandoned. And the lay brothers will credit what I say.'

'And St Giles is on our way?' It was a chapel of the abbey, away at the eastern end of the Foregate.

'It is. We'll go south to Sutton, and then bear west and into the forest. You'll have three miles or more to walk back by the shorter way. Without horses we may save a mile or so.'

'I think my legs will hold me up for that distance,' said Beringar demurely. 'After Compline, then, at St Giles.' And without any further word or question he left Cadfael's side, lengthening his easy stride to gain ground; for Aline Siward was just emerging from the doorway of her house and turning towards the abbey gateway on her way to church. Before she had gone many yards Beringar was at her elbow; she raised her head and smiled confidingly into his face. A creature quite without guile, but by no means without proper pride or shrewd sense, and she opened like a flower at sight of this young man devious as a serpent, whatever else of good or ill might be said of him.

That, thought Cadfael, watching them walk before him in animated conversation, ought to signify something in his favour? Or was it only proof of her childlike trustfulness? Blameless young women have before now been taken in by black-hearted villains, even murderers; and black-hearted villains and murderers have been deeply devoted to blameless young women, contradicting their own nature in this one perverse tenderness.

Cadfael was consoled and cheered by the sight of Godith in church, nobody's fool, nudging and whispering among the boys, and flicking him one rapid, questioning blue glance, which he answered with a reassuring nod and smile. None too well-founded reassurance, but somehow he would make it good. Admirable as Aline was, Godith was the girl for him. She reminded him of Arianna, the Greek boat-girl, long ago, skirts kilted above the knee, short hair a cloud of curls, leaning on her long oar and calling across the water to him . . .

Ah, well! The age he had been then, young Torold had not even reached yet. These things are for the young. Meantime, tonight after Compline, at St Giles!

CHAPTER SEVEN

The ride out through Sutton into the Long Forest, dense and primitive through all but the heathy summits of its fifteen square miles, was like a sudden return visit to aspects of his past, night raids and desperate ambushes once so familiar to him as to be almost tedious, but now, in this shadowy, elderly form, as near excitement as he wished to come. The horse under him was lofty and mettlesome and of high pedigree, he had not been astride such a creature for nearly twenty years, and the flattery and temptation reminded him he was mortal and fallible. Even the young man who rode beside him, accepting his directions without hesitation, reminded him of days past, when exalted and venturesome companions made all labours and privations pleasurable.

Hugh Beringar, once away from the used roads and into the trees and the night shadows, seemed to have no cares in the world, certainly no fear of any treachery on his companion's part. He chattered, even, to pass the time along the way, curious about Brother Cadfael's uncloistral past, and about the countries he had known as well as he knew this forest.

'So you lived in the world all those years, and saw so much of it, and never thought to marry? And half the world women, they say?' The light voice, seemingly idle and faintly mocking, nevertheless genuinely questioned and required an answer.

'I had thought to marry, once,' said Cadfael honestly, 'before I took the Cross, and she was a very fair woman, too, but to say truth, I forgot her in the east, and in the west she forgot me. I was away too long, she gave up waiting and married another man, small blame to her.'

'Have you ever seen her again?' asked Hugh.

'No, never. She has grandchildren by now, may they be good to her. She was a fine woman, Richildis.'

'But the east was also made up of men and women, and you a young crusader. I cannot but wonder,' said Beringar dreamily.

'So, wonder! I also wonder about you,' said Cadfael mildly.

'Do you know any human creatures who are not strangers, one to another?'

A faint gleam of light showed among the trees. The lay brothers sat up late with a reed dip, Cadfael suspected playing at dice. Why not? The tedium here must be extreme. They were bringing these decent brothers a little diversion, undoubtedly welcome.

That they were alive and alert to the slightest sound of an unexpected approach was soon proved, as both emerged ware and ready in the doorway. Brother Anselm loomed huge and muscular, like an oak of his own fifty-five years, and swung a long staff in one hand. Brother Louis, French by descent but born in England, was small and wiry and agile, and in this solitude kept a dagger by him, and knew how to use it. Both of them came forth prepared for anything, placid of face and watchful of eye; but at sight of Brother Cadfael they fell to an easy grinning.

'What, is it you, old comrade? A pleasure to see a known face, but we hardly looked for you in the middle of the night. Are you biding over until tomorrow? Where's your errand?' They looked at Beringar with measuring interest, but he left it to Cadfael to do the dealing for him here, where the abbey's writ ran with more force than the king's.

'Our errand's here, to you,' said Cadfael, lighting down. 'My lord here asks that you'll give stabling and shelter for a few days to these two beasts, and keep them out of the public eye.' No need to hide the reason from these two, who would have sympathised heartily with the owner of such horseflesh in his desire to keep it. 'They're commandeering baggage horses for the army, and that's no fit life for these fellows, they'll be held back to serve in a better fashion.'

Brother Anselm ran an appreciative eye over Beringar's mount, and an affectionate hand over the arched neck. 'A long while since the stable here had such a beauty in it! Long enough since it had any at all, barring Prior Robert's mule when he visited, and he does that very rarely now. We expect to be recalled, to tell truth, this place is too isolated and unprofitable to be kept much longer. Yes, we'll give you house-room, my fine lad, gladly, and your mate, too. All the more gladly, my lord, if you'll let me get my leg across him now and again by way of exercise.'

'I think he may carry even you without trouble,' acknowledged Beringar amiably. 'And surrender them to no one but myself or Brother Cadfael.'

'That's understood. No one will set eyes on them here.' They led the horses into the deserted stable, very content with the break in their tedious existence, and with Beringar's open-handed largesse for their services. 'Though we'd have taken them in for the pleasure of it,' said Brother Louis truthfully. 'I was groom once in Earl Robert of Gloucester's household, I love a fine horse, one with a gloss and a gait to do me credit.'

Cadfael and Hugh Beringar turned homeward together on foot. 'An hour's walking, hardly more,' said Cadfael, 'by the way I'll take you. The path's too overgrown in parts for the horses, but I know it well, it cuts off the Foregate. We have to cross the brook, well upstream from the mill, and can enter the abbey grounds from the garden side, unnoticed, if you're willing to wade.'

'I believe,' said Beringar reflectively, but with complete placidity, 'you are having a game with me. Do you mean to lose me in the woods, or drown me in the mill-race?'

'I doubt if I should succeed at either. No, this will be a most amicable walk together, you'll see. And well worth it, I trust.'

And curiously, for all each of them knew the other was making use of him, it was indeed a pleasant nocturnal journey they made, the elderly monk without personal ambitions, and the young man whose ambitions were limitless and daring. Probably Beringar was working hard at the puzzle of why Cadfael had so readily accommodated him, certainly Cadfael was just as busy trying to fathom why Beringar had ever invited him to conspire with him thus; it did not matter, it made the contest more interesting. And which of them was to win, and to get the most out of the tussle, was very much in the balance.

Keeping pace thus on the narrow forest path they were much of a height, though Cadfael was thickset and burly, and Beringar lean and lissome and light of foot. He followed Cadfael's steps attentively, and the darkness, only faintly alleviated by starlight between the branches, seemed to bother him not at all. And lightly and freely he talked.

'The king intends to move down into Gloucester's country again, in more strength, hence this drive for men and horses. In a few more days he'll surely be moving.'

'And you go with him?' Since he was minded to be talkative, why not encourage him? Everything he said would be calculated, of course, but sooner or later even he might make a miscalculation.

'That depends on the king. Will you credit it, Brother Cadfael, the man distrusts me! Though in fact I'd liefer be put in charge of my own command here, where my lands lie. I've made myself as assiduous as I dare – to see the same face too constantly might have the worst effect, not to see it in attendance at all would be fatal. A nice question of judgment.'

'I feel,' said Cadfael, 'that a man might have considerable confidence in your judgment. Here we are at the brook, do you hear it?' There were stones there by which to cross dry-shod, though the water was low and the bed narrowed, and Beringar, having rested his eyes a few moments to assay the distance and the ground, crossed in a nicely balanced leap that served to justify Cadfael's pronouncement.

'Do you indeed?' resumed the young man, falling in beside him again as they went on. 'Have a high opinion of my judgment? Of risks and vantages only? Or, for instance, of men? – And women?'

'I can hardly question your judgment of men,' said Cadfael drily, 'since you've confided in me. If I doubted, I'd hardly be likely to own it.'

'And of women?' They were moving more freely now through open fields.

'I think they might all be well advised to beware of you. And what else is gossiped about in the king's court, besides the next campaign? There's no fresh word of FitzAlan and Adeney being sighted?'

'None, nor will be now,' said Beringar readily. 'They had luck, and I'm not sorry. Where they are by now there's no knowing, but wherever it is, it's one stage on the way to France.'

There was no reason to doubt him; whatever he was about he was making his dispositions by way of truth, not lies. So the news for Godith's peace of mind was still good, and every day better, as the distance between her father and Stephen's vengeance lengthened. And now there were two excellent horses well positioned on an escape road for Godith and Torold, in the care of two stalwart brothers who would release them at Cadfael's word. The first step was accomplished. Now to recover the saddle-bags from the river, and start them on their way. Not so simple a matter, but surely not impossible.

'I see now where we are,' said Beringar, some twenty minutes later. They had cut straight across the mile of land enclosed by the brook's wanderings, and stood again on the bank; on the other side the stripped fields of pease whitened in the starlight, and beyond their smooth rise lay the gardens, and the great range of abbey buildings. 'You have a nose for country, even in the dark. Lead the way, I'll trust you for an unpitted ford, too.'

Cadfael had only to kilt his habit, having nothing but his sandals to get wet. He strode into the water at the point opposite the low roof of Godith's hut, which just showed above the trees and bushes and the containing wall of the herbarium. Beringar plunged in after him, boots and hose and all. The water was barely knee-deep, but clearly he cared not at all. And Cadfael noted how he moved, gently and steadily, hardly a ripple break-ing from his steps. He had all the intuitive gifts of wild creatures, as alert by night as by day. On the abbey bank he set off instinctively round the edge of the low stubble of pease-haulms, to avoid any rustle among the dry roots soon to be dug in.

'A natural conspirator,' said Cadfael, thinking aloud; and that he could do so was proof of a strong, if inimical, bond between them.

Beringar turned on him a face suddenly lit by a wild smile. 'One knows another,' he said. They had grown used to exchang-ing soundless whispers, and yet making them clear to be heard. 'I've remembered one rumour that's making the rounds, that I forgot to tell you. A few days ago there was some fellow hunted into the river by night, said to be one of FitzAlan's squires. They say an archer got him behind the left shoulder, maybe through the heart. However it was, he went down, somewhere by Atcham his body may be cast up. But they caught a riderless horse, a good saddle-horse, the next day, sure to be his.'

'Do you tell me?' said Cadfael, mildly marvelling. 'You may speak here, there'll be no one prowling in my herb-garden by night, and they're used to me rising at odd times to tend my brews here.'

'Does not your boy see to that?' asked Hugh Beringar innocently.

'A boy slipping out of the dortoir,' said Brother Cadfael,

'would soon have cause to rue it. We take better care of our children here, my lord, than you seem to think.'

'I'm glad to hear it. It's well enough for seasoned old soldiers turned monk to risk the chills of the night, but the young things ought to be protected.' His voice was sweet and smooth as honey. 'I was telling you of this odd thing about the horses . . . A couple of days later, if you'll believe it, they rounded up another saddle-horse running loose, grazing up in the heathlands north of the town, still saddled. They're thinking there was a single body-guard sent out from the castle, when the assault came, to pick up Adeney's daughter from wherever she was hidden, and escort her safely out of the ring round Shrewsbury. They think the attempt failed,' he said softly, 'when her attendant took to the river to save her. So she's still missing, and still thought to be somewhere here, close in hiding. And they'll be looking for her, Brother Cadfael – they'll be looking for her now more eagerly than ever.'

They were up at the edge of the inner gardens by then. Hugh Beringar breathed an almost silent 'Good night!' and was gone like a shadow towards the guest house.

Before he slept out the rest of the night, Brother Cadfael lay awake long enough to do some very hard thinking. And the longer he thought, the more convinced he became that someone had indeed approached the mill closely enough and silently enough to catch the last few sentences spoken within; and that the someone was Hugh Beringar, past all doubt. He had proved how softly he could move, how instinctively he adapted his movements to circumstances, he had provoked a shared expedition committing each of them to the other's discretion, and he had uttered a number of cryptic confidences calculated to arouse suspicion and alarm, and possibly precipitate unwise action – though Cadfael had no intention of giving him that last satisfaction. He did not believe the listener had been within earshot long. But the last thing Cadfael himself had said gave away plainly enough that he intended somehow to get hold of two horses, retrieve the hidden treasury, and see Torold on his way with 'her'. If Beringar had been at the door just a moment earlier, he must also have heard the girl named; but even without that he must surely have had his suspicions. Then just what game was he playing, with his own best horses, with the fugitives he could betray at any moment, yet had not so far betrayed, and with Brother Cadfael? A better and larger prize offered than merely one young man's capture, and the exploitation of a girl against whom he had no real grudge. A man like Beringar might prefer to risk all and play for all, Torold, Godith and treasure in one swoop. For himself alone, as once before, though without success? Or for the king's gain and favour? He was indeed a young man of infinite possibilities.

Cadfael thought about him for a long time before he slept, and one thing, at least, was clear. If Beringar knew now that Cadfael had as good as undertaken to recover the treasury, then from this point on he would hardly let Cadfael out of his sight, for he needed him to lead him to the spot. A little light began to dawn, faint but promising, just before sleep came. It seemed no more than a moment before the bell was rousing him with the rest for Prime.

'Today,' said Cadfael to Godith, in the garden after breakfast, 'do all as usual, go to the Mass before chapter, and then to your schooling. After dinner you should work a little in the garden, and see to the medicines, but after that you can slip away to the old mill, discreetly, mind, until Vespers. Can you dress Torold's wound without me? I may not be seen there today.'

'Surely I can,' she said blithely. 'I've seen it done, and I know the herbs now. But . . . If someone, if *he*, was spying on us yesterday, how if he comes today?' She had been told of the night's expedition, briefly, and the implications at once heartened and alarmed her.

'He will not,' said Cadfael positively. 'If all goes well, wherever *I* am today, there *he* will be. That's why I want you away from me, and why you may breathe more easily away from me. And there's something I may want you and Torold to do for me, late tonight, if things go as I expect. When we come to Vespers, then I'll tell you, yes or no. If it's yes, that's all I need say, and this is what you must do . . .'

She listened in glowing silence throughout, and nodded eager comprehension. 'Yes, I saw the boat, leaning against the wall of the mill. Yes, I know the thicket of bushes at the beginning of the garden, close under the end of the bridge . . . Yes, of course we can do it, Torold and I together!'

'Wait long enough to be sure,' cautioned Cadfael. 'And now run off to the parish Mass, and your lessons, and look as like the other boys as you can, and don't be afraid. If there should be any cause for fear, I intend to hear of it early, and I'll be with you at once.'

A part of Cadfael's thinking was rapidly proved right. He made it his business to be very active about the precincts that Sunday, attendant at every service, trotting on various errands from gate house to guest house, to the abbot's lodging, the infirmary, the gardens; and everywhere that he went, somewhere within view, unobtrusive but present, was Hugh Beringar. Never before had that young man been so constantly at church, in attendance even when Aline was not among the worshippers. Now let's see, thought Cadfael, with mild malice, whether I can lure him from the lists even when she does attend, and leave the field open for the other suitor. For Aline would certainly come to the Mass after chapter, and his last foray to the gate house had shown him Adam Courcelle, dressed for peace and piety, approaching the door of the small house where she and her maid were lodged.

It was unheard of for Cadfael to be absent from Mass, but for once he invented an errand which gave him fair excuse. His skills with medicines were known in the town, and people often asked for his help and advice. Abbot Heribert was indulgent to such requests, and lent his herbalist freely. There was a child along the Foregate towards St Giles who had been under his care from time to time for a skin infection, and though he was growing out of it gradually, and there was no great need for a visit this day, no one had the authority to contradict Cadfael when he pronounced it necessary to go.

In the gateway he met Aline Siward and Adam Courcelle entering, she slightly flushed, certainly not displeased with her escort, but perhaps a little embarrassed, the king's officer devoutly attentive and also warmly flushed, clearly in his case with pleasure. If Aline was expecting to be accosted by Beringar, as had become usual by this time, for once she was surprised. Whether relieved or disappointed there was no telling. Beringar was nowhere to be seen.

Proof positive, thought Cadfael, satisfied, and went on his physicianly visit serenely and without haste. Beringar was discretion itself in his surveillance, he contrived not to be seen at all until Cadfael, on his way home again, met him ambling out gently for exercise on one of his remaining horses, and whistling merrily as he rode.

He saluted Cadfael gaily, as though no encounter could have been more unexpected or more delightful. 'Brother Cadfael, you astray on a Sunday morning?'

Very staidly Cadfael rehearsed his errand, and reported its satisfactory results.

'The range of your skills is admirable,' said Beringar, twinkling. 'I trust you had an undisturbed sleep after your long working day yesterday?'

'My mind was over-active for a while,' said Cadfael, 'but I slept well enough. And thus far you still have a horse to ride, I see.'

'Ah, that! I was at fault, I should have realised that even if the order was issued on a Sunday, they would not move until the sabbath was over. Tomorrow you'll see for yourself.' Unquestionably he was telling the truth, and certain of his information. 'The hunt is likely to be very thorough,' he said, and Cadfael knew he was not talking only of the horses and the provisions. 'King Stephen is a little troubled about his relations with the church and its bishops. I ought to have known he would hold back on Sunday. Just as well, it gives us a day's credit and grace. Tonight we can stay blamelessly at home in all men's sight, as the innocent should. Eh, Cadfael?' And he laughed, and leaned to clap a hand on Brother Cadfael's shoulder, and rode on, kicking his heels into his horse's sides and rousing to a trot towards St Giles.

Nevertheless, when Cadfael emerged from the refectory after dinner, Beringar was visible just within the doorway of the guest-hall opposite, seemingly oblivious but well aware of everything within his field of vision. Cadfael led him harmlessly to the cloister, and sat down there in the sun, and dozed contentedly until he was sure that Godith would be well away and free from surveillance. Even when he awoke he sat for a while, to make quite sure, and to consider the implications

No question but all his movements were being watched very narrowly, and by Beringar in person. He did not delegate such work to his men-at-arms, or to any other hired eyes, but did the duty himself, and probably took pleasure in it, too. If he was willing to surrender Aline to Courcelle, even for an hour, then maximum importance attached to what he was doing instead. I am elected, thought Cadfael, as the means to the end he desires, and that is FitzAlan's treasury. And his surveillance is going to be relentless. Very well! There's no way of evading it. The only thing to do is to make use of it.

Do not, therefore, tire out the witness too much, or alert him too soon of activities planned. He has you doing a deal of guessing, now keep him guessing.

So he betook himself to his herbarium, and worked conscientiously on all his preparations there, brewing and newly begun, all that afternoon until it was time to repair to church for Vespers. Where Beringar secreted himself he did not trouble to consider, he hoped the vigil was tedious in the extreme to a man so volatile and active.

Courcelle had either stayed – the opportunity being heaven-sent, and not to be wasted – or returned for the evening worship, he came with Aline demure and thoughtful on his arm. At sight of Brother Cadfael sallying forth from the gardens he halted, and greeted him warmly.

'A pleasure to see you in better circumstances than when last we met, brother. I hope you may have no more such duties. At least Aline and you, between you, lent some grace to what would otherwise have been a wholly ugly business. I wish I had some way of softening his Grace's mind towards your house, he still keeps a certain grudge that the lord abbot was in no hurry to come to his peace.'

'A mistake a great many others also made,' said Cadfael philosophically. 'No doubt we shall weather it.'

'I trust so. But as yet his Grace is in no mind to extend any privileges to the abbey above the other townsfolk. If I should be compelled to enforce, even within your walls, orders I'd rather see stop at the gates, I hope you'll understand that I do it reluctantly, and have no choice about it.'

He is asking pardon in advance, thought Cadfael, enlightened, for tomorrow's invasion. So it's true enough, as I supposed, and he has been given the ill work to do, and is making it clear beforehand that he dislikes the business and would evade it if he could. He may even be making rather more than he need of his repugnance, for the lady's benefit.

'If that should happen,' he said benignly, 'I'm sure every man of my order will realise that you do only what you must, like any soldier under orders. You need not fear that any odium will attach to you.'

'So I have assured Adam many times,' said Aline warmly, and flushed vividly at hearing herself call him by his Christian name. Perhaps it was for the first time. 'But he's hard to convince. No, Adam, it is true – you take to yourself blame which is not your due, as if you had killed Giles with your own hand, which you know is false. How could I even blame the Flemings? They were under orders, too. In such dreadful times as these no one can do more than choose his own road according to his conscience, and bear the consequences of his choice, whatever they may be.'

'In no times, good or bad,' said Cadfael sententiously, 'can man do more or better than that. Since I have this chance, lady, I should render you account of the alms you trusted to me, for all are bestowed, and they have benefited three poor, needy souls. For want of names, which I did not enquire, say some prayer for three worthy unfortunates who surely pray for you.'

And so she would, he reflected as he watched her enter the church on Courcelle's arm. At this crisis season of her life, bereaved of kin, left mistress of a patrimony she had freely dedicated to the king's service, he judged she was perilously hesitant between the cloister and the world, and for all he had chosen the cloister in his maturity, he heartily wished her the world, if possible a more attractive world than surrounded her now, to employ and fulfil her youth.

Going in to take his place among his brothers, he met Godith making for her own corner. Her eyes questioned brightly, and he said softly: 'Yes! Do all as I told you.'

So now what mattered was to make certain that for the rest of the evening he led Beringar into pastures far apart from where Godith operated. What Cadfael did must be noted, what she did must go unseen and unsuspected. And that could not be secured by adhering faithfully to the evening routine. Supper was always a brief meal, Beringar would be sure to be somewhere within sight of the refectory when they emerged. Collations in the chapter house, the formal reading from the lives of the saints, was a part of the day that Cadfael had been known to miss on other occasions, and he did so now, leading his unobtrusive attendant first to the infirmary, where he paid a brief visit to

Brother Reginald, who was old and deformed in the joints, and welcomed company, and then to the extreme end of the abbot's own garden, far away from the herbarium, and farther still from the gate house. By then Godith would be freed from her evening lesson with the novices, and might appear anywhere between the hut and the herbarium and the gates, so it was essential that Beringar should continue to concentrate on Cadfael, even if he was doing nothing more exciting than trimming the dead flowers from the abbot's roses and clove-pinks. By that stage Cadfael was checking only occasionally that the watch on his movements continued; he was quite certain that it would, and with exemplary patience. During the day it seemed almost casual, hardly expecting action, except that Cadfael was a tricky opponent, and might have decided to act precisely when it was unexpected of him. But it was after dark that things would begin to happen.

When Compline was over there was always, on fine evenings, a brief interlude of leisure in the cloister or the gardens, before the brothers went to their beds. By then it was almost fully dark, and Cadfael was satisfied that Godith was long since where she should be, and Torold beside her. But he thought it best to delay yet a while, and go to the dortoir with the rest. Whether he emerged thence by way of the night stairs into the church, or the outer staircase, someone keeping watch from across the great court, where the guest hall lay, would be able to pick up his traces without trouble.

He chose the night stairs and the open north door of the church, and slipped round the east end of the Lady Chapel and the chapter house to cross the court into the gardens. No need to look round or listen for his shadow, he knew it would be there, moving at leisure, hanging well back from him but keeping him in sight. The night was reasonably dark, but the eyes grew accustomed to it soon, and he knew how securely Beringar could move in darkness. He would expect the night-wanderer to leave by the ford, as they had returned together the previous night. Someone bound on secret business would not pass the porter on the gate, whatever his normal authority.

After he had waded the brook, Cadfael did pause to be sure Beringar was with him. The breaks in the rhythm of the water were very slight, but he caught them, and was content. Now to follow the course of the brook downstream on this side until nearing its junction with the river. There was a little footbridge there, and then it was only a step to the stone bridge that crossed into Shrewsbury. Over the road, and down the slope into the main abbey gardens, and he was already under the shadow of the first archway of the bridge, watching the faint flashes of light from the eddies where once a boat-mill had been moored. In this corner under the stone pier the bushes grew thick, such an awkward slope of ground was not worth clearing for what it would bear. Half-grown willows leaned, trailing leaves in the water, and the bushy growth under their branches would have hidden half a dozen well-screened witnesses.

The boat was there, afloat and tied up to one of the leaning branches, though it was of the light, withy-and-hide type that could be ported easily overland. This time there was good reason it should not, as it usually would, be drawn ashore and turned over in the turf. There was, Cadfael hoped, a solid bundle within it, securely tied up in one or two of the sacks from the mill. It would not have done for him to be seen to be carrying anything. Long before this, he trusted, he had been clearly seen to be empty-handed.

He stepped into the boat and loosed the mooring-rope. The sacking bundle was there, and convincingly heavy when he cautiously tested. A little above him on the slope, drawn into the edge of the bushes, he caught the slight movement of a deeper shadow as he pushed off with the long paddle into the flow under the first archway.

In the event it proved remarkably easy. No matter how keen Hugh Beringar's sight, he could not possibly discern everything that went on under the bridge, detail by detail. However sharp his hearing, it would bring him only a sound suggesting the rattling of a chain drawn up against stone, with some considerable weight on the end, the splash and trickle of water running out from something newly drawn up, and then the iron rattle of the chain descending; which was exactly what it was, except that Cadfael's hands slowed and muted the descent, to disguise the fact that the same weight was still attached, and only the bundle concealed in the boat had been sluiced in the Severn briefly, to provide the trickle of water on the stone ledge. The next part might be more risky, since he was by no means certain he had read Beringar's mind correctly. Brother Cadfael was staking his own life and those of others upon his judgment of men.

So far, however, it had gone perfectly. He paddled his light craft warily ashore, and above him a swift-moving shadow withdrew to higher ground, and, he surmised, went to earth close to the roadway, ready to fall in behind him whichever way he took. Though he would have wagered that the way was already guessed at, and rightly. He tied up the boat again, hastily but securely; haste was a part of his disguise that night, like stealth. When he crept cautiously up to the highroad again, and loomed against the night sky for a moment in stillness, ostensibly waiting to be sure he could cross unnoticed, the watcher could hardly miss seeing that he had now a shape grossly humped by some large bundle he carried slung over his shoulder.

He crossed, rapidly and quietly, and returned by the way he had come, following the brook upstream from the river after passing the ford, and so into the fields and woods he had threaded with Beringar only one night past. The bundle he carried, mercifully, had not been loaded with the full weight it was supposed to represent, though either Torold or Godith had seen fit to give it a convincing bulk and heft. More than enough, Cadfael reflected ruefully, for an ageing monk to carry four miles or more. His nights were being relentlessly curtailed. Once these young folk were wafted away into relative safety he would sleep through Matins and Lauds, and possibly the next morning's Prime, as well, and do fitting penance for it.

Now everything was matter for guesswork. Would Beringar take it for granted where he was bound, and turn back too soon, and with some residue of suspicion, and ruin everything? No! Where Cadfael was concerned he would take nothing for granted, not until he was sure by his own observation where this load had been bestowed in safe-keeping, and satisfied that Cadfael had positively returned to his duty without it. But would he, by any chance, intercept it on the way? No, why should he? To do so would have been to burden himself with it, whereas now he had an old fool to carry it for him, to where he had his horses hidden to convey it with ease elsewhere.

Cadfael had the picture clear in his mind now, the reckoning at its worst. If Beringar had killed Nicholas Faintree in the attempt to possess himself of the treasury, then his aim now would be not only to accomplish what he had failed to do then, but also something beyond, a possibility which had been revealed to him only since that attempt. By letting Brother Cadfael stow away for him both horses and treasure at an advantageous place, he had ensured his primary objective; but in addition, if he waited for Cadfael to convey his fugitives secretly to the same spot, as he clearly intended to do, then Beringar could remove the only witness to his former murder, and capture his once affianced bride as hostage for her father. What an enormous boon to bestow on King Stephen! His own favoured place would be assured, his crime buried for ever.

So much, of course, for the worst. But the range of possibilities was wide. For Beringar might be quite innocent of Faintree's death, but very hot on the trail of FitzAlan's valuables, now he had detected their whereabouts; and an elderly monk might be no object to his plans for his own enrichment, or, if he preferred to serve his interests in another way, his means of ingratiating himself with the king. In which case Cadfael might not long survive his depositing this infernal nuisance he carried, on shoulders already aching, at the grange where the horses were stabled. Well, thought Cadfael, rather exhilarated than oppressed, we shall see!

Once into the woods beyond the coil of the brook, he halted, and dropped the load with a huge grunt from his shoulders, and sat down on it, ostensibly to rest, actually to listen for the soft sounds of another man halting, braced, not resting. Very soft they were, but he caught them, and was happy. The young man was there, tireless, serene, a born adventurer. He saw a dark, amused, saturnine face ready for laughter. He was reasonably sure, then, how the evening would end. With a little luck – better, with God's blessing, he reproved! – he would be back in time for Matins.

There was no perceptible light in the grange when he reached it, but it needed only the rustle and stir of footsteps, and Brother Louis was out with a little pine-flare in one hand and his dagger in the other, as wide awake as at midday, and more perilous.

'God bless you, brother,' said Cadfael, easing the load gratefully from his back. He would have something to say to young Torold when next he talked to him! Someone or something other than his own shoulders could carry this the next time. 'Let me within, and shut the door to.'

'Gaily!' said Brother Louis, and haled him within and did as he was bid.

109

On the way back, not a quarter of an hour later, Brother Cadfael listened carefully as he went, but he heard nothing of anyone following or accompanying him, certainly of no menace. Hugh Beringar had watched him into the grange from cover, possibly even waited for him to emerge unburdened, and then melted away into the night to which he belonged, and made his own lightsome, satisfied way home to the abbey. Cadfael abandoned all precautions and did the same. He was certain, now, where he stood. By the time the bell rang for Matins he was ready to emerge with the rest of the dortoir, and proceed devoutly down the night-stairs to give due praise in the church.

CHAPTER EIGHT

Before dawn on that Monday morning in August the king's officers had deployed small parties to close every road out of Shrewsbury, while at every section within the town wall others stood ready to move methodically through the streets and search every house. There was more in the wind than the commandeering of horses and provisions, though that would certainly be done as they went, and done thoroughly.

'Everything shows that the girl must be in hiding somewhere near,' Prestcote had insisted, reporting to the king after full enquiries. 'The one horse we found turned loose is known to be from FitzAlan's stables, and this young man hunted into the Severn certainly had a companion who has not yet been run to earth. Left alone, she cannot have got far. All your advisers agree, your Grace cannot afford to let the chance of her capture slip. Adeney would certainly come back to redeem her, he has no other child. It's possible even FitzAlan could be forced to return, rather than face the shame of letting her die.'

'Die?' echoed the king, bristling ominously. 'Is it likely I'd take the girl's life? Who spoke of her dying?'

'Seen from here,' said Prestcote drily, 'it may be an absurdity to speak of any such matter, but to an anxious father waiting for better news it may seem all too possible. Of course you would do the girl no harm. No need even to harm her father if you get him into your hands, or even FitzAlan. But your Grace must consider that you should do everything possible to prevent their services from reaching the empress. It's no longer a matter of revenge for Shrewsbury, but simply of a sensible measure to conserve your own forces and cut down on your enemy's.'

'That's true enough,' admitted Stephen, without overmuch enthusiasm. His anger and hatred had simmered down into his more natural easiness of temperament, not to say laziness. 'I am not sure that I like even making such use of the girl.' He remembered that he had as good as ordered young Beringar to track down his affianced bride if he wanted to establish himself in royal favour, and the young man, though respectfully attendant since, if somewhat sporadically, had never yet produced any evidence of zeal in the search. Possibly, thought the king, he read my mind better than I did myself at the time.

'She need come by no injury, and your Grace would be saved having to contend with any forces attached to her father's standard, if not also his lord's. If you can cut off all those levies from the enemy, you will have saved yourself great labour, and a number of your men their lives. You cannot afford to neglect such a chance.'

It was sound advice, and the king knew it. Weapons are where you find them, and Adeney could sit and kick his heels in an easy imprisonment enough, once he was safe in captivity.

'Very well!' he said. 'Make your search and make it thoroughly.'

The preparations were certainly thorough. Adam Courcelle descended upon the Abbey Foregate with his own command and a company of the Flemings. And while Willem Ten Heyt went ahead and established a guard-post at St Giles, to question every rider and search every cart attempting to leave the town, and his lieutenant posted sentries along every path and by every possible crossing-place along the riverside, Courcelle took possession, civilly but brusquely, of the abbey gate house, and ordered the gates closed to all attempting to enter or leave. It was then about twenty minutes before Prime, and already daylight. There had been very little noise made, but Prior Robert from the dortoir had caught the unusual stir and disquiet from the gate house, on which the window of his own chamber looked down, and he came out in haste to see what was afoot.

Courcelle made him a reverence that deceived nobody, and asked with respect for privileges everyone knew he was empowered to take; still, the veil of courtesy did something to placate the prior's indignation.

'Sir, I am ordered by his Grace King Stephen to require of your house free and orderly entry everywhere, a tithe of your stores for his Grace's necessary provision, and such serviceable horses as are not already in the use of people in his Grace's commission. I am also commanded to search and enquire everywhere for the girl Godith, daughter of his Grace's traitor Fulke Adeney, who is thought to be still in hiding here in Shrewsbury.'

Prior Robert raised his thin, silver brows and looked down his long, aristocratic nose. 'You would hardly expect to find such a person within our precincts? I assure you there is none such in the guest house, where alone she might becomingly be found.'

'It is a formality here, I grant you,' said Courcelle, 'but I have my orders, and cannot treat one dwelling more favourably than another.'

There were lay servants listening by then, standing apart silent and wary, and one or two of the boy pupils, sleepy-eyed and scared. The master of the novices came to herd his strays back into their quarters, and stayed, instead, to listen with them.

'This should be reported at once to the abbot,' said the prior with admirable composure, and led the way at once to Abbot Heribert's lodging. Behind them, the Flemings were closing the gates and mounting a guard, before turning their practical attention to the barns and the stables.

Brother Cadfael, having for two nights running missed the first few hours of his rest, slept profoundly through all the earliest manifestations of invasion, and awoke only when the bell rang for Prime, far too late to do anything but dress in haste and go down with the rest of the brothers to the church. Only when he heard the whispers passed from man to man, and saw the closed gates, the lounging Flemings, and the subdued and huge-eyed boys, and heard the businesslike bustle and clatter of hooves from the stable-yard, did he realise that for once events had overtaken him, and snatched the initiative from his hands. For nowhere among the scared and anxious youngsters in church could he see any sign of Godith. As soon as Prime was over, and he was free to go, he hurried away to the hut in the herbarium. The door was unlatched and open, the array of drying herbs and mortars and bottles in shining order, the blankets had been removed from the bench-bed, and a basket of newly gathered lavender and one or two bottles arranged innocently along it. Of Godith there was no sign, in the hut, in the gardens, in the pease-fields along the brook, where at one side the great stack of dried haulms loomed pale as flax, waiting to be carted away to join the hay in the barns. Nor was there any trace of a large bundle wrapped in sacking and probably damp from seeping river-water, which had almost certainly spent the night under that bleached pile, or the small boat which should have been turned down upon it and carefully covered over. The boat, FitzAlan's treasury, and Godith had all vanished into thin air.

Godith had awakened somewhat before Prime, uneasily aware of the heavy responsibility that now lay upon her, and gone out without undue alarm to find out what was happening at the gate house. Though all had been done briskly and quietly, there was something about the stirring in the air and the unusual voices, lacking the decorous monastic calm of the brothers, that disturbed her mind. She was on the point of emerging from the walled garden when she saw the Flemings dismounting and closing the gates, and Courcelle advancing to meet the prior. She froze at the sound of her own name thus coolly spoken. If they were bent upon a thorough search, even here, they must surely find her. Questioned like the other boys, with all those enemy eyes upon her, she could not possibly sustain the performance. And if they found her, they might extend the search and find what she had in her charge. Besides, there was Brother Cadfael to protect, and Torold. Torold had returned faithfully to his mill once he had seen her safely home with the treasure. Last night she had almost wished he could have stayed with her, now she was glad he had the whole length of the Gaye between him and this dawn alarm, and woods not far from his back, and quick senses that would pick up the signs early, and give him due warning to vanish.

Last night had been like a gay, adventurous dream, for some reason inexpressibly sweet, holding their breath together in cover until Cadfael had led his shadow well away from the bridge, loosing the little boat, hauling up the dripping saddle-bags, swathing them in dry sacks to make another bundle the image of Cadfael's; their hands together on the chain, holding it away from the stone, muting it so that there should be no further sound, then softly paddling the short way upstream to the brook, and round to the pease-fields. Hide the boat, too, Cadfael had said, for we'll need it tomorrow night, if the chance offers. Last night's adventure had been the dream, this morning was the awakening, and she needed the boat now, this moment.

There was no hope of reaching Brother Cadfael for orders, what she guarded must be got away from here at once, and it certainly could not go out through the gates. There was no one to tell her what to do, this fell upon her shoulders now. Blessedly, the Flemings were not likely to ransack the gardens until they had looted stables and barns and stores; she had a little time in hand.

114

She went back quickly to the hut, folded her blankets and hid them under the bench behind a row of jars and mortars, stripped the bed and turned it into a mere shelf for more such deceits, and set the door wide open to the innocent daylight. Then she slipped away to the stack of haulms, and dragged out the boat from its hiding-place, and the sacking bundle with it. A godsend that the gentle slope of the field was so glazed with the cropped stems, and the boat so light, that it slid down effortlessly into the brook. She left it beached, and returned to drag the treasury after it, and hoist it aboard. Until last night she had never been in such a boat, but Torold had shown her how to use the paddle, and the steady flow of the brook helped her.

She already knew what she would do. There was no hope at all of escaping notice if she went downstream to the Severn; with such a search in hand, there would be watchers on the main road, on the bridge, and probably along the banks. But only a short way from her launching-place a broad channel was drawn off to the right, to the pool of the main abbey mill, where the mill-race, drawn off upstream through the abbey pool and the fish ponds, turned the wheel and emptied itself again into the pond, to return to the main stream of the brook and accompany it to the river. Just beyond the mill the three grace houses of the abbey were ranged, with little gardens down to the water, and three more like them protected the pond from open view on the other side. The house next to the mill was the one devoted to the use of Aline Siward. True, Courcelle had said he was to search for his fugitive everywhere; but if there was one place in this conventual enclosure that would receive no more than a formal visit from him, it was certainly the house where Aline was living.

What if we are on opposite sides, thought Godith, plying her paddle inexpertly but doggedly at the turn, and sailing into wider, smoother water, she can't throw me to the wolves, it isn't in her, with a face like hers! And are we on opposite sides? Are we on either side, by this time? She places everything she has at the king's disposal, and he hangs her brother! My father stakes life and lands for the empress, and I don't believe she cares what happens to him or any of his like, provided she gets her own way. I daresay Aline's brother was more to her than King Stephen will ever be, and I know I care more for my father and Torold than for the Empress Maud, and I wish the old king's son hadn't drowned when that awful ship went down, so that there'd have been no argument over who inherited, and Stephen and Maud alike could have stayed in their own manors, and left us alone!

The mill loomed on her right, but the wheel was still today, and the water of the race spilled over freely into the pond that opened beyond, with slow counter-currents flowing along the opposite bank to return to the brook. The bank here was sheer for a couple of feet, to level as much ground as possible for the narrow gardens; but if she could heave the bundle safely ashore, she thought she could drag up the boat. She caught at a naked root that jutted into the water from a leaning willow, and fastened her mooring-line to it, before she dared attempt to hoist her treasure up to the edge of the grass. It was heavy for her, but she rolled it on to the thwart, and thence manipulated it into her arms. She could just reach the level rim of turf without tilting the boat too far. The weight rested and remained stable, and Godith leaned her arms thankfully either side of it, and for the first time tears welled out of her eyes and ran down her face.

Why, she wondered rebelliously, why am I going to such trouble for this rubbish, when all I care about is Torold, and my father? And Brother Cadfael! I should be failing him if I tipped it down into the pond and left it there. He went to all sorts of pains to get it to this point, and now I have to go on with the work. And Torold cares greatly that he should carry out the task he was given. That's more than gold. It isn't this lump that matters!

She scrubbed an impatient and grubby hand over her cheeks and eyes, and set about climbing ashore, which proved tricky, for the boat tended to withdraw from under her foot to the length of its mooring; when at last she had scrambled to safety, swearing now instead of crying, she could not draw it up after her, she was afraid of holing it on the jagged roots. It would have to ride here. She lay on her stomach and shortened the mooring, and made sure the knot was fast. Then she towed her detested incubus up into the shadow of the house, and hammered at the door.

It was Constance who opened it. It was barely eight o'clock, Godith realised, and it was Aline's habit to attend the Mass at ten, she might not even be out of her bed yet. But the general disquiet in the abbey had reached these retired places also, it seemed, for Aline was up and dressed, and appeared at once behind her maid's shoulder.

'What is it, Constance?' She saw Godith, soiled and tousled and breathless, leaning over a great sacking bundle on the ground, and came forward in innocent concern. 'Godric! What's the matter? Did Brother Cadfael send you? Is anything wrong?'

'You know the boy, do you, madam?' said Constance, surprised.

'I know him, he's Brother Cadfael's helper, we have talked together.' She cast one luminous glance over Godith from head to foot, took in the smudged marks of tears and the heaving bosom, and put her maid quickly aside. She knew desperation when she saw it, even when it made no abject appeal. 'Come within, come! Here, let me help you with this, whatever it may be. Now, Constance, close the door!' They were safe within, the wooden walls closed them round, the morning sun was warm and bright through an eastern window left open.

They stood looking at each other, Aline all woman in a blue gown, her golden hair loosed about her in a cloud, Godith brown and rumpled, and arrayed unbecomingly in an over-large cotte and ill-fitting hose, short hair wild, and face strained and grubby from soil, grass and sweat.

'I came to ask you for shelter,' said Godith simply. 'The king's soldiers are hunting for me. I'm worth quite a lot to them if they find me. I'm not Godric, I'm Godith. Godith Adeney, Fulke Adeney's daughter.'

Aline let her glance slide, startled and touched, from the fine-featured oval face, down the drab-clad and slender limbs. She looked again into the challenging, determined face, and a spark started and glowed in her eyes.

'You'd better come through here,' she said practically, with a glance at the open window, 'into my own sleeping-chamber, away from the road. Nobody will trouble you there – we can talk freely. Yes, bring your belongings, I'll help you with them.' FitzAlan's treasury was woman-handled between them into the inner room, where not even Courcelle, certainly not any other, would dare to go. Aline closed the door very softly. Godith sat down on a stool by the bed, and felt every sinew in her grown weak, and every stress relaxing. She leaned her head against the wall, and looked up at Aline.

'You do realise, lady, that I'm reckoned the king's enemy? I

117

don't want to trick you into anything. You may think it your duty to give me up.'

'You're very honest,' said Aline, 'and I'm not being tricked into anything. I'm not sure even the king would think the better of me if I gave you up to him, but I'm sure God would not, and I know I should not think the better of myself. You can rest safe here. Constance and I between us will see to it that no one comes near you.'

Brother Cadfael preserved a tranquil face through Prime, and the first conventual Mass, and a greatly abbreviated chapter meeting, while mentally he was racking his brain and gnawing his knuckles over his own inexplicable complacence, which had let him sleep on while the opposing powers stole a march on him. The gates were fast shut, there was no way out there. He could not pass, and certainly by that route Godith had not passed. He had seen no soldiers on the other side of the brook, though they would certainly be watching the river bank. If Godith had taken the boat, where had she gone with it? Not upstream, for the brook was open to view for some way, and beyond that flowed through a bed too uneven and rocky to accommodate such craft. Every moment he was waiting for the outcry that would signal her capture, but every moment that passed without such an alarm was ease to him. She was no fool, and she seemed to have got away, though heaven knew where, with the treasure they were fighting to retain and speed on its way.

At chapter Abbot Heribert made a short, weary, disillusioned speech in explanation of the occupation that had descended upon them, instructed the brothers to obey whatever commands were given them by the king's officers with dignity and fortitude, and to adhere to the order of their day faithfully so far as they were permitted. To be deprived of the goods of this world should be no more than a welcome discipline to those who had aspired beyond the world. Brother Cadfael could at least feel some complacency concerning his own particular harvest; the king was not likely to demand tithes of his herbs and remedies, though he might welcome a cask or two of wine. Then the abbot dismissed them with the injunction to go quietly about their own work until High Mass at ten.

Brother Cadfael went back to the gardens and occupied himself distractedly with such small tasks as came to hand, his mind still busy elsewhere. Godith could safely have forded the brook by broad daylight, and taken to the nearest patch of woodland, but she could not have carried the unwieldy bundle of treasure with her, it was too heavy. She had chosen rather to remove all the evidence of irregular activities here, taking away with her both the treasure and the boat. He was sure she had not gone as far as the confluence with the river, or she would have been captured before this. Every moment without the evil news provided another morsel of reassurance. But wherever she was, she needed his help.

And there was Torold, away beyond the reaped fields, in the disused mill. Had he caught the meaning of these movements in good time, and taken to the woods? Devoutly Cadfael hoped so. In the meantime there was nothing he could do but wait, and give nothing away. But oh, if this inquisition passed before the end of the day, and he could retrieve his two strays after dark, this very night he must see them away to the west. This might well be the most favourable opportunity, with the premises already scoured, the searchers tired and glad to forget their vigilance, the community totally absorbed with their grievances and comparing notes on the army's deprivations, the brothers devoted wholly to fervent prayers of thanks for an ordeal ended.

Cadfael went out to the great court in good time for Mass. There were army carts being loaded with sacks from the barns, and a great bustle of Flemings about the stables. Dismayed guests, caught here in mid-journey with horses worth commandeering, came out in great agitation to argue and plead for their beasts, but it did them no good, unless the owners could prove they were in the king's service already. Only the poor hacks were spared. One of the abbey carts was also taken, with its team, and loaded with the abbey's wheat.

Something curious was happening at the gates, Cadfael saw. The great carriage doors were closed, and guarded, but someone had had the calm temerity to knock at the wicket and ask for entry. Since it could have been one of their own, a courier from the guard-post at St Giles, or from the royal camp, the wicket was opened, and in the narrow doorway appeared the demure figure of Aline Siward, prayer-book in hand, her gold hair covered decently by the white mourning cap and wimple.

'I have permission,' she said sweetly, 'to come in to church.' And seeing that the guards who confronted her were not at home in English, she repeated it just as amiably in French. They were not disposed to admit her, and were on the point of closing the door in her face when one of their officers observed the encounter, and came in haste.

'I have permission,' repeated Aline patiently, 'from Messire Courcelle to come in to Mass. My name is Aline Siward. If you are in doubt, ask him, he will tell you.'

It seemed that she had indeed secured her privilege, for after some hurried words the wicket was opened fully, and they stood back and let her pass. She walked through the turmoil of the great court as though nothing out of the ordinary were happening there, and made for the cloister and the south door of the church. But she slowed her pace on the way, for she was aware of Brother Cadfael weaving his way between the scurrying soldiers and the lamenting travellers to cross her path just at the porch. She gave him a demure public greeting, but in the moment when they were confidingly close she said privately and low:

'Be easy, Godric is safe in my house.'

'Praise to God and you!' sighed Cadfael as softly. 'After dark I'll come for her.' And though Aline had used the boyish name, he knew by her small, secret smile that the word he had used was no surprise to her. 'The boat?' he questioned soundlessly.

'At the foot of my garden, ready.'

She went on into the church, and Cadfael, with a heart suddenly light as thistledown, went decorously to take his place among the procession of his brothers.

Torold sat in the fork of a tree at the edge of the woods east of Shrewsbury castle, eating the remains of the bread he had brought away with him, and a couple of early apples stolen from a tree at the limit of the abbey property. Looking westward across the river he could see not only the great cliff of the castle walls and towers, but further to the right, just visible between the crests of trees, the tents of the royal camp. By the numbers busy about the abbey and the town, the camp itself must be almost empty at this moment.

Torold's body was coping well enough with this sudden crisis, to his satisfaction and, if he would have admitted it, surprise. His mind was suffering more. He had not yet walked very far, or exerted himself very much, apart from climbing into this comfortable and densely leafed tree, but he was delighted with the response of his damaged muscles, and the knit of the gash in his thigh, which hardly bothered him, and the worse one in his shoulder, which had neither broken nor greatly crippled his use of his arm. But all his mind fretted and ached for Godith, the little brother so suddenly transmuted into a creature half sister, half something more. He had confidence in Brother Cadfael, of course, but it was impossible to unload all the responsibility for her on to one pair of cloistered shoulders, however wide and sustaining. Torold fumed and agonised, and yet went on eating his stolen apples. He was going to need all the sustenance he could muster.

There was a patrol moving methodically along. the bank of the Severn, between him and the river, and he dared not move again until they had passed by and withdrawn from sight towards the abbey and the bridge. And how far round the outskirts of the town he would have to go, to outflank the royal cordon, was something he did not yet know.

He had awakened to the unmistakable sounds from the bridge, carried by the water, and insistent enough in their rhythm to break his sleep. Many, many men, mounted and foot, stamping out their presence and their passage upon a stone bow high above water, the combination sending echoes headlong down the river's course. The timber of the mill, the channels of water feeding it, carried the measure to his ears. He had started up and dressed instinctively, gathering everything that might betray his having been there, before he ventured out to look. He had seen the companies fan out at the end of the bridge, and waited to see no more, for this was a grimly thorough operation. He had wiped out all traces of his occupation of the mill, throwing into the river all those things he could not carry away with him, and then had slipped away across the limit of abbey land, away from the advancing patrol on the river bank, into the edge of the woodlands opposite the castle.

He did not know for whom or what this great hunt had been launched, but he knew all too well who was likely to be taken in it, and his one aim now was to get to Godith, wherever she might be, and stand between her and danger if he could. Better still, to take her away from here, into Normandy, where she would be safe.

Along the river bank the men of the patrol separated to beat a way through the bushes where Godith had first come to him.

They had already searched the abandoned mill, but thank God they would find no traces there. Now they were almost out of sight, he felt safe in swinging down cautiously from his tree and withdrawing deeper into the belt of woodland. From the bridge to St Giles the king's highway, the road to London, was built up with shops and dwellings, he must keep well clear. Was it better to go on like this, eastward, and cross the highroad somewhere beyond St Giles, or to wait and go back the way he had come, after all the tumult was over? The trouble was that he did not know when that was likely to be, and his torment for Godith was something he did not want prolonged. He would have to go beyond St Giles, in all probability, before he dared cross the highroad, and though the brook, after that, need be no obstacle the approach to the spot opposite the abbey gardens would still be perilous. He could lie up in the nearest cover and watch, and slip over into the stack of pease-haulms when the opportunity offered, and thence, if all remained quiet, into the herbarium, where he had never yet been, and the hut where Godith had slept the last seven nights in sanctuary. Yes, better go forward and make that circle. Backward meant braving the end of the bridge, and there would be soldiers there until darkness fell, and probably through the night.

It proved a tedious business, when he was longing for swift action. The sudden assault had brought out all the inhabitants in frightened and indignant unrest, and Torold had to beware of any notice in such conditions, since he was a young fellow not known here, where neighbour knew neighbour like his own kin, and any stranger was liable to be accosted and challenged out of sheer alarm. Several times he had to draw off deeper into cover, and lie still until danger passed. Those who lived close to the highway, and had suffered the first shocks, tended to slip away into any available solitude. Those who were daily tending stock or cultivating land well away from the road heard the uproar, and gravitated close enough to satisfy their curiosity about what was going on. Caught between these two tides, Torold passed a miserable day of fretting and waiting; but it brought him at last well beyond Willem Ten Heyt's tight and brutal guard-post, which by then had amassed a great quantity of goods distrained from agitated travellers, and a dozen sound horses. Here the last houses of the town ended, and fields and hamlets stretched beyond. Traffic on the road, half a mile beyond the post, was thin and easily evaded. Torold crossed, and went to earth once more in a thicket above the brook, while he viewed the lie of the land.

The brook was dual here, the mill-race having been drawn off at a weir somewhat higher upstream. He could see both silver streaks in a sunlight now declining very slightly towards the west. It must be almost time for Vespers. Surely King Stephen had finished with the abbey by now, with all Shrewsbury to ransack?

The valley here was narrow and steep, and no one had built on it, the grass being given over to sheep. Torold slid down into the cleft, easily leaping the mill-race, and picking his way over the brook from stone to stone. He began to make his way downstream from one patch of cover to another, until about the time of Vespers he had reached the smoother meadows opposite Brother Cadfael's gleaned pease-fields. Here the ground was all too open, he had to withdraw further from the brook to find a copse to hide in while he viewed the way ahead. From here he could see the roofs of the convent buildings above the garden walls, and the loftier tower and roof of the church, but nothing of the activity within. The face that was presented to him looked placid enough, the pale slope stripped of its harvest, the stack of haulms where Godith and he had hidden boat and treasure barely nineteen hours ago, the russet wall of the enclosed garden beyond, the steep roof of a barn. He would have to wait some time for full daylight to pass, or else take a risk and run for it through the brook, and into the straw-stack beyond, when he saw his opportunity. And here there were people moving from time to time about their legitimate business, a shepherd urging his flock towards the home pasture, a woman coming home from the woods with mushrooms, two children driving geese. He might very well have strolled past all these with a greeting, and been taken for granted, but he could not be seen by any of them making a sudden dash for it through the ford and into the abbey gardens. That would have been enough to call their attention and raise an alarm, and there were sounds of unusual activity, shouts and orders and the creaking of carts and harness, still echoing distantly from beyond the gardens. Moreover, there was a man on horseback in sight on his side the brook, some distance away downstream but drawing gradually nearer, patrolling this stretch of meadows as though he had been posted here to secure the one unwalled exit from the enclave. As probably he had, though he seemed to be taking the duty very easily, ambling his mount along the green at leisure. One man only, but one was enough. He had only to shout, or whistle shrilly on his fingers, and he could bring a dozen Flemings swarming.

Torold went to ground among the bushes, and watched him approach. A big, rawboned, powerful but unhandsome horse, dappled from cream to darkest grey, and the rider a young fellow black-haired and olive-complexioned, with a thin, assured, saturnine face and an arrogantly easy carriage in the saddle. It was this light, elegant seat of his, and the striking colouring of the horse, that caught Torold's closer attention. This was the very beast he had seen leading the patrol along the riverside at dawn, and this same man had surely lighted down from his mount and gone first into Torold's abandoned sanctuary at the mill. Then he had been attended by half a dozen footmen, and had emerged to loose them in after him, before they all mustered again and moved on. Torold was sure of this identification; he had had good reason to watch very closely, dreading that in spite of his precautions they might yet find some detail to arouse suspicion. This was the same horse, and the same man. Now he rode past upstream, apparently negligent and unobservant, but Torold knew better. There was nothing this man missed as he rode, those were lively, witty, formidable eyes that cast such seemingly languid looks about him.

But now his back was turned, and no one else moved at the moment in these evening fields. If he rode on far enough, Torold might attempt the crossing. Even if he misjudged in his haste and soaked himself, he could not possibly drown in this stream, and the night would be warm. Go he must, and find his way to Godith's bed, and somehow get some reassurance.

The king's officer rode on, oblivious, to the limit of the level ground, never turning his head. And no other creature stirred. Torold picked himself up and ran for it, across the open mead, into the brook, picking his footing by luck and instinct well enough, and out upon the pale, shaven fields on the other side. Like a mole burrowing into earth, he burrowed into the stack of haulms. In the turmoil of this day it was no surprise to find boat and bundle vanished, and he had no time to consider whether the omen was bad or good. He drew the disturbed stems about him, a stiff, creamy lace threaded by sunlight and warmth, and lay quivering, his face turned to peer through the network to where the enemy rode serenely.

And the enemy had also turned, sitting the dappled horse motionless, gazing downstream as though some pricking of his thumbs had warned him. For some minutes he remained still, as easy as before, and yet as alert; then he began the return journey, as softly as he had traced it upstream.

Torold held his breath and watched him come. He made no haste, but rode his beat in idle innocence, having nothing to do, and nothing but this repeated to and fro to pass the time here. But when he drew opposite the pease-fields he reined in, and sat gazing across the brook long and steadily, and his eyes homed in upon the loose stack of haulms, and lingered. Torold thought he saw the dark face melt into a secret smile; he even thought the raised bridle-hand made a small movement that could have been a salute. Though that was idiocy, he must have imagined it! For the horseman was moving on downstream on his patrol, gazing towards the outflow from the mill and the confluence with the river beyond. Never a glance behind.

Torold lay down under his weightless covering, burrowed his tired head into his arms, and his hips into the springy turf of the headland, and fell asleep in sheer, exhausted reaction. When he awoke it was more than half dark, and very quiet. He lay for a while listening intently, and then wormed his way out into a pallid solitude above a deserted valley, and crept furtively up the slope into the abbey gardens, moving alone among the myriad sun-warmed scents of Cadfael's herbs. He found the hut, its door hospitably open to the twilight, and peered almost fearfully into the warm silence and gloom within.

'Praise God!' said Brother Cadfael, rising from the bench to haul him briskly within. 'I thought you'd aim for here, I've been keeping an eye open for you every half-hour or so, and at last I have you. Here, sit down and ease your heart, we've come through well enough!'

Urgent and low, Torold asked the one thing that mattered: *'Where is Godith?'*

CHAPTER NINE

Godith, if he had but known it, was at that moment viewing her own reflection in Aline's glass, which Constance was holding well away from her to capture more of the total image. Washed and combed and arrayed in one of Aline's gowns, brocaded in brown and gold thread, with a thin gold bandeau of Aline's round her curls, she turned this way and that to admire herself with delight at being female again, and her face was no longer that of an urchin, but of an austere young gentlewoman aware of her advantages. The soft candlelight only made her more mysterious and strange in her own eyes.

'I wish he could see me like this,' she said wistfully, forgetting that so far she had not mentioned any he except Brother Cadfael, and could not now, even to Aline, reveal anything concerning Torold's person and errand beyond his name. Concerning herself she had told almost everything, but that was the acknowledgement of a debt.

'There is a he?' asked Aline, sparkling with sympathetic curiosity. 'And he will escort you? Wherever you are going? No, I mustn't ask you anything, it would be unfair. But why shouldn't you wear the dress for him? Once away, you can as well travel as yourself as you can in boy's clothes.'

'I doubt it,' said Godith ruefully. 'Not the way we shall be travelling.'

'Then take it with you. You could put it in that great bundle of yours. I have plenty, and if you are going with nothing, then you'll need a gown for when you reach safety.'

'Oh, if you knew how you tempt me! You are kind! But I couldn't take it. And we shall have weight enough to carry, the first miles. But I do thank you, and I shall never forget.'

She had tried on, for pure pleasure, Constance assisting with relish, every dress Aline had with her, and in every one she had imagined herself confronting Torold, without warning, and studying his astonished and respectful face. And somehow, in spite of not knowing where he was or how he was faring, she had spent a blissful afternoon, unshaken by doubts. Certainly he

126

would see her in her splendour, if not in this in other fine gowns, in jewels, with her hair, grown long again, plaited and coiled upon her head in a gold circlet like this one. Then she recalled how she had sat beside him, the two of them companionably eating plums and committing the stones to the Severn through the floorboards of the mill, and she laughed. What use would it ever be, putting on airs with Torold?

She was in the act of lifting the circlet from her head when they all heard the sudden but circumspect knocking on the outer door, and for a moment froze into wary stillness, looking at one another aghast.

'Do they mean to search here, after all?' wondered Godith in a shocked whisper. 'Have I brought you into danger?'

'No! Adam assured me I should not be disturbed, this morning, when they came.' Aline rose resolutely. 'You stay here with Constance, and bolt the door. I'll go. Can it be Brother Cadfael come for you already?'

'No, surely not yet, they'll still be on the watch.'

It had sounded the most deferential of knocks, but all the same, Godith sat very still behind the bolted door, and listened with strained attention to the snatches of voices that reached her from without. Aline had brought her visitor into the room. The voice that alternated with hers was a man's, low-pitched and ardently courteous.

'Adam Courcelle!' Constance mouthed silently, and smiled her knowing smile. 'So deep in love, he can't keep away!'

'And she – Aline?' whispered Godith curiously.

'Who knows! Not *she* – not yet!'

Godith had heard the same voice that morning, addressing the porter and the lay servants at the gate in a very different tone. But such duties can surely give no pleasure, and may well make even a decent man ill-humoured and overbearing. This devout and considerate soul enquiring tenderly after Aline's peace of mind might be his proper self.

'I hope you have not been too much put out by all this stir,' he was saying. 'There'll be no more disturbances, you may rest now.'

'I haven't been molested at all,' Aline assured him serenely. 'I have no complaint, you have been considerate indeed. But I'm sorry for those who have had goods distrained. Is the same thing happening in the town?'

'It is,' he said ruefully, 'and will go on tomorrow, but the abbey may be at peace now. We have finished here.'

'And you did not find her? The girl you had orders to search for?'

'No, we have not found her.'

'What would you say,' asked Aline deliberately, 'if I said that I was glad?'

'I should say that I would expect nothing else from you, and I honour you for it. I know you could not wish danger or pain or captivity to any creature, much less a blameless girl. I've learned so much of you, Aline.' The brief silence was charged, and when he resumed: 'Aline –' his voice sank so low that Godith could not distinguish the words. She did not want to, the tone was too intimate and urgent. But in a few moments she heard Aline say gently:

'You must not ask me to be very receptive tonight, this has been a harrowing day for so many. I can't help but feel almost as weary as they must be. And as you! Leave me to sleep long tonight, there will be a better time for talking of these matters.'

'True!' he said, resuming the soldier on duty as though he squared his shoulders to a load again. 'Forgive me, this was not the time. Most of my men are out of the gates by now, I'll follow them, and let you rest. You may hear marching and the carts rolling for a quarter of an hour or so, after that it will be quiet.'

The voices receded, towards the outer door. Godith heard it opened, and after a few exchanged and inaudible words, closed again. She heard the bolt shot, and in a few moments more Aline tapped at the bedroom door. 'You can safely open, he's gone.'

She stood in the doorway, flushed and frowning, rather in private perplexity than displeasure. 'It seems,' she said, and smiled in a way Adam Courcelle would have rejoiced to see, 'that in sheltering you I've done him no wrong. I think he's relieved at *not* finding you. They're all going. It's over. Now we have only to wait for Brother Cadfael and full darkness.'

In the hut in the herbarium Brother Cadfael fed, reassured and doctored his patient. Torold, once the first question had been answered so satisfactorily, lay down submissively on Godith's bed, and let his shoulder be dressed again, and the gash in his thigh, already healed, nevertheless be well bandaged and padded.

'For if you're to ride into Wales this night,' said Cadfael, 'we don't want any damage or delays, you could all too easily break that open again.'

'Tonight?' said Torold eagerly. 'Is it to be tonight? She and I together?'

'It is, it must, and high time, too. I don't think I could stand this sort of thing much longer,' said Cadfael, though he sounded almost complacent about it. 'Not that I've had too much of the pair of you, you understand, but all the same, I'll be relieved when you're well away towards Owain Gwynedd's country, and what's more, I'll give you a token from myself to the first Welsh you encounter. Though you already have FitzAlan's commendation to Owain, and Owain keeps his word.'

'Once mounted and started,' vowed Torold heartily, 'I'll take good care of Godith.'

'And so will she of you. I'll see she has a pot of this salve I've been using on you, and a few things she may need.'

'And she took boat and load and all with her!' mused Torold, fond and proud. 'How many girls could have kept their heads and done as well? And this other girl took her in! And brought you word of it, and so wisely! I tell you, Brother Cadfael, we breed fine women here in Salop.' He was silent for a moment, and grew thoughtful. 'Now how are we to get her out? They may have left a guard. And anyhow, I can hardly be seen to walk out at the gate house, seeing the porter will know I never walked in that way. And the boat is there, not here.'

'Hush a while,' said Cadfael, finishing off his bandage neatly, 'while I think. What about your own day? You've done well, it seems to me, and come out of it none the worse. And you must have left all open and innocent, for there's been no whisper about the old mill. You caught the wind of them soon, it seems.'

Torold told him about the whole long, dangerous and yet inexpressibly tedious day of starting and stopping, running and hiding, loitering and hurrying. 'I saw the company that combed the river bank and the mill, six armed men on foot, and an officer riding. But I'd made sure there was no sign of me left there. The officer went in first, alone, and then turned his men into it. I saw the same fellow again,' he recalled, suddenly alert to the coincidence, 'this evening, when I crossed the ford and dived into the stack. He was riding the far bank up and down, between river and mill-race, alone. I knew him by his seat in the saddle, and the horse he was riding. I'd made the crossing behind his back, and when he rode back downstream he halted right opposite, and sat and gazed straight at where I was hiding. I could have sworn he'd seen me. He seemed to be staring directly at me. And smiling! I was sure I was found out. But then he rode on. He can't have seen me, after all.'

Cadfael put away his medicines very thoughtfully. He asked mildly: 'And you knew him by his horse again? What was so notable about it?'

'The size and colour. A great, gaunt, striding beast, not beautiful but strong, and dappled clean through from creamy belly to a back and quarters all but black.'

Cadfael scrubbed at his blunt brown nose, and scratched his even browner tonsure. 'And the man?'

'A young fellow hardly older than I. Black-avised, and a light build to him. All I saw of him this morning was the clothes he wore and the way he rode, very easy on what I should guess might be a hard-mouthed brute. But I saw his face tonight. Not much flesh, and bold bones, and black eyes and brows. He whistles to himself,' said Torold, surprised at remembering this. 'Very sweetly!'

So he did! Cadfael also remembered. The horse, too, he recalled, left behind in the abbey stables when two better and less noticeable had been withdrawn. Two, their owner had said, he might be willing to sacrifice, but not all four, and not the pick of the four. Yet the cull had been made, and still he rode one of the remaining two, and doubtless the other, also, was still at his disposal. So he had lied. His position with the king was already assured, he had even been on duty in today's raiding. Very selective duty? And if so, who had selected it?

'And you thought he had seen you cross?'

'When I was safe hidden I looked, and he'd turned my way. I thought he'd seen me moving, from the corner of his eye.'

That one, thought Cadfael, has eyes all round his head, and what he misses is not worth marking. But all he said to Torold was: 'And he halted and stared across at you, and then rode on?'

'I even thought he lifted his bridle-hand a thought to me,' owned Torold, grinning at his own credulity. 'By that time I doubt I was seeing visions at every turn, I was so wild to get to Godith. But then he just turned and rode on, easy as ever. So he can't have seen me, after all.'

Cadfael pondered the implications of all this in wonder and admiration. Light was dawning as dusk fell into night. Not complete darkness yet, simply the departure of the sun, afterglow and all, leaving a faint greenish radiance along the west; not complete dawn, but a promising confirmation of the first elusive beams.

'He can't have, can he?' demanded Torold, fearful that he might have drawn danger after him all too near to Godith.

'Never a fear of it,' said Cadfael confidently. 'All's well, child, don't fret, I see my way. And now it's time for me to go to Compline. You may drop the bolt after me, and lie down here on Godith's bed and get an hour or so of sleep, for by dawn you'll be needing it. I'll come back to you as soon as service is over.'

He did, however, spare the few minutes necessary to amble through the stables, and was not surprised to note that neither the dapple-grey nor its companion, the broad-backed brown cob, was in its stall. An innocent visit to the guest hall after Compline further confirmed that Hugh Beringar was not there in the apartments for gentlefolk, nor were his three men-at-arms present among the commonalty. The porter recalled that the three retainers had gone forth soon after Beringar had ridden in from his day's duties at the end of the hunt, about the time that Vespers ended, and Beringar himself had followed, in no apparent haste, an hour or so later.

So that's how things stand, is it? thought Cadfael. He's staked his hand that it's to be tonight, and is willing to stand or fall on his wager. Well, since he's so bold and so shrewd to read my mind, let's see how good I am at reading his, and I'll stake just as boldly.

Well, then: Beringar knew from the first that his service with the king was accepted and his horses safe enough, therefore he wanted them removed for some other purpose of his own. And made a fellow-conspirator of me! Why? He could have found a refuge for himself if he'd really needed one. No, he wanted me to know just where the horses were, available and inviting. He knew I had two people to deliver out of this town and out of the king's hold, and would jump at his offer for my own ends. He offered me the bait of two horses so that I should transfer the treasury to the same place, ready for flight. And finally, he had no need to hunt for his fugitives, he had only to sit back and leave it to me to bring them to the grange as soon as I could, and then he had everything in one spot, ready to be gathered in. It follows, therefore, that tonight he'll be waiting for us, and this time with his armed men at his back.

There were still details that baffled the mind. If Beringar had indeed turned a blind eye to Torold's hiding-place this evening, for what purpose? Granted he did not know at this moment where Godith was, and might choose to let one bird fly in order to secure its mate also. But now that Cadfael came to consider all that had passed there was no escaping the possibility, to put it no higher, that throughout, Beringar had been turning a similarly blind and sparkling eye to Godith's boyish disguise, and had had a very shrewd idea of where his missing bride was to be found. In that case, if he had known Godric was Godith, and that one of FitzAlan's men was in hiding in the old mill, then as soon as he had satisfied himself that Cadfael had recovered the treasure for him he could simply have gone in force and gathered in all three prizes, and delivered them to a presumably delighted and grateful king. If he had not done so, but chosen this furtive way, it must mean something different. As, for instance, that his intent was to secure Godith and Torold and duly hand them over for his reward, but despatch FitzAlan's gold, not back to Shrewsbury, but by his own men, or indeed in person, to his own home manor, for his own private use. In which case the horses had been moved not only to fool a simple old monk, but to transfer the treasure direct to Maesbury in complete secrecy, without having to go near Shrewsbury.

That, of course, was all supposing Beringar was not Nicholas Faintree's murderer. If he was, the plan differed in one important aspect. He would see to it that though Godith went back to bait the trap for her father, Torold Blund was taken, not alive, but dead. Dead, and therefore silent. A second murder to bury the first.

Altogether a grim prospect, thought Cadfael, surprisingly undisturbed by it. Except, of course, that it could all mean something very different. Could, and does! or my name is not Cadfael, and I'll never pick a fight with a clever young man again!

He went back to the herbarium, settled in his mind and ready for another restless night. Torold was awake and alert, quick to lift the bolt as soon as he was sure who came.

'Is it time yet? Can we get round to the house on foot?' He was on thorns until he could actually see and touch her, and know that she was safe and free, and had taken no harm.

'There are always ways. But it's neither dark enough nor quiet enough yet, so sit down and rest while you may, for you'll have a share of the weight on the way, until we get to the horses. I must go to the dortoir with the rest, and to my bed. Oh, never fret, I'll be back. Once we're in our own cells, leaving is no great problem. I'm next to the night-stairs, and the prior sleeps at the far end, and sleeps like the dead. And have you forgotten the church has a parish door, on to the Foregate? The only door not within the walls. From there to Mistress Siward's house is only a short walk, and if it passes the gate house, do you think the porter takes account of every citizen abroad somewhat late?'

'So this girl Aline could very well have gone to Mass by that door, like the rest of the laity,' Torold realised, marvelling.

'So she could, but then she would have had no chance to speak to me, and besides, she chose to exert her privilege with Courcelle, and show the Flemings she was to be reckoned with, the clever girl. Oh, you have a fine girl of your own, young Torold, and I hope you'll be good to her, but this Aline is only just stretching her powers to find out what she's worth, and what she can do, and trust me, she'll make such another as our Godith yet.'

Torold smiled in the warm darkness within the hut, sure even in his anxiety that there was but one Godric-Godith. 'You said the porter was hardly likely to pay much attention to citizens making for home late,' he reminded, 'but he may very well have a sharp eye for any such in a Benedictine habit.'

'Who said anything about Benedictine habits drifting abroad so late? *You*, young man, shall go and fetch Godith. The parish door is never closed, and with the gate house so close seldom needs to be. I'll let you out there when the time comes. Go to the last little house, beside the mill, and bring Godith and the boat down from the pond to where the water flows back into the brook, and I shall be there, waiting.'

'The third house of the three on our side,' whispered Torold, glowing even in the dark. 'I know it. I'll go!' The warmth of his gratitude and pleasure filled the hut, and set the herbal fragrances stirring headily, because it would be he, and no other, who would come to fetch Godith away, more wildly and wonderfully than in any mere runaway marriage. 'And you'll be on the abbey bank, when we come down to the brook?'

'I will so, and go nowhere without me! And now lie down for an hour, or less, and leave the latch in case you sleep too soundly, and I'll come for you when all's quiet.'

Brother Cadfael's plans worked smoothly. The day having been so rough, all men were glad to close the shutters, put out the lights, barricade themselves in from the night, and sleep. Torold was awake and waiting before Cadfael came for him. Through the gardens, through the small court between guest hall and abbot's lodging, into the cloister, and in through the south door of the church, they went together in such a silence and stillness as belonged neither to night nor day, only to this withdrawn world between services. They never exchanged a word until they were in the church, shoulder to shoulder under the great tower and pressed against the west door. Cadfael eased the huge door ajar, and listened. Peering carefully, he could see the abbey gates, closed and dark, but the wicket gallantly open. It made only a very small lancet of twilight in the night.

'All's still. Go now! I'll be at the brook.'

The boy slid through the narrow opening, and swung lightly away from the door into the middle of the roadway, as though coming from the lanes about the horse-fair. Cadfael closed the door inch by inch in silence. Without haste he withdrew as he had come, and strolled under the solitary starlight through the garden and down the field, bearing to the right along the bank of the brook until he could go no further. Then he sat down in the grass and vetches and moth-pasture of the bank to wait. The August night was warm and still, just enough breeze to rustle the bushes now and then, and make the trees sigh, and cover with slight sounds the slighter sounds made by careful and experienced men. Not that they would be followed tonight. No need! The one who might have been following was already in position at the end of the journey, and waiting for them.

Constance opened the door of the house, and was startled and silenced by the apparition of this young, secular person, instead of the monk she had expected. But Godith was there, intent and burning with impatience at her shoulder, and flew past her with a brief, wordless, almost soundless cry, into his arms and on to his heart. She was Godric again, though for him she would never now be anyone but Godith, whom he had never yet seen in her own proper person. She clung to him, and laughed, and wept, hugged, reviled, threatened him all in a breath, felt tenderly at his swathed shoulder, demanded explanations and cancelled all her demands, finally lifted to him an assuaged face in sudden silence, and waited to be kissed. Stunned and enlightened, Torold kissed her.

'You must be Torold,' said Aline from the background, so serenely that she must have known rather more about their relationship, by now, than he knew himself. 'Close the door, Constance, all's well.' She looked him over, with eyes alert to a young man's qualities by reason of certain recent experiences of her own, and thought well of him. 'I knew Brother Cadfael would send. She wanted to go back as she came this morning, but I said no. He said he would come. I didn't know he would be sending you. But Cadfael's messenger is very welcome.'

'She has told you about me?' enquired Torold, a little flushed at the thought.

'Nothing but what I needed to know. She is discretion itself, and so am I,' said Aline demurely. She, too, was flushed and glittering, but with excitement and enjoyment of her own plotting, half-regretful that her share must end here. 'If Brother Cadfael is waiting, we mustn't lose time. The farther you get by daybreak, the better. Here is the bundle Godith brought. Wait here within, until I see if everything is quiet below in the garden.'

She slipped away into the soft darkness, and stood by the edge of the pond, listening intently. She was sure they had left no guard behind, for why should they, when they had searched everywhere, and taken all they had been sent to take? Yet there might still be someone stirring in the houses opposite. But all were in darkness, she thought even the shutters were closed, in spite of the warm night, for fear some solitary Fleming should return to help himself to what he could find, under cover of the day's official looting. Even the willow leaves hung motionless here, sheltered from the faint breeze that stirred the grasses along the river bank.

'Come!' she whispered, opening the door narrowly. 'All's

quiet. Follow where I step, the slope is rough.' She had even thought to change her pale gown for a dark one since afternoon, to be shadowy among the shadows. Torold hoisted FitzAlan's treasury in its sacking shroud by the rope that secured it, and put off Godith firmly when she would have reached to share the weight with him. Surprisingly, she yielded meekly, and went before him very quickly and quietly to where the boat rode on its short mooring, half-concealed by the stooping willow branches. Aline lay down at the edge of the bank, and leaned to draw the boat in and hold it steady, for there was a two-foot hollow of undercut soil between them and the water. Very quickly and happily this hitherto cloistered and dutiful daughter was learning to be mistress of her own decisions and exploiter of her own powers.

Godith slid down into the boat, and lent both arms to steady the sacking bundle down between the thwarts. The boat was meant for only two people at most, and settled low in the water when Torold also was aboard, but it was buoyant and sturdy, and would get them as far as they needed to go, as it had done once before.

Godith leaned and embraced Aline, who was still on her knees at the edge of the grass. It was too late for spoken thanks then, but Torold kissed the small, well-tended hand held out to him, and then she loosed the end of the mooring-rope, and tossed it aboard, and the boat slipped out softly from under the bank and drifted across in the circling eddies of the outflow, back towards the brook from which the pool had been drawn. The spill from the head-race of the mill caught them and brisked their pace like a gentle push, and Torold sat with paddle idle, and let the silent flow take them out from the pond. When Godith looked back, all she could see was the shape of the willow, and the unlighted house beyond.

Brother Cadfael rose from among the long grasses as Torold paddled the boat across to the abbey shore. 'Well done!' he said in a whisper. 'And no trouble? No one stirring?'

'No trouble. Now you're the guide.'

Cadfael rocked the boat thoughtfully with one hand. 'Put Godith and the load ashore opposite, and then fetch me. I may as well go dry-shod.' And when they were all safely across to the other side of the brook, he hauled the boat out of the water into the grass, and Godith hurried to help him carry it into hiding

136

in the nearest copse. Once in cover, they had leisure to draw breath and confer. The night was still and calm around them, and five minutes well spent here, as Cadfael said, might save them much labour thereafter.

'We may speak, but softly. And since no other eyes, I hope, are to see this burden of ours until you're well away to the west, I think we might with advantage open it and split the load again. The saddle-bags will be far easier to sling on our shoulders than this single lump.'

'I can carry one pair,' said Godith, eager at his elbow.

'So you can, for a short spell, perhaps,' he said indulgently. He was busy disentangling the two pairs of linked bags from the sacks that had swathed them. They had straps comfortably broad for the shoulder, and the weights in them had been balanced in the first place for the horses. 'I had thought we might save ourselves half a mile or so by making use of the river for the first part of the way,' he said, 'but with three of us and only this hazel-shell we should founder. And it's not so far we have to go, loaded – something over three miles, perhaps.'

He shook one pair of bags into the most comfortable position over his shoulder, and Torold took the other pair on his sound side. 'I never carried goods to this value before in my life,' said Cadfael as he set off, 'and now I'm not even to see what's within.'

'Bitter stuff to me,' said Torold at his back, 'it cost Nick his life, and I'm to have no chance to avenge him.'

'You give thought to your own life and bear your own burdens,' said Cadfael. 'He will be avenged. Better you should look to the future, and leave Nick to me.'

The ways by which he led his little convoy differed from those he had used in Beringar's company. Instead of crossing the brook and making directly for the grange beyond Pulley, he bore more strongly to the west, so that by the time they were as far south as the grange they were also a good mile west of it, nearer to Wales, and in somewhat thicker forest.

'How if we should be followed?' wondered Godith.

'We shall not be followed.' He was so positive about it that she accepted the reassurance gladly, and asked nothing more. If Brother Cadfael said it, it was so. She had insisted on carrying Torold's load for half a mile or so, but he had taken it back from her at the first sign of quickening breath or faltering step.

A lace-work of sky showed paler between the branches ahead. They emerged cautiously into the edge of a broad forest ride that crossed their path on good turf at an oblique angle. Beyond it, their own track continued, a little more open to the night than up to this point.

'Now pay good heed,' said Cadfael, halting them within cover, 'for you have to find your way back without me to this spot. This ride that crosses us here is a fine, straight road the old Romans made. Eastward, here to our left, it would bring us to the Severn bridge at Atcham. Westward, to our right, it will take you two straight as an arrow for Pool and Wales, or if you find any obstacle on the way, you may bear further south at the end for the ford at Montgomery. Once you're on this, you can ride fast enough, though in parts it may be steep. Now we cross it here, and have another half-mile to go to the ford of the brook. So pay attention to the way.'

Here the path was clearly better used, horses could travel it without great difficulty. The ford, when they reached it, was wide and smooth. 'And here,' said Cadfael, 'we leave our loads. One tree among so many trees you might well lose, but one tree beside the only ford along the path, and you can't lose it.'

'Leave them?' wondered Torold. 'Why, are we not going straight to where the horses are? You said yourself we should not be followed tonight.'

'Not followed, no.' When you know where your quarry must come, and are sure of the night, you can be there waiting. 'No, waste no more time, trust me and do as I say.' And he let down his own half of the burden, and looked about him, in the dimness to which by now their eyes were accustomed, for the best and safest concealment. In the thicket of bushes close to the ford, on their right, there was a gnarled old tree, one side of it dead, and its lowest branch deep in the cover of the bushes. Cadfael slung his saddle-bags over it, and without another word Torold hoisted his own beside them, and drew back to assure himself that only those who had hidden here were likely ever to find. The full leafage covered all.

'Good lad!' said Cadfael contentedly. 'Now, from here we bear round to the east somewhat, and this path we're on will join the more direct one I used before. For we must approach the grange from the right direction. It would never do for any curious person to suppose we'd been a mile nearer Wales.'

Unburdened now, they drew together and went after him hand in hand, trusting as children. And now that they were drawing nearer to the actual possibility of flight, they had nothing at all to say, but clung to each other and believed that things would go right.

Their path joined the direct one only some minutes' walk from the small clearing where the stockade of the grange rose. The sky paled as the trees fell back. There was a small rush-light burning somewhere within the house, a tiny, broken gleam showed through the pales. All round them the night hung silent and placid.

Brother Anselm opened to them, so readily that surely some aggrieved traveller from Shrewsbury must have brought word even here of the day's upheaval, and alerted him to the possibility that anyone running from worse penalties might well take warning, and get out at once. He drew them within thankfully and in haste, and peered curiously at the two young fellows at Cadfael's back, as he closed the gate.

'I thought it! My thumbs pricked. I felt it must be tonight. Things grow very rough your way, so we've heard.'

'Rough enough,' admitted Cadfael, sighing. 'I'd wish any friend well out of it. And most of all these two. Children, these good brothers have cared for your trust, and have it here safe for you. Anselm, this is Adeney's daughter, and this FitzAlan's squire. Where is Louis?'

'Saddling up,' said Brother Anselm, 'the moment he saw who came. We had it in mind the whole day that you'd have to hurry things. I've put food together, in case you came. Here's the scrip. It's ill to ride too far empty. And a flask of wine here within.'

'Good! And these few things I brought,' said Cadfael, emptying his own pouch. 'They're medicines. Godith knows how to use them.'

Godith and Torold listened and marvelled. The boy said, almost tongue-tied with wondering gratitude: 'I'll go and help with the saddling.' He drew his hand from Godith's and made for the stables, across the small untended court. This forest assart, unmanageable in such troubled times, would soon be forest again, these timber buildings, always modest enough, would moulder into the lush growth of successive summers. The Long Forest would swallow it without trace in three years, or four.

'Brother Anselm,' said Godith, running an awed glance from head to foot of the giant, 'I do thank you with all my heart, for both of us, for what you have done for us two – though I think it was really for Brother Cadfael here. He has been my master eight days now, and I understand. This and more I would do for him, if ever I might. I promise you Torold and I will never forget, and never debase what you've done for us.'

'God love you, child,' said Brother Anselm, charmed and amused, 'you talk like a holy book. What should a decent man do, when a young woman's threatened, but see her safe out of her trouble? And her young man with her!'

Brother Louis came from the stables leading the roan Beringar had ridden when first these two horses of his were brought here by night. Torold followed with the black. They shone active and ready in the faint light, excellently groomed and fed, and well rested.

'And the baggage,' said Brother Anselm significantly. 'That we have safe. For my own part I would have parted it into two, to balance it better on a beast, but I thought I had no right to open it, so it stays as you left it, in one. I should hoist it to the crupper with the lighter weight as rider, but as you think fit.'

They were away, the pair of them, to haul out the sack-bound bundle Cadfael had carried here some nights ago. It seemed there were some things they had not been told, just as there were things Torold and Godith had accepted without understanding. Anselm brought the burden from the house on his huge shoulders, and dumped it beside the saddled horses. 'I brought thongs to buckle it to the saddle.' They had indeed given some thought to this, they had fitted loops of cord to the rope bindings, and were threading their thongs into these when a blade sliced down through the plaited cords that held the latch of the gate behind them, and a clear, assured voice ordered sharply:

'Halt as you stand! Let no man move! Turn hither, all, and slowly, and keep your hands visible. For the lady's sake!'

Like men in a dream they turned as the voice commanded, staring with huge, wary eyes. The gate in the stockade stood wide open, lifted aside to the pales. In the open gateway stood Hugh Beringar, sword in hand; and over either shoulder leaned a bended long-bow, with a braced and competent eye and hand behind it; and both of them were aimed at Godith. The light was faint but steady. Those used to it here were well able to use it to shoot home.

'Admirable!' said Beringar approvingly. 'You have understood me very well. Now stay as you are, and let no man move, while my third man closes the gates behind us.'

CHAPTER TEN

They had all reacted according to their natures. Brother Anselm looked round cautiously for his cudgel, but it was out of reach, Brother Louis kept both hands in sight, as ordered, but the right one very near the slit seam of his gown, beneath which he kept his dagger. Godith, first stunned into incredulous dismay, very quickly revived into furious anger, though only the set whiteness of her face and the glitter of her eyes betrayed it. Brother Cadfael, with what appeared to be shocked resignation, sat down upon the sacking bundle, so that his skirts hid it from sight if it had not already been noted and judged of importance. Torold, resisting the instinct to grip the hilt of Cadfael's poniard at his belt, displayed empty hands, stared Beringar in the eye defiantly, and took two long, deliberate paces to place himself squarely between Godith and the two archers. Brother Cadfael admired, and smiled inwardly. Probably it had not occurred to the boy, in his devoted state, that there had been ample time for both arrows to find their target before his body intervened, had that been the intention.

'A very touching gesture,' admitted Beringar generously, 'but hardly effective. I doubt if the lady is any happier with the situation that way round. And since we're all sensible beings here, there's no need for pointless heroics. For that matter, Matthew here could put an arrow clean through the pair of you at this distance, which would benefit nobody, not even me. You may as well accept that for the moment I am giving the orders and calling the tune.'

And so he was. However his men had held their hands when they might have taken his order against any movement all too literally, it remained true that none of them had the slightest chance of making any effective attack upon him and changing the reckoning. There were yards of ground between, and no dagger is ever going to outreach an arrow. Torold stretched an arm behind him to draw Godith close, but she would not endure it. She pulled back sharply to free herself, and eluding the hand

142

that would have detained her, strode forward defiantly to confront Hugh Beringar.

'What manner of tune,' she demanded, 'for me? If I'm what you want, very well, here I am, what's your will with me? I suppose I still have lands of my own, worth securing? Do you mean to stand on your rights, and marry me for them? Even if my father is dispossessed, the king might let my lands and me go to one of his new captains! Am I worth that much to you? Or is it just a matter of buying Stephen's favour, by giving me to him as bait to lure better men back into his power?'

'Neither,' said Beringar placidly. He was eyeing her braced shoulders and roused, contemptuous face with decided appreciation. 'I admit, my dear, that I never felt so tempted to marry you before – you're greatly improved from the fat little girl I remember. But to judge by your face, you'd as soon marry the devil himself, and I have other plans, and so, I fancy, have you. No, provided everyone here acts like a sensible creature, we need not quarrel. And if it needs saying for your own comfort, Godith, I have no intention of setting the hounds on your champion's trail, either. Why should I bear malice against an honest opponent? Especially now I'm sure he finds favour in your eyes.'

He was laughing at her, and she knew it, and took warning. It was not even malicious laughter, though she found it an offence. It was triumphant, but it was also light, teasing, almost affectionate. She drew back a step; she even cast one appealing glance at Brother Cadfael, but he was sitting slumped and apparently apathetic, his eyes on the ground. She looked up again, and more attentively, at Hugh Beringar, whose black eyes dwelt upon her with dispassionate admiration.

'I do believe,' she said slowly, wondering, 'that you mean it.'

'Try me! You came here to find horses for your journey. There they are! You may mount and ride as soon as you please, you and the young squire here. No one will follow you. No one else knows you're here, only I and my men. But you'll ride the faster and safer if you lighten your loads of all but the necessaries of life,' said Beringar sweetly. 'That bundle Brother Cadfael is so negligently sitting on, as if he thought he'd found a convenient stone – that I'll keep, by way of a memento of you, my sweet Godith, when you're gone.'

Godith had just enough self-control not to look again at Brother Cadfael when she heard this. She had enough to do keeping command of her own face, not to betray the lightning-stroke of understanding, and triumph, and laughter, and so, she knew, had Torold, a few paces behind her, and equally dazzled and enlightened. So that was why they had slung the saddle-bags on the tree by the ford, a mile to the west, a mile on their way into Wales. This prize here they could surrender with joyful hearts, but never a glimmer of joy must show through to threaten the success. And now it lay with her to perfect the coup, and Brother Cadfael was leaving it to her. It was the greatest test she had ever faced, and it was vital to her self-esteem for ever. For this man fronting her was more than she had thought him, and suddenly it seemed that giving him up was almost as generous a gesture as this gesture of his, turning her loose to her happiness with another man and another cause, only distraining the small matter of gold for his pains. For two fine horses, and a free run into Wales! And a kind of blessing, too, secular but valued.

'You mean that,' she said, not questioning, stating. 'We may go!'

'And quickly, if I dare advise. The night is not old yet, but it matures fast. And you have some way to go.'

'I have mistaken you,' she said magnanimously. 'I never knew you. You had a right to try for this prize. I hope you understand that we had also a right to fight for it. In a fair win and a fair defeat there should be no heart-burning. Agreed?'

'Agreed!' he said delightedly. 'You are an opponent after my own heart, and I think your young squire had better take you hence, before I change my mind. As long as you leave the baggage . . .'

'No help for it, it's yours,' said Brother Cadfael, rising reluctantly from his seat on guard. 'You won it fairly, what else can I say?'

Beringar surveyed without disquiet the mound of sacking presented to view. He knew very well the shape of the hump Cadfael had carried here from Severn, he had no misgivings.

'Go, then, and good speed! You have some hours of darkness yet.' And for the first time he looked at Torold, and took his time about studying him, for Torold had held his peace and let her have her head in circumstances he could not be expected to understand, and with admirable self-restraint. 'I ask your pardon, I don't know your name.'

'My name is Torold Blund, a squire of FitzAlan's.'

'I'm sorry that we never knew each other. But not sorry that we never had ado in arms, I fear I should have met my overmatch.' But he was very sunny about it, having got his way, and he was not really much in awe of Torold's longer reach and greater height. 'You take good care of your treasure, Torold, I'll take care of mine.'

Sobered and still, watching him with great eyes that still questioned, Godith said: 'Kiss me and wish me well! As I do you!'

'With all my heart!' said Beringar, and turned her face up between his hands, and kissed her soundly. The kiss lasted long, perhaps to provoke Torold, but Torold watched and was not dismayed. These could have been brother and sister saying a fond but untroubled farewell. 'Now mount, and good speed!'

She went first to Brother Cadfael, and asked his kiss also, with a frantic quiver in her voice and her face that no one else saw or heard, and that might have been of threatened tears, or of almost uncontrollable laughter, or of both together. The thanks she said to him and to the lay brothers were necessarily brief, being hampered by the same wild mixture of emotions. She had to escape quickly, before she betrayed herself. Torold went to hold her stirrup, but Brother Anselm hoisted her between his hands and set her lightly in the saddle. The stirrups were a little long for her, he bent to shorten them to her comfort, and then she saw him look up furtively and flash her a grin, and she knew that he, too, had fathomed what was going on, and shared her secret laughter. If he and his comrade had been let into the whole plot from the beginning, they might not have played their parts so convincingly; but they were very quick to pick up all the undercurrents.

Torold mounted Beringar's roan, and looked down from the saddle at the whole group within the stockade. The archers had unstrung their bows, and stood by looking on with idle interest and some amusement, while the third man opened the gate wide to let the travellers pass.

'Brother Cadfael, everything I owe to you. I shall not forget.'

'If there's anything owing,' said Cadfael comfortably, 'you can repay it to Godith. And see you mind your ways with her until you bring her safe to her father,' he added sternly. 'She's in your care as a sacred charge, beware of taking any advantage.'

Torold's smile flashed out brilliantly for an instant, and was gone; and the next moment so was Torold himself, and Godith after him, trotting out briskly through the open gate into the luminosity of the clearing, and thence into the shadowy spaces between the trees. They had but a little way to go to the wider path, and the ford of the brook, where the saddle-bags waited. Cadfael stood listening to the soft thudding of hooves in the turf, and the occasional rustling of leafy branches, until all sounds melted into the night's silence. When he stirred out of his attentive stillness, it was to find that every other soul there had been listening just as intently. They looked at one another, and for a moment had nothing to say.

'If she comes to her father a virgin,' said Beringar then, 'I'll never stake on man or woman again.'

'It's my belief,' said Cadfael drily, 'she'll come to her father a wife, and very proper, too. There are plenty of priests between here and Normandy. She'll have more trouble persuading Torold he has the right to take her, unapproved, but she'll have her own ways of convincing him.'

'You know her better than I,' said Beringar. 'I hardly knew the girl at all! A pity!' he added thoughtfully.

'Yet I think you recognised her the first time you ever saw her with me in the great court.'

'Oh, by sight, yes – I was not sure then, but within a couple of days I was. She's not so changed in looks, only fined into such a springy young fellow.' He caught Cadfael's eye, and smiled. 'Yes, I did come looking for her, but not to hand her over to any man's use. Nor that I wanted her for myself, but she was, as you said, a sacred charge upon me. I owed it to the alliance others made for us to see her into safety.'

'I trust,' said Cadfael, 'that you have done so.'

'I, too. And no hard feelings upon either side?'

'None. And no revenges. The game is over.' He sounded, he realised suddenly, appropriately subdued and resigned, but it was only the pleasant weariness of relief.

'Then you'll ride back with me to the abbey, and keep me company on the way? I have two horses here. And these lads of mine have earned their sleep, and if your good brothers will give them house-room overnight, and feed them, they may make their way back at leisure tomorrow. To sweeten their welcome, there's two flasks of wine in my saddle-bags, and a pasty. I feared we might have a longer wait, though I was sure you'd come.'

'I had a feeling,' said Brother Louis, rubbing his hands with satisfaction, 'for all the sudden alarm, that there was no real mischief in the wind tonight. And for two flasks of wine and a pasty we'll offer you beds with pleasure, and a game of tables if you've a mind for it. We get very little company here.'

One of the archers led in from the night Beringar's two remaining horses, the tall, rangy dapple-grey and the sturdy brown cob, and placidly lay brothers and men-at-arms together unloaded the food and drink, and at Beringar's orders made the unwieldy, sacking-wrapped bundle secure on the dapple's croup, well balanced and fastened with Brother Anselm's leather straps, provided with quite another end in view. 'Not that I wouldn't trust it with you on the cob,' Beringar assured Cadfael, 'but this great brute will never even notice the weight. And his rider needs a hard hand, for he has a hard mouth and a contrary will, and I'm used to him. To tell truth, I love him. I parted with two better worth keeping, but this hellion is my match, and I wouldn't change him.'

He could not better have expressed what Cadfael was thinking about him. This hellion is my match, and I wouldn't change him! He did his own spying, he gave away generously two valuable horses to discharge his debt to a bride he never really wanted, and he went to all manner of patient, devious shifts to get the girl safe and well out of his path, and lay hand upon the treasury, which was fair game, as she was not. Well, well, we live and learn in the book of our fellow-men!

They rode together, they two alone, by the same road as once before, and even more companionably than then. They went without haste, unwinding the longer way back, the way fitter for horses, the way they had first approached the grange. The night was warm, still and gentle, defying the stormy and ungentle times with its calm assertion of permanent stability.

'I am afraid,' said Hugh Beringar with compunction, 'you have missed Matins and Lauds, and the fault is mine. If I had not delayed everything, you might have been back for midnight. You and I should share whatever penance is due.'

'You and I,' said Cadfael cryptically, 'share a penance already.

Well, I could not wish for more stimulating company. We may compound my offence by riding at ease. It is not often a man gets such a night ride, and safely, and at peace.'

Then they were silent for some way, and thought their own thoughts, but somewhere the threads tangled, for after a while Beringar said with assurance: 'You will miss her.' It was said with brisk but genuine sympathy. He had, after all, been observing and learning for some days.

'Like a fibre gone from my heart,' owned Brother Cadfael without dismay, 'but there'll be others will fill the place. She was a good girl, and a good lad, too, if you'll grant me the fancy. Quick to study, and a hard worker. I hope she'll make as good a wife. The young man's a fair match for her. You saw he favoured one shoulder? One of the king's archers did his best to slice the round of it off him, but with Godith's care now he'll do well enough. They'll reach France.' And after a moment's thought he asked, with candid curiosity: 'What would you have done if any one of us had challenged your orders and made a fight of it?'

Hugh Beringar laughed aloud. 'I fancy I should have looked the world's fool, for of course my men knew better than to shoot. But the bow is a mighty powerful persuader, and after all, an unchancy fellow like me *might* be in earnest. Why, you never thought I'd harm the girl?'

Cadfael debated the wisdom of answering that truthfully as yet, and temporised: 'If I ever thought of it, I soon realised I was wrong. They could have killed before ever Torold stepped between. No, I soon gave up that error.'

'And it does not surprise you that I knew what you had brought to the grange, and what you came to fetch tonight?'

'No revelation of your cunning can surprise me any longer,' said Cadfael. 'I conclude that you followed me from the river the night I brought it. Also that you had procured me to help you place the horses there for a dual purpose, to encourage me to transfer the treasure from wherever it was hidden, and to make it possible for those youngsters to escape, while the gold stayed here. The right hand duelling against the left, that fits you well. Why were you so sure it would be tonight?'

'Faith, if I'd been in your shoes *I* would have got them away with all the haste I could, at this favourable time, when search had been made and failed. You would have had to be a fool to let the chance slip. And as I have found long ago, you are no fool, Brother Cadfael.'

'We have much in common,' agreed Cadfael gravely. 'But once you knew that lump you're carrying there was safe in the grange, why did you not simply remove it, and make sure of it? You could still have let the children depart without it, just as they've done now.'

'And sleep in my bed while they rode away? And never make my peace with Godith, but let her go into France believing me her enemy, and capable of such meanness? No, that I could not stomach. I have my vanity. I wanted a clean end, and no grudges. I have my curiosity, too. I wanted to see this young fellow who had taken her fancy. The treasure was safe enough until you chose to get them away, why should I be uneasy about it? And this way was far more satisfying.'

'That,' agreed Cadfael emphatically, 'it certainly was.'

They were at the edge of the forest, and the open road at Sutton, and were turning north towards St Giles, all in amicable ease, which seemed to surprise neither of them.

'This time,' said Beringar, 'we'll ride in at the gate house like orderly members of the household, even if the time is a little unusual. And if you have no objection, we may as well take this straight to your hut in the garden, and sit out the rest of the night, and see what we have here. I should like to see how Godith has been living in your care, and what skills she's been acquiring. I wonder how far they'll be by now?'

'Halfway to Pool, or beyond. Most of the way it's a good road. Yes, come and see for yourself. You went enquiring for her in the town, did you not? At Edric Flesher's. Petronilla had the worst opinion of your motives.'

'She would,' agreed Beringar, laughing. 'No one would ever have been good enough for her chick, she hated me from the start. Ah, well, you'll be able to put her mind at rest now.'

They had reached the silent Abbey Foregate, and rode between the darkened houses, the ring of hooves eerie in the stillness. A few uneasy inhabitants opened their shutters a crack to look out as they passed, but their appearance was so leisured and peaceful that no one could suspect them of harmful intent. The wary citizens went back to bed reassured. Over the high, enclosing wall the great church loomed on their left hand, and the narrow opening of the wicket showed in the dark bulk of the gate. The porter was a lay brother, a little surprised at being roused to let in two horsemen at such an hour, but satisfied, on recognising both of them, that they must have been employed on some legitimate errand, no great marvel in such troublous times. He was incurious and sleepy, and did not wait to see them cross to the stables, where they tended their horses first, as good grooms should, before repairing to the garden hut with their load.

Beringar grimaced when he hoisted it. 'You carried this on your back all that way?' he demanded with raised brows.

'I did,' said Cadfael truthfully, 'and you witnessed it.'

'Then I call that a noble effort. You would not care to shoulder it again these few paces?'

'I could not presume,' said Cadfael. 'It's in your charge now.'

'I was afraid of that!' But he was in high good humour, having fulfilled his idea of himself, made his justification in Godith's eyes, and won the prize he wanted; and he had more sinew in his slenderness than anyone would have thought, for he lifted and carried the weight lightly enough the short way to the herbarium.

'I have flint and tinder here somewhere,' said Cadfael, going first into the hut. 'Wait till I make you a light, there are breakables all round us here.' He found his box, and struck sparks into the coil of charred cloth, and lit the floating wick in his little dish of oil. The flame caught and steadied, and drew tall and still, shedding a gentle light on all the strange shapes of mortars and flasks and bottles, and the bunches of drying herbs that made the air aromatic.

'You are an alchemist,' said Beringar, impressed and charmed. 'I am not sure you are not a wizard.' He set down his load in the middle of the floor, and looked about him with interest. 'This is where she spent her nights?' He had observed the bed, still rumpled from Torold's spasmodic and unquiet sleep. 'You did this for her. You must have found her out the very first day.'

'So I did. It was not so difficult. I was a long time in the world. Will you taste my wine? It's made from pears, when the crop's good.'

'Gladly! And drink to your better success – against all opponents but Hugh Beringar.'

He was on his knees by then, unknotting the rope that bound his prize. One sack disgorged another, the second a third. It could not be said that he was feverish in his eagerness, or showed any particular greed, only a certain excited curiosity. Out of the third sack rolled a tight bundle of cloth, dark-coloured, that fell apart as it was freed from constriction, and shed two unmistakable sleeves across the earth floor. The white of a shirt showed among the tangle of dark colours, and uncurled to reveal three large, smooth stones, a coiled leather belt, a short dagger in a leather sheath. Last of all, out of the centre something hard and small and bright rolled and lay still, shedding yellow flashes as it moved, burning sullenly gold and silver when it lay still at Beringar's feet.

And that was all.

On his knees, he stared and stared, in mute incomprehension, his black brows almost elevated into his hair, his dark eyes round with astonishment and consternation. There was nothing more to be read, in a countenance for once speaking volubly, no recoil, no alarm, no guilt. He leaned forward, and with a sweep of his hand parted all those mysterious garments, spread them abroad, gaped at them, and fastened on the stones. His eyebrows danced, and came down to their normal level, his eyes blazing understanding; he cast one glittering glance at Cadfael, and then he began to laugh, a huge, genuine laughter that shook him where he kneeled, and made the bunches of herbs bob and quiver over his head. A good, open, exuberant sound it was; it made Cadfael, even at this moment, shake and laugh with him.

'And I have been commiserating with you,' gasped Beringar, wiping tears from his eyes with the back of his hand, like a child, 'all this time, while you had this in store for me! What a fool I was, to think I could out-trick you, when I almost had your measure even then.'

'Here, drink this down,' urged Cadfael, offering the beaker he had filled. 'To your own better success – with all opponents but Cadfael!'

Beringar took it, and drank heartily. 'Well, you deserve that. You have the last laugh, but at least you lent it to me a while, and I shall never enjoy a better. What was it you did? How was it done? I swear I never took my eyes from you. You *did* draw up what that young man of yours had drowned there, I heard it rise, I heard the water run from it on the stone.'

'So I did, and let it down again, but very softly. This one I

151

had ready in the boat. The other Godith and her squire drew up as soon as you and I were well on our way.'

'And have it with them now?' asked Beringar, momentarily serious.

'They have. By now, I hope, in Wales, where Owain Gwynedd's hand will be over them.'

'So all the while you knew that I was watching and following you?'

'I knew you must, if you wanted to find your treasure. No one else could lead you to it. If you cannot shake off surveillance,' said Brother Cadfael sensibly, 'the only thing to do is make use of it.'

'That you certainly did. My treasure!' echoed Beringar, and looked it over and laughed afresh. 'Well, now I understand Godith better. In a fair win and a fair defeat, she said, there should be no heartburning! And there shall be none!' He looked again, more soberly, at the things spread before him on the earth floor, and after some frowning thought looked up just as intently at Cadfael. 'The stones and the sacks, anything to make like for like,' he said slowly, 'that I understand. But why these? What are these things to do with me?'

'You recognise none of them – I know. They are nothing to do with you, happily for you and for me. These,' said Cadfael, stooping to pick up and shake out shirt and hose and cotte, 'are the clothes Nicholas Faintree was wearing when he was strangled by night, in a hut in the woods above Frankwell, and thrown among the executed under the castle wall, to cover up the deed.'

'Your one man too many,' said Beringar, low-voiced.

'The same. Torold Blund rode with him, but they were separated when this befell. The murderer was waiting also for him, but with the second one he failed. Torold won away with his charge.'

'That part I know,' said Beringar. 'The last he said to you, and you to him, that evening in the mill, that I heard, but no more.'

He looked long at the poor relics, the dark brown hose and russet cotte, a young squire's best. He looked up at Cadfael, and eyed him steadily, very far from laughter now. 'I understand. You put these together to spring upon me when I was unprepared – when I looked for something very different. For me to see, and recoil from my own guilt. If this happened the night after the town fell, I had ridden out alone, as I recall. And I had been in the town that same afternoon, and to say all, yes, I did gather more than she bargained for from Petronilla. I knew this was in the wind, that there were two in Frankwell waiting for darkness before they rode. Though what I was listening for was a clue to Godith, and that I got, too. Yes, I see that I might well be suspect. But do I seem to you a man who would kill, and in so foul a fashion, just to secure the trash those children are carrying away with them into Wales?'

'Trash?' echoed Cadfael, mildly and thoughtfully.

'Oh, pleasant to have, and useful, I know. But once you have enough of it for your needs, the rest of it is trash. Can you eat it, wear it, ride it, keep off the rain and the cold with it, read it, play music on it, make love to it?'

'You can buy the favour of kings with it,' suggested Cadfael, but very placidly.

'I have the king's favour. He blows too many ways as his advisers persuade him, but left alone he knows a man when he finds one. And he demands unbecoming services when he's angry and vengeful, but he despises those who run too servilely to perform, and never leave him time to think better of his vindictiveness. I was with him in his camp a part of that evening, he has accepted me to hold my own castles and border for him, and raise the means and the men in my own way, which suits me very well. Yes, I would have liked, when such a chance offered, to secure FitzAlan's gold for him, but losing it is no great matter, and it was a good fight. So answer me, Cadfael, do I seem to you a man who would strangle his fellow-man from behind for money?'

'No! There were the circumstances that made it a possibility, but long ago I put that out of mind. You are no such man. You value yourself too high to value a trifle of gold above your self-esteem. I was as sure as man could well be, before I put it to the test tonight,' said Cadfael, 'that you wished Godith well out of her peril, and were nudging my elbow with the means to get her away. To try at the same time for the gold was fair dealing enough. No, you are not my man. There is not much,' he allowed consideringly, 'that I would put out of your scope, but killing by stealth is one thing I would never look for from you, now that I know you. Well, so you can't help me. There's nothing here to shake you, and nothing for you to recognise.'

'Not recognise – no, not that.' Beringar picked up the yellow topaz in its broken silver claw, and turned it thoughtfully in his hands. He rose, and held it to the lamp to examine it better. 'I never saw it before. But for all that, my thumbs prick. This, after a fashion, I think I may know. I watched with Aline while she prepared her brother's body for burial. All his things she put together and brought them, I think, to you to be given as alms, all but the shirt that was stained with his death-sweat. She spoke of something that was not there, but should have been there – a dagger that was hereditary in her family, and went always to the eldest son when he came of age. As she described it to me, I do believe this may be the great stone that tipped the hilt.' He looked up with furrowed brows. 'Where did you find this? Not on your dead man!'

'Not on him, no. But trampled into the earth floor, where Torold had rolled and struggled with the murderer. And it does not belong to any dagger of Torold's. There is only one other who can have worn it.'

'Are you saying,' demanded Beringar, aghast, 'that it was Aline's brother who slew Faintree? Has she to bear that, too?'

'You are forgetting, for once, your sense of time,' said Brother Cadfael reassuringly. 'Giles Siward was dead several hours before Nicholas Faintree was murdered. No, never fear, there's no guilt there can touch Aline. No, rather, whoever killed Nicholas Faintree had first robbed the body of Giles, and went to his ambush wearing the dagger he had contemptibly stolen.'

Beringar sat down abruptly on Godith's bed, and held his head hard between his hands. 'For God's sake, give me more wine, my mind no longer works.' And when his beaker was refilled he drank thirstily, picked up the topaz again and sat weighing it in his hand. 'Then we have some indication of the man you want. He was surely present through part, at any rate, of that grisly work done at the castle, for there, if we're right, he lifted the pretty piece of weaponry to which this thing belongs. But he left before the work ended, for it went on into the night, and by then, it seems, he was lurking in ambush on the other side Frankwell. How did he learn of their plans? May not one of those poor wretches have tried to buy his own life by betraying them? Your man was there when the killing began, but left well before the end. Prestcote was there surely, Ten Heyt and his Flemings were there and did the work, Courcelle, I hear, fled the business as soon as he could, and took to the cleaner duties of scouring the town for FitzAlan, and small blame to him.'

'Not all the Flemings,' Cadfael pointed out, 'speak English.'

'But some do. And among those ninety-four surely more than half spoke French just as well. Any one of the Flemings might have taken the dagger. A valuable piece, and a dead man has no more need of it. Cadfael, I tell you, I feel as you do about this business, such a death must not go unavenged. Don't you think, since it can't be any further grief or shame to her, I might show this thing to Aline, and make certain whether it is or is not from the hilt she knew?'

'I think,' said Cadfael, 'that you may. And after chapter we'll meet again here, if you will. If, that is, I am not so loaded with penance at chapter that I vanish from men's sight for a week.'

In the event, things turned out very differently. If his absence at Matins and Lauds had been noticed at all, it was clean forgotten before chapter, and no one, not even Prior Robert, ever cast it up at him or demanded penance. For after the former day's excitement and distress, another and more hopeful upheaval loomed. King Stephen with his new levies, his remounts and his confiscated provisions, was about to move south towards Worcester, to attempt inroads into the western stronghold of Earl Robert of Gloucester, the Empress Maud's half-brother and loyal champion. The vanguard of his army was to march the next day, and the king himself, with his personal guard, was moving today into Shrewsbury castle for two nights, to inspect and secure his defences there, before marching after the vanguard. He was well satisfied with the results of his foraging, and disposed to forget any remaining grudges, for he had invited to his table at the castle, this Tuesday evening, both Abbot Heribert and Prior Robert, and in the flurry of preparation minor sins were overlooked.

Cadfael repaired thankfully to his workshop, and lay down and slept on Godith's bed until Hugh Beringar came to wake him. Hugh had the topaz in his hand, and his face was grave and tired, but serene.

'It is hers. She took it in her hands gladly, knowing it for her own. I thought there could not be two such. Now I am going to the castle, for the king's party are already moving in there, and Ten Heyt and his Flemings will be with him. I mean to find the man, whoever he may be, who filched that dagger after Giles was dead. Then we shall know we are not far from your murderer. Cadfael, can you not get Abbot Heribert to bring you with him to the castle this evening? He must have an attendant, why not you? He turns to you willingly, if you ask, he'll jump at you. Then if I have anything to tell, you'll be close by.'

Brother Cadfael yawned, groaned and kept his eyes open unwillingly on the young, dark face that leaned over him, a face of tight, bright lines now, fierce and bleak, a hunting face. He had won himself a formidable ally.

'A small, mild curse on you for waking me,' he said, mumbling, 'but I'll come.'

'It was your own cause,' Beringar reminded him, smiling.

'It *is* my cause. Now for the love of God, go away and let me sleep away dinner, and afternoon and all, you've cost me hours enough to shorten my life, you plague.'

Hugh Beringar laughed, though it was a muted and burdened laugh this time, marked a cross lightly on Cadfael's broad brown forehead, and left him to his rest.

CHAPTER ELEVEN

A server for every plate was required at the king's supper. It was no problem to suggest to Abbot Heribert that the brother who had coped with the matter of the mass burial, and even talked with the king concerning the unlicensed death, should be on hand with him to be questioned at need. Prior Robert took with him his invariable toady and shadow, Brother Jerome, who would certainly be indefatigable with finger-bowl, napkin and pitcher throughout, a great deal more assiduous than Cadfael, whose mind might well be occupied elsewhere. They were old enemies, in so far as Brother Cadfael entertained enmities. He abhorred a sickly-pale tonsure.

The town was willing to put on a festival face, not so much in the king's honour as in celebration of the fact that the king was about to depart, but the effect was much the same. Edric Flesher had come down to the high street from his shop to watch the guests pass by, and Cadfael flashed him a ghost of a wink, by way of indication that they would have things to discuss later, things so satisfactory that they could well be deferred. He got a huge grin and a wave of a meaty hand in response, and knew his message had been received. Petronilla would weep for her lamb's departure, but rejoice for her safe delivery and apt escort. I must go there soon, he thought, as soon as this last duty is done.

Within the town gate Cadfael had seen the blind old man sitting almost proudly in Giles Siward's good cloth hose, holding out his palm for alms with a dignified gesture. At the high cross he saw the little old woman clasping by the hand her feeble-wit grandson with his dangling lip, and the fine brown cotte sat well on him, and gave him an air of rapt content by its very texture. Oh, Aline, you ought to give your own charity, and see what it confers, beyond food and clothing!

Where the causeway swept up from the street to the gate of the castle, the beggars who followed the king's camp had taken up new stations, hopeful and expectant, for the king's justiciar, Bishop Robert of Salisbury, had arrived to join his master, and brought a train of wealthy and important clerics with him. In the lee of the gate-house wall Lame Osbern's little trolley was drawn up, where he could beg comfortably without having to move. The worn wooden pattens he used for his callused knuckles lay tidily beside him on the trolley, on top of the folded black cloak he would not need until night fell. It was so folded that the bronze clasp at the neck showed up proudly against the black, the dragon of eternity with his tail in his mouth.

Cadfael let the others go on through the gates, and halted to say a word to the crippled man. 'Well, how have you been since last I saw you by the king's guard-post? You have a better place here.'

'I remember you,' said Osbern, looking up at him with eyes remarkably clear and innocent, in a face otherwise as misshapen as his body. 'You are the brother who brought me the cloak.'

'And has it done you good service?'

'It has, and I have prayed for the lady, as you asked. But, brother, it troubles me, too. Surely the man who wore it before me is dead. Is it so?'

'He is,' said Cadfael, 'but that should not trouble you. The lady who sent it to you is his sister, and trust me, her giving blesses the gift. Wear it, and take comfort.'

He would have walked on then, but a hasty hand caught at the skirt of his habit, and Osbern besought him pleadingly: 'But, brother, I go in dread that I bear some guilt. For I saw the man, living, with this cloak about him, hale as I . . .'

'You *saw* him?' echoed Cadfael on a soundless breath, but the anxious voice had ridden over him and rushed on.

'It was in the night, and I was cold, and I thought to myself, I wish the good God would send me such a cloak to keep me warm! Brother, thought is also prayer! And no more than three days later God did indeed send me this very cloak. You dropped it into my arms! How can I be at peace? The young man gave me a groat that night, and asked me to say a prayer for him on the morrow, and so I did. But how if my first prayer made the second of none effect? How if I have prayed a man into his grave to get myself a cloak to wear?'

Cadfael stood gazing at him amazed and mute, feeling the chill of ice flow down his spine. The man was sane, clear of mind and eye, he knew very well what he was saying, and his trouble of heart was real and deep, and must be the first consideration, whatever else followed.

158

'Put all such thoughts out of your mind, friend,' said Cadfael firmly, 'for only the devil can have sent them. If God gave you the thing for which you wished, it was to save one morsel of good out of a great evil for which you are no way to blame. Surely your prayers for the former wearer are of aid even now to his soul. This young man was one of FitzAlan's garrison here, done to death after the castle fell, at the king's orders. You need have no fears, his death is not at your door, and no sacrifice of yours could have saved him.'

Osbern's uplifted face eased and brightened, but still he shook his head, bewildered. 'FitzAlan's man? But how could that be, when I saw him enter and leave the king's camp?'

'You saw him? You are sure? How do you know this is the same cloak?'

'Why, by this clasp at the throat. I saw it clearly in the fire-light when he gave me the groat.'

He could not be mistaken, then, there surely were not two such designs exactly alike, and Cadfael himself had seen its match on the buckle of Giles Siward's sword-belt.

'When was it that you saw him?' he asked gently. 'Tell me how it befell.'

'It was the night before the assault, around midnight. I had my place then close to the guard-post for the sake of the fire, and I saw him come, not openly, but like a shadow, among the bushes. He stood when they challenged him, and asked to be taken to their officer, for he had something to tell, to the king's advantage. He kept his face hidden, but he was young. And afraid! But who was not afraid, then? They took him away within, and afterwards I saw him return, and they let him out. He said he had orders to go back, for there must be no suspicion. That was all I heard. He was in better heart then, not so frightened, so I asked him for alms, and he gave, and asked my prayers in return. Say some prayer for me tomorrow, he said – and on the morrow, you tell me, he died! This I'm sure of, when he left me he was not expecting to die.'

'No,' said Cadfael, sick with pity and grief for all poor, frightened, breakable men, 'surely he was not. None of us knows the day. But pray for him you may, and your prayers will benefit his soul. Put off all thought that ever you did him harm, it is not so. You never wished him ill, God hears the heart. Never wished him any, never did him any.'

He left Osbern reassured and comforted, but went on into the castle carrying with him the load of discomfort and depression the lame man had shed. So it always is, he thought, to relieve another you must burden yourself. And such a burden! He remembered in time that there was one more question he should have asked, the must urgent of all, and turned back to ask it.

'Do you know, friend, who was the officer of the guard, that night?'

Osbern shook his head. 'I never saw him, he never came out himself. No, brother, that I can't tell you.'

'Trouble no more,' said Cadfael. 'Now you have told it freely, and you know the cloak came to you with a blessing, not a bane. Enjoy it freely, as you deserve.'

'Father Abbot,' said Cadfael, seeking out Heribert in the court-yard, 'if you have no need of me until you come to table, there is work here I have still to do, concerning Nicholas Faintree.'

With King Stephen holding audience in the inner ward, and the great court teeming with clerics, bishops, the small nobility of the county, even an earl or so, there was no room, in any case, for the mere servitors, whose duties would begin when the feast began. The abbot had found a friend in the bishop of Salisbury, and readily dismissed Cadfael to whatever pursuit he chose. He went in search of Hugh Beringar with Osbern's story very heavy on his mind, and the last question still unanswered, though so many sad mysteries were now made plain. It was not a terrified prisoner with the rope already round his neck who had broken down and betrayed the secret of FitzAlan's plans for his treasury. No, that betrayal had taken place a day previously, when the issue of battle was still to be decided, and the thing had been done with forethought, to save a life it yet had failed to save. He came by stealth, and asked to be taken to the officer of the guard, for he had something to tell to the king's advantage! And when he left he told the guard he had orders to go back, so that there could be no suspicion, but then he was in better heart. Poor wretch, not for long!

By what means or on what pretext he had managed to get out of the castle – perhaps on pretence of reconnoitring the enemy's position? – certainly he had obeyed his instructions to return and keep all suspicion lulled. He had returned only to confront the death he had thought he was escaping.

Hugh Beringar came out and stood on the steps of the great hall, craning round him for one person among all that shifting throng. The black Benedictine habits showed here and there in strong contrast to the finery of lordlings in their best, but Cadfael was shorter than many of those about him, and saw the man he was seeking before he was himself seen. He began to weave his way towards him, and the keen black eyes sweeping the court beneath drawn brows lit upon him, and glittered. Beringar came down to take him by the arm and draw him away to a quieter place.

'Come away, come up on to the guard-walk, there'll be no one there but the sentry. How can we talk here?' And when they had mounted to the wall, he found a corner where no one could approach them without being seen, he said, eyeing Cadfael very earnestly: 'You have news in your face. Tell it quickly, and I'll tell you mine.'

Cadfael told the story as briefly as it had been told to him, and it was understood as readily. Beringar stood leaning against the merlon of the wall as though bracing his back for a dour defence. His face was bitter with dismay.

'Her brother! No escaping it, this can have been no other. He came by night out of the castle, by stealth, hiding his face, he spoke with the king's officer, and returned as he had come. So that there might be no suspicion! Oh, I am sick!' said Beringar savagely. 'And all for nothing! His treason fell victim to one even worse. You don't know yet, Cadfael, you don't know all! But that of all people it should be *her brother*!'

'No help for it,' said Cadfael, 'it was he. In terror for his life, regretting an ill-judged alliance, he went hurrying to the besiegers to buy his life, in exchange – for what? Something of advantage to the king! That very evening they had held conference and planned the removal of FitzAlan's gold. That was how someone learned in good time of what Faintree and Torold carried, and the way they were to go. Someone who never passed that word on, as I think, to king or any, but acted upon it himself, and for his own gain. Why else should it end as it did? The young man, so says Osbern, went back under orders, relieved and less afraid.'

'He had been promised his life,' said Beringar bitterly, 'and probably the king's favour, too, and a place about him, no wonder he went back the happier in that belief. But what was

161

really intended was to send him back to be taken and slaughtered with the rest, to make sure he should not live to tell the tale. For listen, Cadfael, to what I got out of one of the Flemings who was in that day's murderous labour from first to last. He said that after Arnulf of Hesdin was hanged, Ten Heyt pointed out to the executioners a young man who was to be the next to go, and said the order came from above. And it was done. They found it a huge jest that he was dragged to his death incredulous, thinking at first, no doubt, they were putting up a pretence to remove him from the ranks, and then he saw it was black reality, and he screamed that they were mistaken, that he was not to die with the rest, that he had been promised his life, that they should send and ask – '

'Send and ask,' said Brother Cadfael, 'of Adam Courcelle.'

'No – I learned no name . . . my man heard none. What makes you hit on that name in particular? He was not by but once, according to this man's account, he came but once to look at the bodies they had already cut down, and it was early, they would be but few. Then he went away to his work in the town, and was seen no more. Weak-stomached, they thought.'

'And the dagger? Was Giles wearing it when they strung him up?'

'He was, for my man had an eye to the thing himself, but when he was relieved for a while, and came back to get it, it was already gone.'

'Even to one with a great prize in view,' said Cadfael sadly, 'a small extra gain by the way may not come amiss.'

They looked at each other mutely for a long moment. 'But why do you say so certainly, Courcelle?'

'I am thinking,' said Cadfael, 'of the horror that fell upon him when Aline came to collect her dead, and he knew what he had done. If I had known, he said, if I had known, I would have saved him for you! No matter at what cost! God forgive me! he said, but he meant: Aline, forgive me! With all his heart he meant it then, though I would not call that repentance. And he gave back, you'll remember, the cloak. I think, truly I do think, he would then have given back also the dagger, if he had dared. But he could not, it was already broken and incomplete. I wonder,' said Cadfael, pondering, 'I wonder what he has done with it now? A man who would take it from the dead in the first place would not part with it too easily, even for a girl's

162

sake, and yet he never dare let her set eyes on it, and he is in earnest in courting her. Would he keep it, in hiding? Or get rid of it?'

'If you are right,' said Beringar, still doubtful, 'we need it, it is our proof. And yet, Cadfael, for God's sake, how are we to deal now? God knows I can find no good to say for one who tried to purchase his own safety so, when his fellows were at their last gasp. But neither you nor I can strip this matter bare, and do so wicked an injury to so innocent and honourable a lady. It's enough that she mourns for him. Let her at least go on thinking that he held by his mistaken choice faithfully to the end, and gave his life for it – not that he died craven, bleating that he was promised grace in return for so base a betrayal. She must not know, now or ever.'

Brother Cadfael could not but agree. 'But if we accuse him, and this comes to trial, surely everything will come out. That we cannot allow, and there lies our weakness.'

'And our strength,' said Beringar fiercely, 'for neither can *he* allow it. He wants his advancement with the king, he wants offices, but he wants Aline – do you think I did not know it? Where would he stand with her if ever a breath of this reached her? No, he will be at least as anxious as we to keep the story for ever buried. Give him but a fair chance to settle the quarrel out of hand, and he'll jump at it.'

'Your preoccupation,' said Cadfael gently, 'I understand, and sympathise with it. But you must also acknowledge mine. I have here another responsibility. Nicholas Faintree must not lie uneasy for want of justice.'

'Trust me, and stand ready to back me in whatever I shall do this night at the king's table,' said Hugh Beringar. 'Justice he shall have, and vengeance, too, but let it be as I shall devise.'

Cadfael went to his duty behind the abbot's chair in doubt and bewilderment, with no clear idea in his mind of what Beringar intended, and no conviction that without the broken dagger any secure case could be made against Courcelle. The Fleming had not seen him take it, what he had cried out to Aline over her brother's body, in manifest pain, was not evidence. And yet there had been vengeance and death in Hugh Beringar's face, as much for Aline Siward's sake as for Nicholas Faintree's. What mattered most in the world to him, at this moment, was that

Aline should never know how her brother had disgraced his blood and his name, and in that cause Beringar would not scruple to spend not only Adam Courcelle's life, but also his own. And somehow, reflected Cadfael ruefully, I have become very much attached to that young man, and I should not like to see any ill befall him. I would rather this case went to law, even if we have to step carefully in drawing up our evidence, and leave out every word concerning Torold Blund and Godith Adeney. But for that we need, we must have, proof positive that Giles Siward's dagger passed into the possession of Adam Courcelle, and preferably the dagger itself, into the bargain, to match with the piece of it I found on the scene of the murder. Otherwise he will simply lie and lie, deny everything, say he never saw the topaz or the dagger it came from, and has nothing to answer; and from the eminence of the position he has won with the king, he will be unassailable.

There were no ladies present that night, this was strictly a political and military occasion, but the great hall had been decked out with borrowed hangings, and was bright with torches. The king was in good humour, the garrison's provisions were assured, and those who had robbed for the royal supplies had done their work well. From his place behind Heribert at the king's high table Cadfael surveyed the full hall, and estimated that some five hundred guests were present. He looked for Beringar, and found him at a lower table, in his finery, very debonair and lively in conversation, as though he had no darker preoccupation. He was master of his face; even when he glanced briefly at Courcelle there was nothing in the look to attract attention, certainly nothing to give warning of any grave purpose.

Courcelle was at the high table, though crowded to its end by the visiting dignitaries. Big, vividly coloured and handsome, accomplished in arms, in good odour with the king, how strange that such a man should feel it necessary to grasp secretly at plunder, and by such degrading means! And yet, in this chaos of civil war, was it so strange after all? Where a king's favour could be toppled with the king, where barons were changing sides according as the fortunes changed, where even earls were turning to secure their own advantage rather than that of a cause that might collapse under their feet and leave them prisoner and ruined! Courcelle was merely a sign of the times;

in a few years there would be duplicates of him in every corner of the realm.

I do not like the way I see England going, thought Cadfael with anxious foreboding, and above all I do not like what is about to happen, for as surely as God sees us, Hugh Beringar is set to sally forth on to a dubious field, half-armed.

He fretted through the long meal, hardly troubled by the demands of Abbot Heribert, who was always abstemious with wine, and ate very frugally. Cadfael served and poured, proffered the finger-bowl and napkin, and waited with brooding resignation.

When the dishes were cleared away, musicians playing, and only the wine on the tables, the servitors in their turn might take their pick of what was left in the kitchens, and the cooks and scullions were already helping themselves and finding quiet corners to sit and eat. Cadfael collected a bread trencher and loaded it with broken meats, and took it out through the great court to Lame Osbern at the gate. There was a measure of wine to go with it. Why should not the poor rejoice for once at the king's cost, even if that cost was handed on down the hierarchies until it fell at last upon the poor themselves? Too often they paid, but never got their share of the rejoicing.

Cadfael was walking back to the hall when his eye fell upon a lad of about twelve, who was sitting in the torchlight on the inner side of the gate house, his back comfortably against the wall, carving his meat into small pieces with a narrow-bladed knife. Cadfael had seen him earlier, in the kitchen, gutting fish with the same knife, but he had not seen the haft of it, and would not have seen it now if the boy had not laid it down beside him on the ground while he ate.

Cadfael halted and gazed, motionless. It was no kitchen knife, but a well-made dagger, and its hilt was a slender shaft of silver, rounded to the hand, showing delicate lines of filigree-work, and glowing round the collar of the blade with small stones. The hilt ended in a twist of silver broken off short. It was hard to believe, but impossible not to believe. Perhaps thought really is prayer.

He spoke to the boy very softly and evenly; the unwitting means of justice must not be alarmed. 'Child, where did you get so fine a knife as that?'

The boy looked up, untroubled, and smiled. When he had

165

gulped down the mouthful with which his cheeks were bulging, he said cheerfully: 'I found it. I didn't steal it.'

'God forbid, lad, I never thought it. Where did you find it? And have you the sheath, too?'

It was lying beside him in the shadow, he patted it proudly. 'I fished them out of the river. I had to dive, but I found them. They really are mine, father, the owner didn't want them, he threw them away. I suppose because this was broken. But it's the best knife for slitting fish I ever had.'

So he threw them away! Not, however, simply because the jewelled hilt was broken.

'You saw him throw it into the river? Where was this, and when?'

'I was fishing under the castle, and a man came down alone from the water-gate to the bank of the river, and threw it in, and went back to the castle. When he'd gone I dived in where I saw it fall, and I found it. It was early in the evening, the same night all the bodies were carried down to the abbey – a week ago, come tomorrow. It was the first day it was safe to go fishing there again.'

Yes, it fitted well. That same afternoon Aline had taken Giles away to St Alkmund's, and left Courcelle stricken and wild with unavailing regrets, and in possession of a thing that might turn Aline against him for ever, if once she set eyes on it. And he had done the only, the obvious thing, consigned it to the river, never thinking that the avenging angel, in the shape of a fisher-boy, would redeem it to confront him when most he believed himself safe.

'You did not know who this man was? What like was he? What age?' For there remained the lingering doubt; all he had to support his conviction was the memory of Courcelle's horrified face and broken voice, pleading his devotion over Giles Siward's body.

The child hoisted indifferent shoulders, unable to picture for another what he himself had seen clearly and memorably. 'Just a man. I didn't know him. Not old like you, father, but quite old.' But to him anyone of his father's generation would be old, though his father might be only a year or two past thirty.

'Would you know him if you saw him again? Could you point him out among many?'

'Of course!' said the boy almost scornfully. His eyes were

young, bright, and very observant, if his tongue was none too fluent, of course he would know his man again.

'Sheathe your knife, child, and bring it, and come with me,' said Cadfael with decision. 'Oh, don't fret, no one will take your treasure from you, or if later you must give it up, you shall be handsomely paid for it. All I need is for you to tell again what you have told to me, and you shan't be the loser.'

He knew, when he entered the hall with the boy beside him, a little apprehensive now but even more excited, that they came late. The music was stilled, and Hugh Beringar was on his feet and striding towards the dais on which the high table stood. They heard his voice raised, high and clear, as he mounted and stood before the king. 'Your Grace, before you depart for Worcester, there is a matter on which I beg you'll hear me and do right. I demand justice on one here in this company, who has abused his position in your confidence. He has stolen from the dead, to the shame of his nobility, and he has committed murder, to the shame of his manhood. I stand on my charges, to prove them with my body. And here is my gage!'

Against his own doubts, he had accepted Cadfael's intuition, to the length of staking his life upon it. He leaned forward, and rolled something small and bright across the table, to clang softly against the king's cup. The silence that had fallen was abrupt and profound. All round the high table heads craned to follow the flash of yellow brilliance that swayed irregularly over the board, limping on its broken setting, and then were raised to stare again at the young man who had launched it. The king picked up the topaz and turned it in his large hands, his face blank with incomprehension at first, and then wary and brooding. He, too, looked long at Hugh Beringar. Cadfael, picking his way between the lower tables, drew the puzzled boy after him and kept his eyes upon Adam Courcelle, who sat at his end of the table stiff and aware. He had command of his face, he looked no more astonished or curious than any of those about him; only the taut hand gripping his drinking-horn betrayed his consternation. Or was even that imagined, to fit in with an opinion already formed? Cadfael was no longer sure of his own judgment, a state he found distressing and infuriating.

'You have bided your time to throw your thunderbolt,' said

the king at length, and looked up darkly at Beringar from the stone he was turning in his hands.

'I was loth to spoil your Grace's supper, but neither would I put off what should not be put off. Your Grace's justice is every honest man's right.'

'You will need to explain much. What is this thing?'

'It is the tip of a dagger-hilt. The dagger to which it belongs is now by right the property of the lady Aline Siward, who has loyally brought all the resources of her house to your Grace's support. It was formerly in the possession of her brother Giles, who was among those who garrisoned this castle against your Grace, and have paid the price for it. I say that it was taken from his dead body, an act not unknown among the common soldiery, but unworthy of knight or gentleman. That is the first offence. The second is murder – that murder of which your Grace was told by Brother Cadfael, of the Benedictine house here in Shrewsbury, after the count of the dead was made. Your Grace and those who carried out your orders were used as a shield for one who strangled a man from behind, as your Grace will well remember.'

'I do remember,' said the king grimly. He was torn between displeasure at having to exert himself to listen and judge, when his natural indolence had wanted only a leisurely and thoughtless feast, and a mounting curiosity as to what lay behind all this. 'What has this stone to do with that death?'

'Your Grace, Brother Cadfael is also present here, and will testify that he found the place where this murder was committed, and found there, broken off in the struggle and trodden into the ground, this stone. He will take oath, as I do, that the man who stole the dagger is the same who killed Nicholas Faintree, and that he left behind him, unnoticed, this proof of his guilt.'

Cadfael was drawing nearer by then, but they were so intent on the closed scene above that no one noticed his approach. Courcelle was sitting back, relaxed and brightly interested, in his place, but what did that mean? Doubtless he saw very well the flaw in this; no need to argue against the claim that whoever stole the dagger slew the man, since no one could trace possession to him. The thing was at the bottom of the Severn, lost for ever. The theory could be allowed to stand, the crime condemned and deplored, provided no one could furnish a name, and proof to back it. Or, on the other hand, this could far more simply be the detachment of an innocent man!

'Therefore,' said Hugh Beringar relentlessly, 'I repeat those charges I have made here before your Grace. I appeal one among us here in this hall of theft and murder, and I offer proof with my body, to uphold my claim in combat upon the body of Adam Courcelle.'

He had turned at the end to face the man he accused, who was on his feet with a leap, startled and shaken, as well he might be. Shock burned rapidly into incredulous anger and scorn. Just so would any innocent man look, suddenly confronted with an accusation so mad as to be laughable.

'Your Grace, this is either folly or villainy! How comes my name into such a diatribe? It may well be true that a dagger was stolen from a dead man, it may even be true that the same thief slew a man, and left this behind as witness. But as for how my name comes into such a tale, I leave it to Hugh Beringar to tell – if these are not simply the lies of an envious man. When did I ever see this supposed dagger? When was it ever in my possession? Where is it now? Has any ever seen me wear such a thing? Send, my lord, and search those soldier's belongings I have here, and if such a thing is found in any ward or lodging of mine, let me know of it!'

'Wait!' said the king imperiously, and looked from one face to the other with frowning brows. 'This is indeed a matter that needs to be examined, and if these charges are made in malice there will be an account to pay. What Adam says is the nub of it. Is the monk indeed present? And does he confirm the finding of this broken ornament at the place where this killing befell? And that it came from that very dagger?'

'I brought Brother Cadfael here with me tonight,' said the abbot, and looked about for him helplessly.

'I am here, Father Abbot,' said Cadfael from below the dais, and advanced to be seen, his arm about the shoulders of the boy, now totally fascinated, all eyes and ears.

'Do you bear out what Beringar says?' demanded King Stephen. 'You found this stone where the man was slain?'

'Yes, your Grace. Trampled into the earth, where plainly there had been a struggle, and two bodies rolling upon the ground.'

'And whose word have we that it comes from a dagger once

belonging to Mistress Siward's brother? Though I grant you it should be easy enough to recognise, once known.'

'The word of Lady Aline herself. It has been shown to her, and she has recognised it.'

'That is fair witness enough,' said the king, 'that whoever is the thief may well be the murderer, also. But why it should follow that either you or Beringar here suppose him to be Adam, that for my life I cannot see. There's never a thread to join him to the dagger or the deed. You might as well cast round here among us, and pick on Bishop Robert of Salisbury, or any one of the squires down below there. Or prick your knife-point into a list of us with eyes closed. Where is the logic?'

'I am glad,' said Courcelle, darkly red and forcing a strained laughter, 'that your Grace puts so firm a finger on the crux of the matter. With goodwill I can go along with this good brother to condemn a mean theft and a furtive killing, but, Beringar, beware how you connect me with either, or any other honest man. Follow your thread from this stone, by all means, if thread there is, but until you can trace this dagger into my hands, be careful how you toss challenges to mortal combat about you, young man, for they may be taken up, to your great consternation.'

'My gage is now lying upon the table,' said Hugh Beringar with implacable calm. 'You have only to take it up. I have not withdrawn it.'

'My lord king,' said Cadfael, raising his voice to ride over the partisan whisperings and murmurings that were running like conflicting winds about the high table, 'it is not the case that there is no witness to connect the dagger with any person. And for proof positive that stone and dagger belong together, here is the very weapon itself. I ask your Grace to match the two with your own hands.'

He held up the dagger, and Beringar at the edge of the dais took it from him, staring like a man in a dream, and handed it in awed silence to the king. The boy's eyes followed it with possessive anxiety, Courcelle's with stricken and unbelieving horror, as if a drowned victim had risen to haunt him. Stephen looked at the thing with an eye appreciative of its workmanship, slid out the blade with rising curiosity, and fitted the topaz in its silver claw to the jagged edge of the hilt.

'No doubt but this belongs. You have all seen?' And he

looked down at Cadfael. 'Where, then, did you come by this?'

'Speak up, child,' said Cadfael encouragingly, 'and tell the king what you told to me.'

The boy was rosy and shining with an excitement that had quite overridden his fear. He stood up and told his tale in a voice shrill with self-importance, but still in the simple words he had used to Cadfael, and there was no man there who could doubt he was telling the truth.

'. . . and I was by the bushes at the edge of the water, and he did not see me. But I saw him clearly. And as soon as he went away I dived in where it had fallen, and found it. I live by the river, I was born by it. My mother says I swam before I walked. I kept the knife, thinking no wrong, since he did not want it. And that is the very knife, my lord, and may I have it back when you are done?'

The king was diverted for a moment from the gravity of the cause that now lay in his hands, to smile at the flushed and eager child with all the good-humour and charm his nature was meant to dispense, if he had not made an ambitious and hotly contested bid for a throne, and learned the rough ways that go with such contests.

'So our fish tonight was gutted with a jewelled knife, was it, boy? Princely indeed! And it was good fish, too. Did you catch it, as well as dress it?'

Bashfully the boy said that he had helped.

'Well, you have done your part very fitly. And now, did you know this man who threw away the knife?'

'No, my lord, I don't know his name. But I know him well enough when I see him.'

'And do you see him? Here in this hall with us now?'

'Yes, my lord,' said the child readily, and pointed a finger straight at Adam Courcelle. 'That was the man.'

All eyes turned upon Courcelle, the king's most dourly and thoughtfully of all, and there was a silence that lasted no more than a long-drawn breath, but seemed to shake the foundations of the hall, and stop every heart within its walls. Then Courcelle said, with arduous and angry calm: 'Your Grace, this is utterly false. I never had the dagger, I could not well toss it into the river. I deny that ever I had the thing in my possession, or ever saw it until now.'

'Are you saying,' asked the king drily, 'that the child lies? At

171

whose instigation? Not Beringar's — it seems to me that he was as taken aback by this witness as I myself, or you. Am I to think the Benedictine order has procured the boy to put up such a story? And for what end?'

'I am saying, your Grace, that this is a foolish error. The boy may have seen what he says he saw, and got the dagger as he claims he got it, but he is mistaken in saying he saw me. I am not the man. I deny all that has been said against me.'

'And I maintain it,' said Hugh Beringar. 'And I ask that it be put to the proof.'

The king crashed a fist upon the table so that the boards danced, and cups rocked and spilled wine. 'There is something here to be probed, and I cannot let it pass now without probing it.' He turned again to the boy, and reined in his exasperation to ask more gently: 'Think and look carefully, now, and say again: are you certain this is the man you saw? If you have any doubt, say so. It is no sin to be mistaken. You may have seen some other man of like build or colour. But if you are sure, say that also, without fear.'

'I am sure,' said the boy, trembling but adamant. 'I know what I saw.'

The king leaned back in his great chair, and thumped his closed fists on the arms, and pondered. He looked at Hugh Beringar with grim displeasure: 'It seems you have hung a mill-stone round my neck, when most I need to be free and to move fast. I cannot now wipe out what has been said, I must delve deeper. Either this case goes to the long processes of court law — no, not for you nor any will I now delay my going one day beyond the morrow's morrow! I have made my plans, I cannot afford to change them.'

'There need be no delay,' said Beringar, 'if your Grace coun-tenances trial by combat. I have appealed Adam Courcelle of murder, I repeat that charge. If he accepts, I am ready to meet him without any ceremony or preparation. Your Grace may see the outcome tomorrow, and march on the following day, freed of this burden.'

Cadfael, during these exchanges, had not taken his eyes from Courcelle's face, and marked with foreboding the signs of gradually recovered assurance. The faint sweat that had broken on his lip and brow dried, the stare of desperation cooled into calculation; he even began to smile. Since he was now cornered, and there were two ways out, one by long examination and questioning, one by simple battle, he was beginning to see in this alternative his own salvation. Cadfael could follow the measuring, narrowed glance that studied Hugh Beringar from head to foot, and understood the thoughts behind the eyes. Here was a younger man, lighter in weight, half a head shorter, much less in reach, inexperienced, over-confident, an easy victim. It should not be any problem to put him out of the world; and that done, Courcelle had nothing to fear. The judgment of heaven would have spoken, no one thereafter would point a finger at him, and Aline would be still within his reach, innocent of his dealings with her brother, and effectively separated from a too-engaging rival, without any blame to Courcelle, the wrongly accused. Oh, no, it was not so grim a situation, after all. It should work out very well.

He reached out along the table, picked up the topaz, and rolled it contemptuously back towards Beringar, to be retrieved and retained.

'Let it be so, your Grace. I accept battle, tomorrow, without formality, without need for practice. Your Grace shall march the following day.' And I with you, his confident countenance completed.

'So be it!' said the king grimly. 'Since you're bent on robbing me of one good man, between you, I suppose I may as well find and keep the better of the two. Tomorrow, then, at nine of the clock, after Mass. Not here within the wards, but in the open – the meadow outside the town gate, between road and river, will do well. Prestcote, you and Willem marshal the lists. See to it! And we'll have no horses put at risk,' he said practically. 'On foot, and with swords!'

Hugh Beringar bowed acquiescence. Courcelle said: 'Agreed!' and smiled, thinking how much longer a reach and stronger a wrist he had for sword-play.

'*À l'outrance!*' said the king with a vicious snap, and rose from the table to put an end to a sullied evening's entertainment.

CHAPTER TWELVE

On the way back through the streets of the town, dark but not quite silent, somehow uneasily astir as if rats ran in a deserted house, Hugh Beringar on his rawboned grey drew alongside Brother Cadfael and walked his mount for some few minutes at their foot-pace, ignoring Brother Jerome's close proximity and attentive ears as though they had not existed. In front, Abbot Heribert and Prior Robert conversed in low and harried tones, concerned for one life at stake, but unable to intervene. Two young men at bitter enmity had declared for a death. Once both contestants had accepted the odds, there was no retreating; he who lost had been judged by heaven. If he survived the sword, the gallows waited for him.

'You may call me every kind of fool,' said Beringar accommodatingly, 'if it will give you any ease.' His voice had still its light, teasing intonation, but Cadfael was not deceived.

'It is not for me, of all men,' he said, 'to blame, or pity – or even regret what you have done.'

'As a monk?' asked the mild voice, the smile in it perceptible to an attentive ear.

'As a man! Devil take you!'

'Brother Cadfael,' said Hugh heartily, 'I do love you. You know very well you would have done the same in my place.'

'I would not! Not on the mere guess of an old fool I hardly knew! How if I had been wrong?'

'Ah, but you were not wrong! He is the man – doubly a murderer, for he delivered her poor coward brother to his death just as vilely as he throttled Faintree. Mind, never a word to Aline about this until all's over – one way or the other.'

'Never a word, unless she speak the first. Do you think the news is not blown abroad all through this town by now?'

'I know it is, but I pray she is deep asleep long ago, and will not go forth to hear this or any news until she goes to High Mass at ten. By which time, who knows, we may have the answer to everything.'

'And you,' said Brother Cadfael acidly, because of the pain he

174

felt, that must have some outlet, 'will you now spend the night on your knees in vigil, and wear yourself out before ever you draw in the field?'

'I am not such a fool as all that,' said Hugh reprovingly, and shook a finger at his friend. 'For shame, Cadfael! You a monk, and cannot trust God to see right done? I shall go to bed and sleep well, and rise fresh to the trial. And now I suppose you will insist on being my deputy and advocate to heaven?'

'No,' said Cadfael grudgingly, 'I shall sleep, and get up only when the bell rings for me. Am I to have less faith than an impudent heathen like you?'

'That's my Cadfael! Still,' conceded Beringar, 'you may whisper a word or two to God on my behalf at Matins and Lauds, if you'll be so kind. If he turns a deaf ear to you, small use the rest of us wearing out our knee-bones.' And he leaned from his tall horse to lay a light hand for an instant on Cadfael's broad tonsure, like a playful benediction, and then set spurs to his horse and trotted ahead, passing the abbot with a respectful reverence, to vanish into the curving descent of the Wyle.

Brother Cadfael presented himself before the abbot immediately after Prime. It did not seem that Heribert was much surprised to see him, or to hear the request he put forward.

'Father Abbot, I stand with this young man Hugh Beringar in this cause. The probing that brought to light the evidence on which his charge rests, that was my doing. And even if he has chosen to take the cause into his own hands, refusing me any perilous part in it, I am not absolved. I pray leave to go and stand trial with him as best I may. Whether I am of help to him or not, I must be there. I cannot turn my back at this pass on my friend who has spoken for me.'

'I am much exercised in mind, also,' admitted the abbot, sighing. 'In spite of what the king has said, I can only pray that this trial need not be pressed to the death.' And I, thought Cadfael ruefully, dare not even pray for that, since the whole object of this wager is to stop a mouth for ever. 'Tell me,' said Heribert, 'is it certain that the man Courcelle killed that poor lad we have buried in the church?'

'Father, it is certain. Only he had the dagger, only he can have left the broken part behind him. There is here a clear contest of right and wrong.'

175

'Go, then,' said the abbot. 'You are excused all duties until this matter is ended.' For such duels had been known to last the day long, until neither party could well see, or stand, or strike, so that in the end one or the other fell and could not rise, and simply bled to death where he lay. And if weapons were broken, they must still fight, with hands, teeth and feet, until one or the other broke and cried for quarter; though few ever did, since that meant defeat, the judgment of heaven convicting, and the gallows waiting, an even more shameful death. A bitter business, thought Cadfael, kilting his habit and going out heavily from the gate house, not worthy of being reverenced as the verdict of God. In this case there was a certain appropriateness about it, however, and the divine utterance might yet be heard in it. If, he thought, I have as much faith as he? I wonder if he did indeed sleep well! And strangely, he could believe it. His own sleep had been fitful and troubled.

Giles Siward's dagger, complete with its lopped topaz, he had brought back with him and left in his cell, promising the anxious fisher-boy either restoration or fair reward, but it was not yet time to speak to Aline in the matter. That must wait the issue of the day. If all went well, Hugh Beringar himself should restore it to her. If not – no, he would not consider any such possibility.

The trouble with me, he thought unhappily, is that I have been about the world long enough to know that God's plans for us, however infallibly good, may not take the form that we expect and demand. And I find an immense potential for rebellion in this old heart, if God, for no matter what perfect end, choose to take Hugh Beringar out of this world and leave Adam Courcelle in it.

Outside the northern gate of Shrewsbury the Castle Foregate housed a tight little suburb of houses and shops, but it ended very soon, and gave place to meadows on either side the road. The river twined serpentine coils on both sides, beyond the fields, and in the first level meadow on the left the king's marshals had drawn up a large square of clear ground, fenced in on every side by a line of Flemings with lances held crosswise, to keep back any inquisitive spectator who might encroach in his excitement, and to prevent flight by either contestant. Where the ground rose slightly, outside the square, a great chair had been placed

176

for the king, and the space about it was kept vacant for the nobility, but on the other three sides there was already a great press of people. The word had run through Shrewsbury like the wind through leaves. The strangest thing was the quietness. Every soul about the square of lances was certainly talking, but in such hushed undertones that the sum of all those voices was no louder than the absorbed buzzing of a hive of bees in sunshine.

The slanting light of morning cast long but delicate shadows across the grass, and the sky above was thinly veiled with haze. Cadfael lingered where guards held a path clear for the procession approaching from the castle, a brightness of steel and sheen of gay colours bursting suddenly out of the dim archway of the gate. King Stephen, big, flaxen-haired, handsome, resigned now to the necessity that threatened to rob him of one of his officers, but none the better pleased for that, and not disposed to allow any concessions that would prolong the contest. To judge by his face, there would be no pauses for rest, and no limitation imposed upon the possible savagery. He wanted it over. All the knights and barons and clerics who streamed after him to his presidential chair were carrying themselves with the utmost discretion, quick to take their lead from him.

The two contestants appeared as the royal train drew aside. No shields, Cadfael noted, and no mail, only the simple protection of leather. Yes, the king wanted a quick end, none of your day-long hacking and avoiding until neither party could lift hand. On the morrow the main army would leave to follow the vanguard, no matter which of these two lay dead, and Stephen had details yet to be settled before they marched. Beringar first, the accuser, went to kneel to the king and do him reverence, and did so briskly, springing up vigorously from his knee and turning to where the ranks of lances parted to let him into the arena. He caught sight of Cadfael then, standing a little apart. In a face tight, grave and mature, still the black eyes smiled.

'I knew,' he said, 'that you would not fail me.'

'See to it,' said Cadfael morosely, 'that you do not fail me.'

'No dread,' said Hugh. 'I'm shriven white as a March lamb.' His voice was even and reflective. 'I shall never be readier. And your arm will be seconding mine.'

At every stroke, thought Cadfael helplessly, and doubted that all these tranquil years since he took the cowl had really made any transformation in a spirit once turbulent, insubordinate and incorrigibly rash. He could feel his blood rising, as though it was he who must enter the lists.

Courcelle rose from his knee and followed his accuser into the square. They took station at opposite corners, and Prestcote, with his marshal's truncheon raised, stood between them and looked to the king to give the signal. A herald was crying aloud the charge, the name of the challenger, and the refutation uttered by the accused. The crowd swayed, with a sound like a great, long-drawn sigh, that rippled all round the field. Cadfael could see Hugh's face clearly, and now there was no smiling, it was bleak, intent and still, eyes fixed steadily upon his opponent.

The king surveyed the scene, and lifted his hand. The truncheon fell and Prestcote drew aside to the edge of the square as the contestants advanced to meet each other.

At first sight, the contrast was bitter. Courcelle was half as big again, half as old again, with height and reach and weight all on his side, and there was no questioning his skill and experience. His fiery colouring and towering size made Beringar look no more than a lean, lightweight boy, and though that lightness might be expected to lend him speed and agility, within seconds it was clear that Courcelle also was very fast and adroit on his feet. At the first clash of steel on steel, Cadfael felt his own arm and wrist bracing and turning the stroke, and swung aside with the very same motion Beringar made to slide out of danger; the turn brought him about, with the arch of the town gate full in view.

Out of the black hollow a girl came darting like a swallow, all swift black and white and a flying cloud of gold hair. She was running, very fleetly and purposefully, with her skirts caught up in her hands almost to the knee, and well behind her, out of breath but making what haste she could, came another young woman. Constance was wasting much of what breath she still had in calling after her mistress imploringly to stop, to come away, not to go near; but Aline made never a sound, only ran towards where two gallants of hers were newly launched on a determined attempt to kill each other. She looked neither to right nor left, but only craned to see over the heads of the crowd. Cadfael hastened to meet her, and she recognised him with a gasp, and flung herself into his arms.

'Brother Cadfael, what is this? What has he done? And you knew, you knew, and you never warned me! If Constance had not gone into town to buy flour, I should never have known . . .'

'You should not be here,' said Cadfael, holding her quivering and panting on his heart. 'What can you do? I promised him not to tell you, he did not wish it. You should not look on at this.'

'But I will!' she said with passion. 'Do you think I'll go tamely away and leave him now? Only tell me,' she begged, 'is it true what they're saying – that he charged Adam with murdering that young man? And that Giles's dagger was the proof?'

'It is true,' said Cadfael. She was staring over his shoulder into the arena, where the swords clashed, and hissed and clashed again, and her amethyst eyes were immense and wild.

'And the charge – that also is true?'

'That also.'

'Oh, God!' she said, gazing in fearful fascination. 'And he is so slight . . . how can he endure it? Half the other's size . . . and he dared try to solve it this way! Oh, Brother Cadfael, how could you let him?'

At least now, thought Cadfael, curiously eased, I know which of those two is 'he' to her, without need of a name. I never was sure until now, and perhaps neither was she. 'If ever you succeed,' he said, 'in preventing Hugh Beringar from doing whatever he's set his mind on doing, then come to me and tell me how you managed it. Though I doubt it would not work for me! He chose this way, girl, and he had his reasons, good reasons. And you and I must abide it, as he must.'

'But we are three,' she said vehemently. 'If we stand with him, we *must* give him strength. I can pray and I can watch, and I will. Bring me nearer – come with me! I must see!'

She was thrusting impetuously through towards the lances when Cadfael held her back by the arm. 'I think,' he said, 'better if *he* does not see *you*. Not now!'

Aline uttered something that sounded like a very brief and bitter laugh. 'He would not see me now,' she said, 'unless I ran between the swords, and so I would, if they'd let me – No!' She took that back instantly, with a dry sob. 'No, I would not do so to him. I know better than that. All I can do is watch, and keep silence.'

The fate of women in a world of fighting men, he thought wryly, but for all that, it is not so passive a part as it sounds. So he drew her to a slightly raised place where she could see, without disturbing, with the glittering gold sheen of her unloosed hair in the sun, the deadly concentration of Hugh Beringar. Who had blood on the tip of his sword by then, though from a mere graze on Courcelle's cheek, and blood on his own left sleeve below the leather.

'He is hurt,' she said in a mourning whisper, and crammed half her small fist in her mouth to stop a cry, biting hard on her knuckles to ensure the silence she had promised.

'It's nothing,' said Cadfael sturdily. 'And he is the faster. See there, that parry! Slight he may seem, but there's steel in that wrist. What he wills to do, he'll do. And he has truth weighting his hand.'

'I love him,' said Aline in a soft, deliberate whisper, releasing her bitten hand for a moment. 'I did not know until now, but I do love him!'

'So do I, girl,' said Cadfael, 'so do I!'

They had been two full hours in the arena, with never a break for breath, and the sun was high and hot, and they suffered, but both went with relentless care, conserving their strength, and now, when their eyes met at close quarters over the braced swords, there was no personal grudge between them, only an inflexible purpose, on the one side to prove truth, on the other to disprove it, and on either side by the only means left, by killing. They had found out by then, if they had been in doubt, that for all the obvious advantages on one side, in this contest they were very evenly matched, equal in skill, almost equal in speed, the weight of truth holding a balance true between them. Both bled from minor wounds. There was blood here and there in the grass.

It was almost noon when Beringar, pressing hard, drove his opponent back with a sudden lunge, and saw his foot slip in blood-stained turf, thinned by the hot, dry summer. Courcelle, parrying, felt himself falling, and threw up his arm, and Hugh's following stroke took the sword almost out of his hand, shivered edge to edge, leaving him sprawled on one hip, and clutching only a bladeless hilt. The steel fell far aside, and lay useless.

Beringar at once drew back, leaving his foe to rise unthreatened. He rested his point against the ground, and looked towards Prestcote, who in turn was looking for guidance to the king's chair.

'Fight on!' said the king flatly. His displeasure had not abated.

Beringar leaned his point into the turf and gazed, wiping sweat from brow and lip. Courcelle raised himself slowly, looked at the useless hilt in his hand, and heaved desperate breath before hurling the thing from him in fury. Beringar looked from him to the king, frowning, and drew off two or three more paces while he considered. The king made no further move, apart from gesturing dourly that they should continue. Beringar took three rapid strides to the rim of the square, tossed his sword beneath the levelled lances, and set hand slowly to draw the dagger at his belt.

Courcelle was slow to understand, but blazed into renewed confidence when he realised the gift that was offered to him.

'Well, well!' said King Stephen under his breath. 'Who knows but I may have been mistaken in the best man, after all?'

With nothing but daggers now, they must come to grips. Length of reach is valuable, even with daggers, and the poniard that Courcelle drew from its sheath at his hip was longer than the decorative toy Hugh Beringar held. King Stephen revived into active interest, and shed his natural irritation at being forced into this encounter.

'He is mad!' moaned Aline at Cadfael's shoulder, leaning against him with lips drawn back and nostrils flaring, like any of her fighting forebears. 'He had licence to kill at leisure. Oh, he is stark mad. And I love him!'

The fearful dance continued, and the sun at its zenith shortened the shadows of the two duellists until they advanced, retreated, side-stepped on a black disc cast by their own bodies, while the full heat beat pitilessly on their heads, and within their leather harness they ran with sweat. Beringar was on the defensive now, his weapon being the shorter and lighter, and Courcelle was pressing hard, aware that he held the advantage. Only Beringar's quickness of hand and eye saved him from repeated slashes that might well have killed, and his speed and agility still enabled him at every assault to spring back out of range. But he was tiring at last; his judgment was less precise and confident, his movement less alert and steady. And Courcelle, whether he had got his second wind or simply gathered all his powers in one desperate effort, to make an end, seemed to have recovered his earlier force and fire. Blood ran on Hugh's right hand, fouled his hilt and made it slippery in his palm. The tatters of Courcelle's left sleeve fluttered at the edge of his vision, a distraction that troubled his concentration. He had tried several darting attacks, and drawn blood in his turn, but length of blade and length of arm told terribly against him. Doggedly he set himself to husband his own strength, by constant retreat if necessary, until Courcelle's frenzied attacks began to flag, as they must at last.

'Oh, God!' moaned Aline almost inaudibly. 'He was too generous, he has given his life away . . . The man is playing with him!'

'No man,' said Cadfael firmly, 'plays with Hugh Beringar with impunity. He is still the fresher of the two. This is a wild spurt to end it, he cannot maintain it long.'

Step by step Hugh gave back, but at each attack only so far as to elude the blade, and step by step, in a series of vehement rushes, Courcelle pursued and drove him. It seemed that he was trying to pen him into a corner of the square, where he would have to make a stand, but at the last moment the attacker's judgment flagged or Hugh's agility swung him clear of the trap, for the renewed pursuit continued along the line of lancers, Beringar unable to break out again into the centre of the arena, Courcelle unable to get through the sustained defence, or prevent this lame progress that seemed likely to end in another corner.

The Flemings stood like rocks, and let battle, like a slow tide, flow painfully along their immovable ranks. And halfway along the side of the square Courcelle suddenly drew back one long, rapid step instead of pursuing, and tossing his poniard from him in the grass, stooped with a hoarse cry of triumph, and reached beneath the levelled lances, to rise again brandishing the sword Hugh Beringar had discarded as a grace to him, more than an hour previously.

Hugh had not even realised that they had come to that very place, much less that he had been deliberately driven here for this purpose. Somewhere in the crowd he heard a woman shriek. Courcelle was in the act of straightening up, the sword in his hand, his eyes, under the broad, streaming brow half-mad with exultation. But he was still somewhat off-balance when Hugh launched himself upon him in a tigerish leap. A second later would have been too late. As the sword swung upward, he flung his whole weight against Courcelle's breast, locked his right arm, dagger and all, about his enemy's body, and caught the threatening sword-arm by the wrist in his left hand. For a moment they

182

heaved and strained, then they went down together heavily in the turf, and rolled and wrenched in a deadlocked struggle at the feet of the indifferent guards.

Aline clenched her teeth hard against a second cry, and covered her eyes, but the next moment as resolutely uncovered them. 'No, I will see all, I must . . . I will bear it! He shall not be ashamed of me! Oh, Cadfael . . . oh, Cadfael . . . What is happening? I can't see. . . .'

'Courcelle snatched the sword, but he had no time to strike. Wait, one of them is rising . . .'

Two had fallen together, only one arose, and he stood half-stunned and wondering. For his enemy had fallen limp and still under him, and relaxed straining arms nervelessly into the grass; and there he lay now, open-eyed to the glare of the sun, and a slow stream of red was flowing sluggishly from under him, and forming a dark pool about him on the trampled ground.

Hugh Beringar looked from the gathering blood to the dagger he still gripped in his right hand, and shook his head in bewilder-ment, for he was very tired, and weak now with this abrupt and inexplicable ending, and there was barely a drop of fresh blood on his blade, and the sword lay loosely clasped still in Courcelle's right hand, innocent of his death. And yet he had his death; his life was ebbing out fast into the thick grass. So what manner of ominous miracle was this, that killed and left both weapons unstained?

Hugh stooped, and raised the inert body by the left shoulder, turning it to see where the blood issued; and there, driven deep through the leather jerkin, was the dead man's own poniard, which he had flung away to grasp at the sword. By the look of it the hilt had lodged downwards in thick grass against the solidly braced boot of one of the Flemings. Hugh's onslaught had flung the owner headlong upon his discarded blade, and their rolling, heaving struggle had driven it home.

I did not kill him, after all, thought Beringar. His own cunning killed him. And whether he was glad or sorry he was too drained to know. Cadfael would be satisfied, at least; Nicholas Faintree was avenged, he had justice in full. His murderer had been accused publicly, and publicly the charge had been justified by heaven. And his murderer was dead; that failing breath was already spent.

Beringar reached down and picked up his sword, which rose

unresisting out of the convicted hand. He turned slowly, and raised it in salute to the king, and walked, limping now and dropping a few trickles of blood from stiffening cuts in hand and forearm, out of the square of lances, which opened silently to let him go free.

Two or three paces he took across the sward towards the king's chair, and Aline flew into his arms, and clasped him with a possessive fervour that shook him fully alive again. Her gold hair streamed about his shoulders and breast, she lifted to him a rapt, exultant and exhausted face, the image of his own, she called him by his name: 'Hugh . . . Hugh . . .' and fingered with aching tenderness the oozing wounds that showed in his cheek and hand and wrist.

'Why did you not tell me? Why? Why? Oh, you have made me die so many times! Now we are both alive again . . . Kiss me!'

He kissed her, and she remained real, passionate and unquestionably his. She continued to caress, and fret, and fawn.

'Hush, love,' he said, eased and restored, 'or go on scolding, for if you turn tender to me now I'm a lost man. I can't afford to droop yet, the king's waiting. Now, if you're my true lady, lend me your arm to lean on, and come and stand by me and prop me up, like a good wife, or I may fall flat at his feet.'

'Am I your true lady?' demanded Aline, like all women wanting guarantees before witnesses.

'Surely! Too late to think better of it now, my heart!'

She was beside him, clasped firmly in his arm, when he came before the king. 'Your Grace,' said Hugh, condescending out of some exalted private place scarcely flawed by weariness and wounds, 'I trust I have proven my case against a murderer, and have your Grace's countenance and approval.'

'Your opponent,' said Stephen, 'proved your case for you, all too well.' He eyed them thoughtfully, disarmed and diverted by this unexpected apparition of entwined lovers. 'But what you have proved may also be your gain. You have robbed me, young man, of an able deputy sheriff of this shire, whatever else he may have been, and however foul a fighter. I may well take reprisal by drafting you into the vacancy you've created. Without prejudice to your own castles and your rights of garrison on our behalf. What do you say?'

184

'With your Grace's leave,' said Beringar, straight-faced, 'I must first take counsel with my bride.'

'Whatever is pleasing to my lord,' said Aline, equally demurely, 'is also pleasing to me.'

Well, well, thought Brother Cadfael, looking on with interest, I doubt if troth was ever plighted more publicly. They had better invite the whole of Shrewsbury to the wedding.

Brother Cadfael walked across to the guest hall before Compline, and took with him not only a pot of his goose-grass salve for Hugh Beringar's numerous minor grazes, but also Giles Siward's dagger, with its topaz finial carefully restored.

'Brother Oswald is a skilled silversmith, this is his gift and mine to your lady. Give it to her yourself. But ask her – as I know she will – to deal generously by the boy who fished it out of the river. So much you will have to tell her. For the rest, for her brother's part, yes, silence, now and always. For her he was only one of the many who chose the unlucky side, and died for it.'

Beringar took the repaired dagger in his hand, and looked at it long and sombrely. 'Yet this is not justice,' he said slowly. 'You and I between us have forced into the light the truth of one man's sins, and covered up the truth of another's.' This night, for all his gains, he was very grave and a little sad, and not only because all his wounds were stiffening, and all his misused muscles groaning at every movement. The recoil from triumph had him fixing honest eyes on the countenance of failure, the fate he had escaped. 'Is justice due only to the blameless? If he had not been so visited and tempted, he might never have found himself mired to the neck in so much infamy.'

'We deal with what is,' said Cadfael. 'Leave what might have been to eyes that can see it plain. You take what's lawfully and honourably won, and value and enjoy it. You have that right. Here are you, deputy sheriff of Salop, in royal favour, affianced to as fine a girl as heart could wish, and the one you set your mind on from the moment you saw her. Be sure I noticed! And if you're stiff and sore in every bone tomorrow – and, lad, you will be! – what's a little disciplinary pain to a young man in your high feather?'

'I wonder,' said Hugh, brightening, 'where the other two are by now.'

'Within reach of the Welsh coast, waiting for a ship to carry them coastwise round to France. They'll do well enough.' As between Stephen and Maud, Cadfael felt no allegiance; but these young creatures, though two of them held for Maud and two for Stephen, surely belonged to a future and an England delivered from the wounds of civil war, beyond this present anarchy.

'As for justice,' said Brother Cadfael thoughtfully, 'it is but half the tale.' He would say a prayer at Compline for the repose of Nicholas Faintree, a clean young man of mind and life, surely now assuaged and at rest. But he would also say a prayer for the soul of Adam Courcelle, dead in his guilt; for every untimely death, every man cut down in his vigour and strength without time for repentance and reparation, is one corpse too many. 'No need,' said Cadfael, 'for you ever to look over your shoulder, or feel any compunction. You did the work that fell to you, and did it well. God disposes all. From the highest to the lowest extreme of a man's scope, wherever justice and retribution can reach him, so can grace.'